BACKDROP OF STARS

Backdrop of Stars

Edited by
HARRY HARRISON

NEW ENGLISH LIBRARY
TIMES MIRROR

For
Kingsley Amis
hearty partisan –
and stern critic

First published in Great Britain in 1968 by Dobson Books Ltd
© 1968 by Harry Harrison

*

FIRST NEL PAPERBACK EDITION MAY 1975

*

NEL Books are published by
New English Library Limited from Barnard's Inn, Holborn, London, E.C.I.
Made and printed in Great Britain by Hunt Barnard Printing Ltd., Aylesbury, Bucks.

45002269 2

CONTENTS

ACKNOWLEDGEMENTS

Judas Danced by Brian W. Aldiss, copyright © 1958 by Ballantine Books, Inc. By permission of the author.

The Last of the Deliverers by Poul Anderson, copyright © 1958 by Mercury Press, Inc. By permission of the author and the author's agents, Scott Meredith Literary Agency, Inc.

Founding Father by Isaac Asimov, copyright © 1965 by Galaxy Publishing Corporation. By permission of the author.

End-Game by J. G. Ballard, copyright © 1963 by *New Worlds SF*. By permission of the author.

Tiger Ride by James Blish and Damon Knight, copyright © 1948 by Street and Smith Publications, Inc. By permission of the authors.

Consumer's Report by Theodore R. Cogswell, copyright © 1955 by *Imagination*. By permission of the author.

Proposal by L. Sprague de Camp, copyright © 1952 by *Startling Stories*. By permission of the author.

Sail On! Sail On! by Philip José Farmer, copyright © 1952 by *Startling Stories* and reprinted by permission of the author and the author's agents, Scott Meredith Literary Agency, Inc.

Missing Link by Frank Herbert, copyright © 1959 by Street and Smith Publications, Inc. By permission of the author.

Myths My Great-granddaughter Taught Me by Fritz Leiber, copyright © 1963 by Mercury Press, Inc. By permission of the author.

Syndrome Johnny by Katherine MacLean, copyright © 1951 by Galaxy Publishing Corporation. By permission of the author.

INTRODUCTION

Art is a winged word, neither to hold nor to bind, ever ready to fly away with a discussion that would fasten it to its own ground and to the work that bears its name. The homely note of the craft allows no such distractions; it holds you fast to the matter in hand, to the thing that has been made and the manner of its making; nor lets you forget that the whole of the matter is contained within the finished form of the thing, and that the form was fashioned by the craft.

Percy Lubbock
from the preface to
The Craft of Fiction

This volume has been fashioned by the writers whose stories it contains, chosen by them despite the barriers and restrictions I placed in their way. I wanted only stories that they liked, that had not been anthologised before, that they had a particular reason for writing, that were of a certain length – and I still reserved the editorial prerogative of rejection, which I exercised freely. The length of the correspondence, in some cases, exceeds the length of the story. This has resulted in an anthology of representative stories by some of the most able practitioners in the science fiction field, a book that may be read for the fiction alone, but has an added dimension in that each contributor has added a comment about his own story. I hope you will also experience the sharp pleasure that I felt when, one by one, these idiosyncratic and personal statements arrived.

Though I have been selective in choosing the fiction, I have attempted no restrictions on the comments. All I asked for was some truth about each story, and I received that in abundance. I gave the maximum length for the comment – which naturally some writers instantly violated. I did not state where the comments were to run – so they came both before and after the stories, and in one case both before *and* after. I hoped for some comment on the craft of science fiction – and received polemics on politics and the finances of writing.

I have enjoyed every word of it. The most exciting part has been the realisation that Percy Lubbock's winged word of art has been brought to ground in these essays on our craft. Art gains a dimension through understanding, and you will find that here. How much more enjoyable *Sail On! Sail On!* is after a plunge into the wonderful possibilities and ramifications of Farmer's imagined universe. And what interesting strings of speculation we can pick up and follow from *Myths My Great-granddaughter Taught Me* after seeing from what a maelstrom of myth the author has plucked his material.

I have no favourites; I like them all, for they are all true statements. Cogswell no truer than the others when he tells the editor off for attempting to analyse the craft of science fiction in this manner. Or Aldiss no less revealing in his glimpse into the intimacies of the creative process. I will not go on, for every entry strikes a common note of sincerity.

My only regret is that this volume could not have been longer, and it is physical limitations alone that have prevented the inclusion of many other writers of importance. The thirteen here are all personal friends whose writing and companionship I have always enjoyed. I have tried to select stories that contain their own individualistic contribution to this form of literature, then attempted to subtly goad them into revealing something about the craft that presents their art. They responded with an enthusiasm for which I will always be grateful.

Here are the results.

HARRY HARRISON

JUDAS DANCED

by
Brian W. Aldiss

It was not a fair trial.

You understand I was not inclined to listen properly, but it was not a fair trial. It had a mistrustful and furtive haste about it. Judge, counsel and jury all took care to be as brief and explicit as possible. I said nothing, but I knew why: everyone wanted to get back to the dances.

So it was not very long before the judge stood up and pronounced sentence:

'Alexander Abel Crowe, this court finds you guilty of murdering Parowen Scryban for the second time.'

I could have laughed out loud. I nearly did.

He went on: 'You are therefore condemned to suffer death by strangulation for the second time, which sentence will be carried out within the next week.'

Round the court ran a murmur of excitement.

In a way, even I felt satisfied. It had been an unusual case: few are the people who care to risk facing death a second time; the first time you die makes the prospect worse, not better. For just a minute, the court was still, then it cleared with almost indecent haste. In a little while, only I was left there.

I, Alex Abel Crowe – or approximately he – came carefully down out of the prisoner's box and limped the length of the dusty room to the door. As I went, I looked at my hands. They weren't trembling.

Nobody bothered to keep a check on me. They knew they could pick me up whenever they were ready to execute sentence. I was unmistakable, and I had nowhere to go. I was the man with the club foot who could not dance; nobody could mistake me for anyone else. Only I could do that.

Outside in the dark sunlight, that wonderful woman stood waiting for me with her husband, waiting on the court steps.

11

The sight of her began to bring back life and hurt to my veins. I raised my hand to her as my custom was.

'We've come to take you home, Alex,' Husband said, stepping towards me.

'I haven't got a home,' I said, addressing her.

'I meant *our* home,' he informed me.

'Elucidation accepted,' I said. 'Take me away, take me away, take me away, Charlemagne. And let me sleep.'

'You need a sleep after all you have been through,' he said. Why, he sounded nearly sympathetic.

Sometimes I called him Charlemagne, sometimes just Charley. Or Cheeps, or Jags, or Jaggers, or anything, as the mood took me. He seemed to forgive me. Perhaps he even liked it – I don't know. Personal magnetism takes you a long way; it has taken me so far I don't even have to remember names.

They stopped a passing taxi and we all climbed in. It was a tumbril, they tell me. You know, French? Circa seventeen-eighty, something. Husband sat one side, Wife the other, each holding one of my arms, as if they thought I should get violent. I let them do it, although the idea amused me.

'Hallo, friends!' I said ironically. Sometimes I called them 'parents', or 'disciples', or sometimes 'patients'. Anything.

The wonderful woman was crying slightly.

'Look at her!' I said to Husband. 'She's lovely when she cries, that I swear. I could have married her, you know, if I had not been dedicated. Tell him, you wonderful creature, tell him how I turned you down!'

Through her sobbing, she said, 'Alex said he had more important things to do than sex.'

'So you've got me to thank for Perdita!' I told him. 'It was a big sacrifice, but I'm happy to see you happy.' Often now I called her Perdita. It seemed to fit her. He laughed at what I had said, and then we were all laughing. Yes, it was good to be alive; I knew I made them feel good to be alive. They were loyal. I had to give them something – I had no gold and silver.

The tumbril stopped outside Charley's place – the Husband Residence, I'd better say. Oh, the things I've called that place! Someone should have recorded them all. It was one of those inverted beehive houses: just room for a door and an elevator on the ground floor, but the fifth floor could hold a ballroom. Topply, topply. Up we went to the fifth. There was no sixth

12

floor; had there been, I should have gone up there, the way I felt. I asked for it anyhow, just to see the wonderful woman brighten up. She liked me to joke, even when I wasn't in a joking mood. I could tell she still loved me so much it hurt her.

'Now for a miracle, ye pampered jades,' I said, stepping forth, clumping into the living room.

I seized an empty vase from a low shelf and spat into it. Ah, the old cunning was still there! It filled at once with wine, sweet and bloody-looking. I sipped and found it good.

'Go on and taste it, Perdy!' I told her.

Wonderful w. turned her head sadly away. She would not touch that vase. I could have eaten every single strand of hair on her head, but she seemed unable to see the wine. I really believe she could not see that wine.

'Please don't go through all that again, Alex,' she implored me wearily. Little faith, you see – the old, old story. (Remind me to tell you a new one I heard the other day.) I put my behind on one chair and my bad foot on another and sulked.

They came and stood by me . . . not too close.

'Come nearer,' I coaxed, looking up under my eyebrows and pretending to growl at them. 'I won't hurt you. I only murder Parowen Scryban, remember?'

'We've got to talk to you about that,' Husband said desperately. I thought he looked as if he had aged.

'I think you look as if you have aged, Perdita,' I said. Often I called him Perdita too; why, man, they sometimes looked so worried you couldn't tell them apart.

'I cannot live forever, Alex,' he replied. 'Now try and concentrate about this killing, will you?'

I waved a hand and tried to belch. At times I can belch like a sinking ship.

'We do all we can to help you, Alex,' he said. I heard him although my eyes were shut; can you do that? 'But we can only keep you out of trouble if you co-operate. It's the dancing that does it; nothing else betrays you like dancing. You've got to promise you'll stay away from it. In fact, we want you to promise that you'll let us restrain you. To keep you away from the dancing. Something about that dancing . . . '

He was going on and on, and I could still hear him. But other things were happening. That word 'dancing' got in the way of all his other words. It started a sort of flutter under my eyelids. I crept my hand out and took the wonderful woman's hand, so soft and lovely, and listened to that word 'dancing' dancing. It brought its own rhythm, bouncing about alike an eyeball inside my head. The rhythm grew louder. He was shouting.

I sat up suddenly, opening my eyes.

W. woman was on the floor, very pale.

'You squeezed too hard, boy,' she whispered.

I could see that her little hand was the only red thing she had.

'I'm sorry,' I said. 'I really wonder you two don't throw me out for good!' I couldn't help it, I just started laughing. I like laughing. I can laugh even when nothing's funny. Even when I saw their faces, I still kept laughing like mad.

'Stop it!' Husband said. For a moment he looked as if he would have hit me. But I was laughing so much I did not recognise him. It must have done them good to see me enjoying myself; they both needed a fillip, I could tell.

'If you stop laughing, I'll take you down to the club,' he said, greasily bribing.

I stopped. I always know when to stop. With all humility, that is a great natural gift.

'The club's the place for me,' I said. 'I've already got a club foot – I'm half-way there!'

I stood up.

'Lead on, my loyal supporters, my liege lords,' I ordered.

'You and I will go alone, Alex,' Husband said. 'The wonderful woman will stay here. She really ought to go to bed.'

'What's in it for her?' I joked. Then I followed him to the elevator. He knows I don't like staying in any one place for long.

When I got to the club, I knew, I would want to be somewhere else. That's the worst of having a mission: it makes you terribly restless. Sometimes I am so restless I could dic. Ordinary people just don't know what the word means. I could have married her if I had been ordinary. They call it destiny.

But the club was good.

We walked there. I limped there. I made sure I limped badly.

The club had a timescreen. That, I must admit, was my only interest in the club. I don't care for women. Or men. Not living women or men. I only enjoy them when they are back in time.

14

This night – I nearly said 'this particular night', but there was nothing particularly particular about it – the timescreen had only been tuned roughly three centuries back into the past. At least, I guessed it was twenty-first-century stuff by the women's dresses and a shot of a power station. A large crowd of people were looking in as Perdita Caesar and I entered, so I started to pretend he had never seen one of the wall screens before.

'The tele-eyes which are projected back into history consume a fabulous amount of power every second,' I told him loudly in a voice which suggested I had swallowed a poker. 'It makes them very expensive. It means private citizens cannot afford screens and tele-eyes, just as once they could not afford their own private cinemas. This club is fortunately very rich. Its members sleep in gold leaf at nights.'

Several people were glancing round at me already. Caesar was shaking his head and rolling his eyes.

'The tele-eyes cannot get a picture further than twenty-seven centuries back,' I told him, 'owing to the limitations of science. Science, as you know, is a system for taking away with one hand while giving with the other.'

He could not answer cleverly. I went on: 'It has also proved impossible, due to the aforesaid limitations, to send human beings further back in time than one week. And that costs so much that only governments can do it. As you may have heard, nothing can be sent ahead into time – there's no future in it!'

I had to laugh at that. It was funny, and quite spontaneous.

Many people were calling out to me, and Caesar Borgia was dragging at my arm, trying to make me be quiet.

'I wouldn't spoil anyone's fun!' I shouted. 'You lot get on with your watching; I'll get on with my speech.'

But I did not want to talk to a lot of feather-bedders like them. So I sat down without saying another word, Boy Borgia collapsing beside me with a sigh of relief. Suddenly I felt very, very sad. Life just is not what is was; once on a time, I could have married this husband's wife.

'Physically, you can go back one week,' I whispered, 'optically, twenty-seven centuries. It's very sad.'

It was very sad. The people on the screen were also sad. They lived in the Entertainment Era, and appeared to be getting little pleasure from it. I tried to weep for them, but failed because at the moment they seemed just animated

15

history. I saw them as period pieces, stuck there a couple of generations before reading and writing had died out altogether and the fetter of literacy fell forever from the world. Little any of them cared for the patterns of history.

'I've had an idea I want to tell you about, Cheezer,' I said. It was a good idea.

'Can't it wait?' he asked. 'I'd like to see this scan. It's all about the European Allegiance.'

'I must tell you before I forget.'

'Come on,' he said resignedly, getting up.

'You are too loyal to me,' I complained. 'You spoil me. I'll speak to St Peter about it.'

As meek as you like, I followed him into an ante-room. He drew himself a drink from an automatic man in one corner. He was trembling. I did not tremble, although at the back of my mind lurked many things to tremble about.

'Go on then, say whatever in hell you want to say,' he told me, shading his eyes with his hand. I have seen him use that trick before; he did it after I killed Parowen Scryban the first time, I remember. There's nothing wrong with my memory, except in patches.

'I had this idea,' I said, trying to recall it. 'This idea – oh, yes. History. I got the idea looking at those twenty-first-century people. Mythology is the key to everything, isn't it? I mean, a man builds his life on a set of myths, doesn't he? Well, in our world, the so-called Western world, those accepted myths were religious until about mid-nineteenth century. By then, a majority of Europeans were literate, or within reach of it, and for a couple of centuries the myths became literary ones: tragedy was no longer the difference between grace and nature but between art and reality.'

Julius dropped his hand. He was interested. I could see he wondered what was coming next. I hardly knew myself.

'Then mechanical aids – television, computers, scanners of every type – abolished literacy,' I said. 'Into the vacuum came the timescreens. Our mythologies are now historical: tragedy has become simply a failure to see the future.'

I beamed at him and bowed, not letting him know I was beyond tragedy. He just sat there. He said nothing. Sometimes such terrible boredom descends on me that I can hardly fight against it.

'Is my reasoning sound?' I asked. (Two women looked into

16

the room, saw me, and left again hurriedly. They must have sensed I did not want them, otherwise they would have come to me; I am young and handsome – I am not thirty-three yet.)

'You could always reason well,' Marcus Aurelius Marconi said, 'but it just never leads anywhere. God, I'm so tired.'

'This bit of reasoning leads somewhere. I beg you to believe it, Holy Roman,' I said, flopping on my knees before him. 'It's the state philosophy I've really been telling you about. That's why although they keep the death penalty for serious crimes – like murdering a bastard called Parowen Scryban – they go back in time the next day and call off the execution. They believe you should die for your crime, you see? But more deeply they believe every man should face his true future. They've – we've all seen too many premature deaths on the timescreen. Romans, Normans, Celts, Goths, English, Israelis. Every race. Individuals – all dying too soon, failing to fulfil – '

Oh, I admit it, I was crying on his knees by then, although bravely disguising it by barking like a dog: a Great Dane. Hamlet. Not in our stars but in ourselves. (I've watched W.S. write that bit.)

I was crying at last to think the police would come without fail within the next week to snuff me out, and then resurrect me again, according to my sentence. I was remembering what it was like last time. They took so long about it.

They took so long. Though I struggled, I could not move; those police know how to hold a man. My windpipe was blocked, as sentence of court demanded.

And then, it seemed, the boxes sailed in. Starting with small ones, they grew bigger. They were black boxes, all of them. Faster they came, and faster, inside me and out. I'm telling you how it felt, my God! And they blocked the whole, whole universe, black and red. With my lungs really crammed tight with boxes, out of the world I went. Dead!

Into limbo I went.

I don't say nothing happened, but I could not grasp what was happening there, and I was unable to participate. Then I was alive again.

It was abruptly the day before the strangulation once more, and the government agent had come back in time and rescued me, so that from one point of view I was not strangled. *But* I still remembered it happening, and the boxes, and limbo. Don't talk to me about paradoxes. The government expended several billion megavolts sending that man back for me, and those megavolts account for all paradoxes. I was dead and then alive again.

Now I had to undergo it all once more. No wonder there was little crime nowadays: the threat of that horrible experience held many a likely criminal back. But I *had* to kill Parowen Scryban; just so long as they went back and resurrected him after I had finished with him, I had to go and do it again. Call it a moral obligation. No one understands. It is as if I were living in a world of my own.

'Get up, get up! You're biting my ankles.'

Where had I heard that voice before? At last I could no longer ignore it. Whenever I try to think, voices interrupt. I stopped chewing whatever I was chewing, unblocked my eyes and sat up. This was just a room; I had been in rooms before. A man was standing over me; I did not recognise him. He was just a man.

'You look as if you have aged,' I told him.

'I can't live forever, thank God,' he said. 'Now get up and let's get you home. You're going to bed.'

'What home?' I asked. 'What bed? Who in the gentle name of anyone may you be?'

He looked sick.

'Just call me Adam,' he said sickly.

I recognised him then and went with him. We had been in some sort of a club; he never told me why. I still don't know why we went to that club.

The house he took me to was shaped like a beehive upside-down, and I walked there like a drunk. A club-footed drunk.

This wonderful stranger took me up in an elevator to a soft bed. He undressed me and put me in that soft bed as gently as if I had been his son. I am really impressed by the kindness strangers show me; personal magnetism, I suppose.

For as long as I could after he had left me, I lay in the bed in the inverted beehive. Then the darkness grew thick and sticky, and I could imagine all the fat, furry bodies, chitinously winged, of the bees on the ceiling. A minute more and I should fall head first into them. Stubbornly, I fought to sweat it out, but a man can only stand so much.

On hands and knees I crawled out of bed and out of the room. Quickly, softly, I clicked the door shut behind me; not a bee escaped.

People were talking in a lighted room along the corridor. I crawled to the doorway, looking and listening. The wonderful stranger talked to the wonderful woman; she was in night attire (pronounced 'nigh ta-ta') with a hand bandaged.

She was saying: 'You will have to see the authorities in the morning and petition them.'

He was saying: 'It'll do no good. I can't get the law changed. You know that. It's hopeless.'

I merely listened.

Sinking on to the bed, he buried his face in his hands, finally looking up to say, 'The law insists on personal responsibility. We've got to take care of Alex. It's a reflection of the time we live in; owing to the timescreens we've got – whether we like it or not – historical perspectives. We can see that the whole folly of the past was due to failures in individual liability. Our laws are naturally framed to correct that, which they do – it just happens to be tough on us.'

He sighed and said, 'The sad thing is, even Alex realises that. He talked quite sensibly to me at the club about not evading the future.'

'It hurts me most when he talks sensibly,' the wonderful double-you said. 'It makes you realise he is still capable of suffering.'

He took her bandaged hand, almost as if they had a pain they hoped to alleviate by sharing it between them.

'I'll go and see the authorities in the morning,' he promised, 'and ask them to let the execution be final – no reprieve afterwards.'

Even that did not seem to satisfy her.

Perhaps, like me, she could not tell what either of them was talking about. She shook her head miserably from side to side.

'If only it hadn't been for his club foot,' she said. 'If only it hadn't been for that, he could have danced the sickness out of himself.'

Her face was growing more and more screwed up.

It was enough. More.

'Laugh and grow fat,' I suggested. I croaked because my throat was dry. My glands are always like bullets. It reminded me of a frog, so I hopped spontaneously into the room. They did not move. I sat on the bed with them.

'All together again,' I said.

They did not move.

19

'Go back to bed, Alex,' she of the wonderfulness said in a low voice.

They were looking at me; goodness knows what they wanted me to say or do. I stayed where I was. A little green clock on a green shelf said nine o'clock.

'Oh, holy heavens!' the double-you said. 'What does the future hold?'

'Double chins for you, double yous for me,' I joked. That green clock said a minute past nine. I felt as if its little hands were slowly, slowly disembowelling me.

If I waited long enough, I knew I should think of something. They talked to me while I thought and waited; what good they imagined they were doing is beyond me, but I would not harm them. They mean well. They're the best people in the world. That doesn't mean to say I have to listen to them.

The thought about the clock arrived. Divine revelation.

'The dancing will be on now,' I said, standing up like a jack knife.

'No!' Husband said.

'No!' Perdita said.

'You look as if you have aged,' I told them. That is my favourite line in all speech.

I ran out of the room, slamming the door behind me, ran step-club-step-club down the passage and hurled myself into the elevator. With infinitesimal delay, I chose the right button and sank to ground level. There, I wedged the lattice door open with a chair; that put the elevator out of action.

People in the street took no notice of me. The fools just did not realise who I was. Nobody spoke to me as I hurried along, and of course I replied in kind.

Thus I came to the dance area.

Every community has its dance area. Think of all that drama, gladiatorial contests, reading, and sport have ever meant in the past; now they are all merged into dance, inevitably, for only by dance – our kind of dance – can history be interpreted. And interpretation of history is our being, because through the timescreens we see that history is life. It lives round us, so we dance it. Unless we have club feet.

Many dances were in progress among the thirty permanent sets. The sets were only casually separated from each other, so that spectators or dancers going from one to another, might

20

get the sense of everything happening at once, which is the sense the timescreens give you.

That is what I savagely love about history. It is not past: it is always going on. Cleopatra lies forever in the sweaty arms of Anthony, Socrates continually gulps his hemlock down. You just have to be watching the right screen or the right dance.

Most of the dancers were amateurs – although the term means little where everyone dances out their roles whenever possible. I stood among a crowd, watching. The bright movements have a dizzying effect; they excite me. To one side of me, Marco Polo sweeps exultantly through Cathay to Kubla Khan. Ahead, four children who represent the satellites of Jupiter, glide out to meet the sombre figure of Galileo Galilei. To the other side, the Persian poet Firdausi leaves for exile in Bagdad. Further still, I catch a glimpse of Heyerdahl turning towards the tide.

And if I cross my eyes, raft, telescope, pagoda, palm all mingle. That is meaning! If I could only dance it!

I cannot stay still. Here is my restlessness again, my only companion. I move, eyes unfocused. I pass round the sets or across them, mingling stiff-legged among the dancers. Something compels me, something I cannot remember. Now I cannot even remember who I am. I've gone beyond mere identity.

Everywhere the dancing is faster, matching my heart. I would not harm anyone, except one person who harmed me eternally. It is he I must find. Why do they dance so fast? The movements drive me like whips.

Now I run into a mirror. It stands on a crowded set. I fight with the creature imprisoned in it, thinking it real. Then I understand that it is only a mirror. Shaking my head, I clear the blood from behind my eyes and regard myself. Yes, that is unmistakably me. And I remember who I am meant to be.

I first found who I was meant to be as a child, when I saw one of the greatest dramas of all. There it was, captured by the timescreens! The soldiers and centurions came and a bragging multitude. The sky drew dark as they banged three crosses into the ground. And when I saw the Man they nailed upon the central cross, I knew I had His face.

Here it is now, that same sublime face, looking at me in pity and pain out of the glass. Nobody believes me; I no longer tell

21

them who I think I am. But one thing I know I have to do. I have to do *it*.

So now I run again clump-trot-clump-trot, knowing just what to look for. All these great sets, pillars and panels of concrete and plastic, I run round them all, looking.

And here it is. Professionals dance out this drama, my drama, so difficult and intricate and sad. Pilate in dove grey, Mary Magdalene moves in green. Hosts of dancers fringe them, representing the crowd who did not care. I care! My eyes burn among them, seeking. Then I have the man I want.

He is just leaving the set to rest out of sight until the cue for his last dance. I follow him, keeping behind cover like a crab in a thicket.

Yes! He looks just like me! He is my living image, and consequently bears That face. Yet it is now overlaid with make-up, pink and solid, so that when he comes out of the bright lights he looks like a corpse.

I am near enough to see the thick muck on his skin, with its runnels and wrinkles caused by sweat and movement. Underneath it all, the true face is clear enough to me, although the make-up plastered on it represents Judas.

To have That face and to play Judas! It is the most terrible of all wickedness. But this is Parowen Scryban, whom I have twice murdered for this very blasphemy. It is some consolation to know that although the government slipped back in time and saved him afterwards, he must still remember those good deaths. Now I must kill him again.

As he turns into a rest room, I have him. Ah, my fingers slip into that slippery pink stuff, but underneath the skin is firm. He is small, slender, tired with the strain of dancing. He falls forward with me on his back.

I kill him now, although in a few hours they will come back and rescue him and it will all not have happened. Never mind the shouting: squeeze. Squeeze, dear God!

When blows fall on my head from behind, it makes no difference. Scryban should be dead by now, the traitor. I roll off him and let many hands tie me into a strait jacket.

Many lights are in my eyes. Many voices are talking. I just lie there, thinking I recognise two of the voices, one a man's, one a woman's.

The man says, 'Yes, Inspector, I *know* that under law parents are responsible for their own children. We look after Alex

22

as far as we can, but he's mad. He's a throwback! I – God, Inspector, I *hate* the creature.'

'You mustn't say that!' the woman cries. 'Whatever he does, he's our son.'

They sound too shrill to be true. I cannot think what they make such a fuss about. So I open my eyes and look at them. She is a wonderful woman but I recognise neither her nor the man; they just do not interest me. Scryban I do recognise.

He is standing rubbing his throat. He looks a real mess with his two faces all mixed together like a Picasso. Because he is breathing, I know they have come back and saved him again. No matter: he will remember.

The man they call Inspector (and who, I ask, would want a name like that?) goes over to speak to Scryban.

'Your father tells me you are actually this madman's brother,' he says to Scryban. Judas hangs his head, though he continues to massage his neck.

'Yes,' he says. He is as quiet as the woman was shrill; strange how folks vary. 'Alex and I are twin brothers. I changed my name years ago – the publicity, you know . . . harmful to my professional career . . .'

How terribly tired and bored I feel.

Who is whose brother, I ask myself, who mothers whom? I'm lucky: I own no relations. These people look sad company. The saddest in the universe.

'I think you all look as if you have aged!' I shout suddenly.

That makes the Inspector come and stand over me, which I dislike. He has knees half-way up his legs. I managed to resemble one of the tritons on one of Benvenuto Cellini's salt cellars, and so he turns away at last to speak to Husband.

'All right,' he says. 'I can see this is just one of those things nobody can be responsible for. I'll arrange for the reprieve to be countermanded. This time, when the devil is dead he stays dead.'

Husband embraces Scryban. Wonderful woman begins to cry. Traitors all! I start to laugh, making it so harsh and loud and horrible it frightens even me.

What none of them understand is this: on the third time I shall rise again.

COMMENT ON
JUDAS DANCED

A writer's stories are the series of disguises he wears. *Judas Danced* is a disguise I no longer need and the crazed Byronic figure of the central character a persona I no longer recognise, but I retain an affection for the story, while it is particularly suitable for the sort of discussion Editor Harrison invites his contributors to make for this anthology.

Judas Danced was not only a disguise for me at a rather frenzied period of my life (I wrote it in April 1957); it is itself about disguises. Alex, the central figure, believes himself to be Christ. His twin brother, who exactly resembles him, disguises himself as Judas. Alex's unconscious incest-motivations prevent him from recognising his parents; he merely sees his mother as a woman he could have married. And the civilisation to which they belong is itself involved in large-scale pretences, with mock-tumbrils in the streets, the elaborate imitations of what is past, and so on.

My intention was to confuse the reader by seeing all this through Alex's eyes, so that he would be forced to work out for himself what was truth, what illusion. It seems a simple enough exercise now although at the time of writing I felt differently. I was in two minds then about giving up writing science fiction. My first story had been published only two years before, and I already found myself unable to imitate the admired giants of the genre. Cheerfulness kept breaking in – and poetry and feeling, and other impurities that were then rare in SF and which I imagined readers did not much value. That may or may not have been true; the moment to check on it is gone, now that SF has gained a wider and more cosmopolitan audience.

Judas Danced represents the phase when, being unable to imitate, I ceased to care about imitating and tried to strike out on my own (or as the less charitable might say, to imitate writers beyond the SF field). With characteristic diffidence, the attempt is disguised under the disguises, while among the story's weaknesses must be accounted the fact that I was unsure of my audience – a fault also of my novel *Nono-Stop* (*Star-Ship* in America) which I had finished the previous month.

Well, so much for the self-confessions. When a story is completed successfully, it is often uncommonly difficult to recall where the notions that buoy it came from; they merge, and in any case were never wholly separate, since one is unable to conceive G before F and E have been cultivated a bit. With Judas, the case was different.

It was different for two reasons: because I had challenged myself loading incompatible notions into the story and because soon after I had finished writing, I did a small article about it for an amateur magazine called *Sphere*.

Some of these notions or trails of thought were as follows: the sadness of greasepaint when an ageing woman applies it thickly so that she may pass for beautiful for five minutes across the footlights (but what if the greasepaint had to conceal beauty?); the suspicion that our civilisation, having passed out of the religion-dominated stage, might be passing out of the literacy-dominated stage (but into a stage dominated by what?); might not an intricate form of dancing represent the highest sort of co-ordination possible to man, involving brain, muscle, instinct, discipline and creativity like no other activity (but what if you were constitutionally unable to dance?); supposing all history were open for us to range over, wouldn't the weaker-minded identify with the great figures, and wouldn't the great dramas become as unreal as soap operas – just as soap operas become as real as life to the weak-minded today?; and so on.

These were the cerebral ingredients . But on the side of sentiment, I had the picture of a man uttering those banal words 'You can't live for ever', which conceal the horrid thought of death in cliché form, and using them genuinely as a solace for himself, so tormented is his lot. That the mixture of all these ingredients came off as well as it had is a miracle – it's a bad way to concoct a story! If an SF story does not have its initial impulse in one centrally felt idea or character, it is liable to decline into a series of episodes that seem the more machine-like because they probably concern machines.

The completed story went to Frederick Pohl in New York, who accepted it for the first issue of *Star Science Fiction* magazine, which Ballantine were preparing to bring out. It was my first acceptance in America. I had been brought up on American magazines; all things American fascinated me; for worse or better, one cannot really claim to be a writer before one has had a story published in New York; after the acceptance of *Judas Danced*, circumstances were never the same for me again.

Of course, earning the right to speak up for oneself – or imagining one has earned it, which is just as useful – is one thing. Knowing what one can say when the right is earned is another. Ever since the sputniks went up, SF has been unsure of its function; which is no bad thing, since before that date it was riding very cockily along predicting the space age, and propaganda and fiction are worse enemies than art and science. But at least the prediction stuff served as a sense of destiny. Now we're in the space age, where do we go?

Perhaps William Burroughs has the most immediately attractive answer: dive into a highly personalised universe where one's own demons can be capitalised as the Nova Mob.

Happily, SF is changing to accommodate this sort of writing, and losing some of its old simon pure nursery air in the process. But I have a feeling the process can only go so far. One of the attractions of SF has long been what Burroughs seems to distrust: a sense of shape, which implies a preference for resolution. SF keeps digging away to try and discover the secret of the universe ('What if the old catographers were right?' Philip José Farmer asks) and to bring, like science itself, order out of chaos. As long as its subject matter is these themes and not merely ones of personal agony – which at present at least more properly belong in mainstream fiction – SF obviously cannot afford to yield itself into chaos or enjoy the excitements of shuffled pages and fold-in methods. It is a probing medium, a highly moral and moralising medium, and moralists never had much time for chaos and old night.

If I were writing *Judas Danced* today, it might be much freer in form, much nearer chaos, nearer Alex; he would be more felt, less reported upon. Half the cerebral ingredients, as I've called them, might go. The result would be the difference between a character drawn by Arnold Bennett and one drawn by Virginia Woolf. We should be right inside Alex – but the result would be rather less SF. Despite all the psychological fantasies, SF is most itself when in hot pursuit of the external world.

Or so I think one must claim when presenting the preceding piece of prose, written in the year of the first sputnik.

BRIAN W. ALDISS

THE LAST OF THE DELIVERERS

by

Poul Anderson

When I was nine years old, we still had a crazy man living in our town. He was very old, almost a hundred I suppose, and all his kin were dead. But in those days every town still had a few people who did not belong to any family.

Uncle Jim was wrong in the head, but harmless. He cobbled for us. His shop was in the front room of his house, always prim and neat, and when you stood there among the good smells of leather and oil, you could see his living room beyond. He did not have many books, but shelf after shelf was loaded with tall bright sheaves cased in plastic – old as himself, and as cracked and yellow with their age. He called them his magazines, and if we children were good he sometimes let us look at the pictures in them, but we had to be very careful. After he was dead I had a chance to read the texts, which didn't make sense. Nobody would worry about the things the people in those magazines made such a fuss over. He also had a big antique television set, though why he kept it when there was nothing to receive but official calls and the town had a perfectly good set for them, I don't know. But he was crazy.

Every morning his long stiff figure went for a walk down Main Street. The Trees there were mostly elms, grown tall enough to overshadow it and speckle the pavement with cool bright sunflecks. Uncle Jim was always dressed in his ancient clothes, no matter how hot the day, and summer in Ohio can get plenty hot. He wore frayed white shirts with scratchy, choky collars, and long trousers and a clumsy kind of jacket, and narrow shoes that pinched his feet. It was ugly, but he kept it painfully clean. We children, being young and therefore cruel, thought at first that because we never saw him unclothed he must be hiding some awful deformity, and teased him about it. But my aunt's brother John made us stop, and Uncle Jim never held it against us. He even used to give us candy he had

27

made himself, till the town dentist complained; then all of us had solemn talks with our fathers and found out that sugar rots the teeth.

Finally we decided that Uncle Jim – we called him that, without saying on which side he was anyone's uncle, because he wasn't really – wore all those clothes as a sort of background for his button that said WIN WITH WILLARD. He told me once, when I asked, that Willard had been the last Republican President of the United States and a very great man who tried to avert disaster but was too late because the people were already far gone in sloth and decadence. That was a big lading for a nine-year-old head, and I still don't really understand it, except that once the towns did not govern themselves and the country was divided between two big groups who were not even clans but who more or less took turns furnishing a President; and the President was not an umpire between towns and states, but ran everything.

Uncle Jim used to creak down Main Street past Townhall and sunpower plant, then turn at the fountain and go by my father's great-uncle Conrad's house to the edge of town where the fields and Trees rolled to the blue rim of the world. At the airport he would turn and come back by Joseph Arakelian's, where he always looked in at the hand looms and sneered with disgust and talked about automatic machinery; though what he had against the looms I don't know, because Joseph's weavery was famous. He also made harsh remarks about our ratty little airport and the town's half-dozen flitters. That wasn't fair: we had a very good airport, surfaced with concrete blocks ripped out of the old highway, and there were enough flitters for all our longer trips. You'd never get more than six groups going anywhere at any one time in a town this size.

But I wanted to tell about the Communist.

This was in the spring. The snow had melted and the ground begun to dry and our farmers were out planting. The rest of our town bustled with preparations for the Fête, cooking and baking, oh such a smell as filled the air, women trading recipes from porch to porch, artisans hammering and sawing and welding, the washlines afire with Sunday-best clothes taken out of winter chests, lovers hand in hand whispering of the festivals to come. Red and Bob and Stinky and I were playing marbles by the airport. It used to be mumbletypeg, but some of the kids flipped their knives into Trees and the Elders made

28

a rule that no kid could carry a knife unless a grown-up was with him.

So it was a fair sweet morning, the sky a dizzy-high arch of blue, sunlight bouncing off puffy white clouds and down to the earth, and the first pale whisper of green had been breathed across the hills. Dust leaped where our marbles hit, a small wind blew up from the south and slid across my skin and rumpled my hair, the world and the season and we were young.

We were about to quit, fetch our guns and take into the woods after rabbit, when a shadow fell across us and we saw Uncle Jim and my mother's cousin Andy. Uncle Jim wore a long coat above all his other clothes, and still shivered as he leaned on his cane, and the shrunken hands were blue with cold. Andy wore a kilt, for the pockets, and sandals. He was our town engineer, a stocky man of forty, but once in the prehistoric past before I was born he had been on an expedition to Mars, and this made him a hero for us kids. We never understood why he was not a swaggering corsair. He owned three thousand books at least, more than twice the average in our town. He spent a lot of time with Uncle Jim too, and I didn't know why. Now I see that he was trying to learn about the past from him, not the dead past mummified in the history books but the people who had once been alive.

The old man looked down at us and said: 'You boys aren't wearing a stitch. You'll catch your death of cold.' He had a high, thin voice, but it was steady. In all the years alone, he must have learned how to be firm with himself.

'Oh, nonsense,' said Andy. 'I'll bet it's sixty in the sun.'

'We was going after rabbits,' I said importantly. 'I'll bring mine to your place and your wife can make us a stew.' Like all children, I spent as much time with kinfolk as I did with my ortho-parents, but I favoured Andy's home. His wife was a wonderful cook, his oldest son was better than most on the guitar, and his daughter's chess was just about my speed, neither too good nor too bad.

I'd won most of the marbles this game, so now I gave them back. 'When I was a boy,' said Uncle Jim, 'we played for keeps.'

'What happened after the best shooter had won all the marbles in town?' asked Stinky. 'It's hard work making a good marble, Uncle Jim. I can't hardly replace all I lost anyway.'

'You could have bought some more,' he told him. 'There

29

were stores where you could buy anything.'

'But who made all those marbles?'

'There were factories – '

Imagine that! Big grown men spending their lives making coloured glass balls!

We were almost ready to leave when the Communist showed up. We saw him as he rounded the clump of Trees at the north quarter-section, which was pasture that year. He was on the Middleton road, and dust scuffed up from his bare feet.

A stranger in town is always big news, and we kids started running to meet him till Andy recalled us with a sharp word and reminded us that he was entitled to proper courtesy. So we waited, with our eyes bugging out, till he reached us.

But this was a woebegone stranger. He was tall and thin, like Uncle Jim, but his cape hung in rags about a narrow chest where you could count all the ribs, and under a bald dome of a head was a dirty white beard down to his waist. He walked heavily, leaning on a staff, heavy as Time, and even then I sensed the loneliness like a weight on his thin shoulders.

Andy stepped forward and bowed. 'Greetings and welcome, Freeborn,' he said. 'I am Andrew Jackson Welles, town engineer, and on behalf of the Folks I bid you stay, rest, and refresh yourself.' He didn't just rattle the words off as he would for someone he knew, but declaimed them with great care.

Uncle Jim smiled then, a smile like thawing after a nine year's winter, for this man was as old as himself and born in the same forgotten world. He trod forth and held out his hand. 'Hello, sir,' he said. 'My name is Robbins. Pleased to meet you.' They didn't have very good manners in his day.

'Thank you, Comrade Welles, Comrade Robbins,' said the stranger. His smile was lost somewhere in that tangled mold of whiskers. 'I'm Harry Miller.'

'*Comrade?*' Uncle Jim spoke it slowly, like a word out of a nightmare, and his hand crept back again. 'What do you mean?'

The newcome wanderer straightened and looked at us in a way that frightened me. 'I meant what I said,' he answered. 'I don't make any bones about it. Harry Miller, of the Communist Party of the United States of America!'

Uncle Jim sucked in a long breath. 'But – ' he stammered, 'but I thought . . . at the very least, I thought all you rats were dead.'

30

'Now hold on,' said Andy. 'Your pardon, Freeborn Miller. Our friend isn't, uh, isn't quite himself. Don't take it personally, I beg you.'

There was a grimness in Miller's chuckle. 'Oh, I don't mind. I've been called worse than that.'

'And deserved it!' I had never seen Uncle Jim angry before. His face got red and he stamped his cane in the dust. 'Andy, this, this man is a traitor. D'you hear? He's a foreign agent!'

'You mean you come clear from Russia?' murmured Andy, and we boys clustered near with our ears stiff in the breeze, because a foreigner was a seldom sight.

'No,' said Miller. 'No, I'm from Pittsburgh. Never been to Russia. Wouldn't want to go. Too awful there – they *had* Communism once.'

'Didn't know anybody was left in Pittsburgh,' said Andy. 'I was there last year with a salvage crew, after steel and copper, and we never saw anything but birds.'

'A few. A few. My wife and I – But she died, and I couldn't stay in that rotting empty shell of a city, so I went out on the road.'

'And you can go back on the road,' snarled Uncle Jim.

'Now, please be quiet,' said Andy. 'Come on into town, Freeborn Miller – Comrade Miller, if you prefer. May I invite you to stay with me?'

Uncle Jim grabbed Andy's arm. He shook like a dead leaf in fall, under the heartless fall winds. 'You can't!' he shrieked. 'Don't you see, he'll poison your minds, he'll subvert you, we'll end up slaves to him and his gang of bandits!'

'It seems you've been doing a little mind-poisoning of your own, Mister Robbins,' said Miller.

Uncle Jim stood for a moment, head bent to the ground, and the quick tears of an old man glimmered in his eyes. Then he lifted his face and pride rang in the words: 'I am a Republican.'

'I thought so.' The Communist glanced around and nodded to himself. 'Typical bourgeois pseudo-culture. Look at those men, each out on his own little tractor in his own field, hugging his own little selfishness to him.'

Andy scratched his head. 'What are you talking about, Freeborn?' he asked. 'Those are town machines. Who wants to be bothered with keeping his own tractor and plough and harvester?'

'Oh . . . you mean – ' I could see a light of wonder in the

31

Communist's eyes, and he half stretched out his hands. They were aged hands, I could see the bones just under the dried-out skin. 'You mean you *do* work the land collectively?'

'Why, no. What on earth would be the point of that?' replied Andy. 'A man's entitled to what he raises himself, isn't he?'

'So the land which should be the property of all the people, is parcelled among those kulaks!' flared Miller.

'How in hell's name can land be anybody's property? It's . . . it's land! You can't put forty acres in your pocket and walk off with them.' Andy took a long breath. 'You must have been pretty well cut off from things in Pittsburgh – ate the ancient canned stuff, didn't you? I thought so. It's easy enough to explain. Look, that section out there is being planted in corn by my mother's cousin Glenn. It's his corn, that he swaps for whatever else he needs. But next year, to conserve the soil, it'll be put in alfalfa, and my sister's son Willy takes care of ·it then. As for garden truck and fruit, most of us raise our own, just to get outdoors each day.'

The light faded in our visitor. 'It doesn't make sense,' said Miller, and I could hear how tired he was. It must have been a long hike from Pittsburgh, living off handouts from gypsies and the Lone Farmers.

'I quite agree,' said Uncle Jim with a stiff kind of smile. 'In my father's day – ' He closed his mouth. I knew his father had died in Korea, in some war when he was just a baby, and Uncle Jim had been left to keep the memory and the sad barren pride of it. I remembered my history, which Freeborn Levinsohn taught in our town because he knew it best, and a shiver crept in my skin. A *Communist!* Why, they had killed and tortured Americans . . . only this was a faded rag of a man, he couldn't kill a puppy. It was very odd.

We started towards Townhall. People saw us and began to crowd around, staring and whispering as much as decorum allowed. I strutted with Red and Bob and Stinky, right next to the stranger, the real live Communist, under the eyes of all the other kids.

We passed Joseph's weavery, and his family and apprentices came out to join the goggle eyes. Miller spat in the street. 'I imagine those people are hired!' he said.

'You don't expect them to work for nothing, do you?' asked Andy.

'They should work for the common good.'

'But they do. Every time somebody needs a garment or a

32

blanket, Joseph gets his boys together and they make one. You can buy better stuff from him than most women can make at home.'

'I knew it. The bourgeois exploiter – '

'I only wish that were the case,' said Uncle Jim, tight-lipped.

'You would,' snapped Miller.

'But it isn't. People don't have any drive these days. No spirit of competition. No desire to improve their living standard. No . . . they buy what they need, and wear it while it lasts – and it's made to last damn near forever.' Uncle Jim waved his cane in the air. 'I tell you, Andy, the country's gone to hell. The economy is stagnant. Business has become a bunch of miserable little shops and people making for themselves what they used to buy!'

'I think we're pretty well fed and clothed and housed,' said Andy.

'But where's your . . . your drive? Where's the get-up-and-go, the hustling, that made America great? Look – your wife wears the same model of gown her mother wore. You use a flitter that was built in your father's time. Don't you want anything *better*?'

'Our machinery works well enough,' said Andy. He spoke in a bored voice, this was an old argument to him while the Communist was new. I saw Miller's tattered cape swirl into Si Johansen's carpenter shop and followed.

Si was making a chest of drawers for George Hulme, who was getting married this spring. He put down his tools and answered politely.

'Yes . . . yes, Freeborn . . . sure, I work here . . . Organise? What *for*? Social-like, you mean? But my apprentices got too damn much social life as it is. Every third day a holiday, damn near . . . No, they *ain't* oppressed. Hell, they're my own kin! . . . But there ain't any people who haven't got good furniture. Not unless they're lousy carpenters and too uppity to get help – '

'But the people all over the world!' screamed Miller. 'Don't you have any heart, man? What about the Mexican peons?'

Si Johansen shrugged. 'What about them? If they want to run things different down there, it's their own business.' He put away his electric sander and hollered to his apprentices that they could have the rest of the day off. They'd have taken it anyway, of course, but Si was a little bit bossy.

Andy got Miller out in the street again, and at Townhall the

Mayor came in from the fields and received him. Since good weather was predicted for the whole week, we decided there was no hurry about the planting and we'd spend the afternoon welcoming our guest.

'Bunch of bums!' snorted Uncle Jim. 'Your ancestors stuck by a job till it was finished.'

'This'll get finished in time,' said the Mayor, like he was talking to a baby. 'What's the rush, Jim?'

'Rush? To get on with it – finish it and go on to something else. Better things for better living!'

'For the benefit of your exploiters,' crackled Miller. He stood on the Townhall steps like a starved and angry rooster.

'What exploiters?' The Mayor was as puzzled as me.

'The . . . the big businessmen, the –'

'There aren't any more businessmen,' said Uncle Jim, and a little more life seemed to trickle out of him as he admitted it. 'Our shopkeepers . . . no. They only want to make a living. They've never heard of making a profit. They're too lazy to expand.'

'Then why haven't you got socialism?' Miller's red eyes glared around as if looking for some hidden enemy. 'It's every family for itself. Where's your solidarity?'

'We get along pretty well with each other, Freeborn,' said the Mayor. 'We got courts to settle any arguments.'

'But don't you want to go on, to advance, to –'

'We got enough,' declared the Mayor, patting his belly. 'I couldn't eat any more than I do.'

'But you could wear more!' said Uncle Jim. He jittered on the steps, the poor crazy man, dancing before all our eyes like the puppets in a travelling show. 'You could have your own car, a new model every year with beautiful chrome plate all over it, and new machines to lighten your labour, and –'

' – and to buy those shoddy things, meant only to wear out, you would have to slave your lives away for the capitalists,' said Miller. 'The People must produce for the People.'

Andy traded a glance with the Mayor. 'Look, Freeborn,' he said gently, 'you don't seem to get the point. We don't *want* all those gadgets. We have enough. It isn't worthwhile scheming and working to get more than we have, not while there are girls to love in springtime and deer to hunt in the fall. And when we do work, we'd rather work for ourselves, not for somebody else, whether you call the somebody else a capitalist

34

or the People. Now let's go sit down and take it easy before lunch.'

Wedged between the legs of the Folks, I heard Si Johansen mutter to Joseph Arakelian: 'I don't get it. What would we do with all this machinery? If I had some damn machine to make furniture for me, what'd I do with my hands?'

Joseph lifted his shoulders. 'Beats me, Si. Personally, I'd go nuts watching two people wear the same identical pattern.'

'It might be kind of nice at that,' said Red to me. 'Having a car like they show in Uncle Jim's ma-gazines.'

'Where'd you go in it?' asked Bob.

'Gee, I dunno. To Canada, maybe. But shucks, I can go to Canada any time I can talk my dad into borrowing a flitter.'

'Sure,' said Bob. 'And if you're going less than a hundred miles, you got a horse, haven't you? Who wants an old car?'

I wriggled through the crowd towards the Plaza, where the women were setting up outdoor tables and bringing food for a banquet. The crowd was so thick around our guest where he sat that I couldn't get near, but Stinky and I skun up into the Plaza Tree, a huge grey oak, and crawled along a branch till we hung just above his head. It was a bare and liver-spotted head, wobbling on a thread of neck, but he darted it around and spoke shrill.

Andy and the Mayor sat near him, puffing their pipes, and Uncle Jim was there too. The Folks had let him in so they could watch the fireworks. That was perhaps a cruel and thoughtless thing to do, but how could we know? Uncle Jim had always been so peaceful, and we'd never had two crazy men in town.

'I was still young,' Comrade Miller was saying, 'I was only a boy, and there were still telecasts. I remember how my mother cried, when we knew the Soviet Union was dissolved. On that night she made me swear to keep faith, and I have, I have, and now I'm going to show you the truth and not a pack of capitalist lies.'

'Whatever did happen to Russia?' wondered Ed Mulligan. He was the town psychiatrist, he'd trained at Menninger clear out in Kansas. 'I never would have thought the Communists would let their people go free, not from what I've read of them.'

'The Communists were corrupted,' said Miller fiercely. 'Filthy bourgeois lies and money.'

'Now that isn't true,' said Uncle Jim. 'They simply got corrupt and easygoing of their own accord. Any tyrant will. And

35

so they didn't foresee what changes the new technology would make, they blithely introduced it, and in the course of one generation their Iron Curtain rusted away. Nobody *listened* to them any more.'

'Pretty correct, Jim,' said Andy. He saw my face among the twigs, and winked at me. 'There was some violence, it was more complicated than you think but that's essentially what happened. Trouble is, you can't seem to realise that it happened in the U.S.A. also.'

Miller shook his withered head. 'Marx proved that technological advances mean inevitable progress towards socialism,' he said. 'Oh, the cause has been set back, but the day is coming.'

'Why, maybe you're right up to a point,' said Andy. 'But you see, science and society went beyond that point. Maybe I can give you a simple explanation.'

'If you wish,' said Miller, grumpy-like.

'Well, I've studied the period. Technology made it possible for a few people and acres to feed the whole country, so there were millions of acres lying idle; you could buy them for peanuts. Meanwhile the cities were over-taxed, under-represented, and choked by their own traffic. Along came the cheap sun-power unit and the high-capacity accumulator. Those made it possible for a man to supply most of his own wants, not work his heart out for someone else to pay the inflated prices demanded by an economy where every single business was subsidised or protected at the taxpayer's expense. Also, by living in the new way, a man cut down his money income to the point where he had to pay almost no taxes – so he actually lived better on a shorter work week.

'More and more, people tended to drift out and settle in small country communities. They consumed less, so there was a great depression, and that drove still more people out to fend for themselves. By the time big business and organised labour realised what was happening and tried to get laws passed against what they called un-American practices, it was too late; nobody was interested. It all happened so gradually, you see . . . but it happened, and I think we're happier now.'

'Ridiculous!' said Miller. 'Capitalism went bankrupt, as Marx foresaw two hundred years ago, but its vicious influence was still so powerful that instead of advancing to collectivism you went back to being peasants.'

'Please,' said the Mayor. I could see he was annoyed, and

thought that maybe peasants were somebody not Freeborn. 'Uh, maybe we can pass the time with a little singing.'

Though he had no voice to speak of, courtesy demanded that Miller be asked to perform first. He stood up and quavered out something about a guy named Joe Hill. It had a nice tune, but even a nine-year-old like me knew it was lousy poetics. A childish *a-b-c-b* scheme of masculine rhymes and not a double metaphor anywhere. Besides, who cares what happened to some little tramp when there are hunting songs and epics about interplanetary explorers to make? I was glad when Andy took over and gave us some music with muscle in it.

Lunch was called, and I slipped down from the Tree and found a seat nearby. Comrade Miller and Uncle Jim glowered at each other across the table, but nothing was said till after the meal, a couple of hours later. People had kind of lost interest in the stranger as they learned he'd spent his life huddled in a dead city, and wandered off for the dancing and games. Andy hung around, not wanting to but because he was Miller's host.

The Communist sighed and got up. 'You've been nice to me,' he said.

'I thought we were all a bunch of capitalists,' sneered Uncle Jim.

'It's man I'm interested in, wherever he is and whatever conditions he has to live under,' said Miller.

Uncle Jim lifted his voice with his cane: 'Man! You claim to care for man, you who only killed and enslaved him?'

'Oh, come off it, Jim,' said Andy. 'That was a long time ago. Who cares at this late date?'

'*I* do!' Uncle Jim started crying, but he looked at Miller and walked up to him, stiff-legged, hands clawed. 'They killed my father! Men died by the tens of thousands for an ideal! And you don't care! The whole damn country has lost its guts!'

I stood under the Tree, one hand on the cool rough comfort of its bark. I was a little afraid, because I did not understand. Surely Andy, who had been sent by the United Townships Research Foundation all the long black way to Mars, just to gather knowledge, was no coward. Surely my father, a gentle man and full of laughter, did not lack guts. What was it we were supposed to want?

'Why, you bootlicking belly-crawling lackey,' yelled Miller, 'it was you who gutted them! It was you who murdered work-

ing men, and roped their sons into your dummy unions, and
. . . and . . . what about the Mexican poens?'

Andy tried to come between them. Miller's staff clattered on
his head. Andy stepped back, wiping the blood off, looking
helpless, as the old crazy men howled at each other. He couldn't
use force – he might hurt them.

Perhaps, in that moment, he realised. 'It's all right, Freeborn,' he said quickly. 'It's all right. We'll listen to you. Look,
you can have a nice debate tonight, right in Townhall, and
we'll all come and – '

He was too late. Uncle Jim and Comrade Miller were already
fighting, thin arms locked and dim eyes full of tears because
they had no strength left to destroy what they hated. But I
think, now, that the hate arose from a baffled love. They both
loved us in a queer maimed fashion, and we did not care, we
did not care.

Andy got some men together and separated the two and
they were led off to different houses for a nap. But when Dr
Simmons looked in on Uncle Jim a few hours later, he was
gone. The doctor hurried off to find the Communist, and he
was gone too.

I only learned that afterward, since I went off to play tag
and pom-pom-pullaway with the other kids down where the
river flowed cool and dark. It was in the same river, next morning, that Constable Thompson found the Communist and the
Republican. Nobody knew what had happened. They met
under the Trees, alone, at dusk when bonfires were being lit
and the Elders making merry around them and lovers stealing
off into the woods. That's all anybody knows. We gave them a
nice funeral.

It was the talk of the town for a week, and in fact the whole
state of Ohio heard about it, but then the talk died and the
old crazy men were forgotten. That was the year the Brother-
hood came into power in the north, and men worried what it
could mean. The next spring they learned, and there was an
alliance made and war went across the hills. For the Brother-
hood gang, just as it had threatened, planted no Trees at all,
and such evil cannot go unpunished.

COMMENT ON
THE LAST OF THE DELIVERERS

This story may surprise a few readers. My attitude towards politics, especially international politics, is pretty hardnosed, and I have been active in the attempt to get a 'forward strategy' adopted. It shows in various fiction pieces, too. So why pick for reprint anything that depicts our opponents as human and says that our conflict with them may one day cease to have meaning?

Well, they *are* human. Antagonisms which are not ended by the obliteration of one side do tend to fade away. Remember the wars of religion and their outcome. Then think what ruin they brought without ever accomplishing their official purpose. My devout hope is that the contest now going on in the world will not erupt into genocide but will slowly dissolve until all men can again see their common humanity. My opinion is that, at present, the only chance for such an outcome lies in creating and maintaining such conditions that totalitarianism has a negative payoff. But I am not fanatic in this belief. Fanaticism is the very thing to be opposed, under any name. The happy ending just might come about through some development which today we cannot predict. We must remain open to any such opportunity, or the blame for catastrophe could fall squarely on us.

Science fiction can be of some small service in keeping us reminded of how unknowable the future really is, how great a need we have for flexibility. The story here suggests one conceivable course of events. The likelihood of its bearing any relation to what is actually going to happen is so minute that I have resisted the temptation to update it. The time can better be devoted to exploring other possibilities.

At the risk of beating to death a point which should perhaps be left implicit in the narrative, let me add something else. (After all, one is not often offered a pulpit like this.) That phrase 'happy ending' is mere shorthand. No doubt Cinderella had a pleasant marriage. But did she not find that a prince's wife has burdens of her own to bear? Struggling to learn the

39

formalities of life at a royal court, did she not, once in a while, feel the least bit nostalgic for her kitchen?

Collectively as well as individually, man is never going to find perfection. Some societies he builds may work better, for the majority anyhow, than others. But all of them will have their built-in drawbacks. Their affairs will always be conducted with a high irreducible minimum of inefficiency. Read: sentimentalism, magical thinking, shortsightedness, vanity, greed, envy, hate, fear – not because we are evil but because we are mortal.

The failure to recognise this has made too much science fiction politically so naïve as to be unbelievable. So has the failure of many authors to understand the day-to-day action of politics. It is not enough to know how a spaceship works; ships have crews and crews have organisation. Engines operate under the laws of economics as well as the laws of thermodynamics. The people who build them reached the decision to do so through decision-making processes. These human mechanisms are known. You can find them in a book or in a visit to City Hall.

I don't claim to have mastered the lesson very well myself. But more of us writers should make the attempt, and more readers should call us on it when we fail.

POUL ANDERSON

INTRODUCTION TO
FOUNDING FATHER

Since early 1958, what with one thing or another, I have scarcely written as many as a dozen science fiction stories, all of them quite short. In the years preceding 1958, on the other hand, I had written up to 200,000 words of science fiction a year, so science fiction editors missed me a bit.

Various devices were used by them to stir me out of my lethargy (or, rather, to divert my energies into the old accustomed channels – for it wasn't that I had stopped writing by any means; it was just that I was writing material other than science fiction).

Some of the devices worked for I have my weaknesses. One is a tearful sentimentality about old times, old friends, old feats. Editors who know this are sometimes quite merciless in their manipulation of said sentimentality.

About a year ago, Fred Pohl, editor of Galaxy decided to squeeze my sentiment. He pointed out that the October 1965 issue of Galaxy would be coming up and that it was the fifteenth anniversary issue.

'The fifteenth anniversary issue,' I said, round-eyed, as fifteen years rolled back in my mind and I was suddenly much younger. 'How could so much time have passed while I was looking the other way.'

'And,' said Fred, impressively, 'we want all the authors who contributed to the first issue to contribute to this one. A matter of sentiment.'

Sentiment! A lump was in my throat at once. My blue eyes misted with tears. 'I'll do it,' I said, brokenly.

'Good,' said Fred, rising to pass on to the next victim. 'Here's the cover illustration. I want a story built around it,' and was gone before I could object.

I was appalled. I know that many authors have written stories to match cover-paintings and that they found no difficulty in doing so. This did not apply to me, however. I was always relieved beyond measure that no editor had ever thought to ask me to do one. To test myself, you see, I had often tried to imagine a story based on some magazine cover before opening the magazine to read the actual story it was based on. The complete failure of my efforts was always humiliating.

But I couldn't refuse this time. My honour was engaged and I have all sorts of peculiar notions about my honour. In fact, I am very sentimental about it.

So I stared at the cover illustration which I will now describe to you. In the foreground was a grave, handsome face behind the glass visor of a space helmet. To his left, in the background, were four rude wooden crosses, fading into the distance against an alien sky. Balanced on the wooden upright of each cross was a space helmet. Leaning against the base of each cross was a pair of oxygen cylinders.

Clearly we had here one live astronaut and four dead astronauts. How did they come to die? Had the living astronaut killed them? Had he tried to save them and failed? Did he know they were there? Did he care?

Nothing came to me at all.

Help! Help! What to do!

Remember, I told myself with despairing sentimentality, this is for good old Galaxy. This is for good old Horace Gold and those good old talks about science fiction plots in the good old days. What would good old Horace Gold have done?

From out the misty past came floating up to me one of good old Horace's favourite comments: 'Stand it on its head,' he used to say. 'When you think of an obvious situation, consider it in reverse. Are you sure that B follows A? Maybe A follows B? Or maybe C follows A?'

So I looked at the cover illustration again. There were the four crosses with the helmets and the oxygen tanks. Did the crosses have to signify death? Maybe they signified life?

Exactly!

So I wrote the story, and here it is!

ISAAC ASIMOV

FOUNDING FATHER

by

Isaac Asimov

The original combination of catastrophes had taken place five years ago – five revolutions of this planet, HC-12549d by the charts, and nameless otherwise. Six-plus revolutions of Earth, but who was counting – any more?

If the men back home knew, they might say it was a heroic fight, an epic of the Galactic Corps; five men against a hostile world, holding their bitter own for five (or six-plus) years. And now they were dying, the battle lost after all. Three were in final coma, a fourth had his yellow-tinged eyeballs still open, and a fifth was yet on his feet.

But it was no question of heroism at all. It had been five men fighting off boredom and despair and maintaining their metallic bubble of livability only for the most unheroic reason that there was nothing else to do while life remained.

If any of them felt stimulated by the battle, he never mentioned it. After the first year, they stopped talking of rescue, and after the second, a moratorium descended on the word, 'Earth'.

But one word remained always present. If unspoken it had to be found in their thoughts: 'Ammonia'.

It had come first while the landing was being scratched out against all odds on limping motors and in a battered space can.

You allow for bad breaks, of course; you expect a certain number – but one at a time. A stellar flare fries out the hyper-circuits – that can be repaired, given time. A meteorite disaligns the feeder-valves – they can be straightened, given time. A trajectory is miscalculated under tension and a momentarily unbearable acceleration tears out the jump-antennae and dulls the senses of every man on board   but antennae can be replaced and senses will recover, given time.

The chances are one in countless many that all three will happen at once; and still less that they will happen during a

43

particularly tricky landing when the one necessary currency for the correction of all errors, time, is the one thing that is most lacking.

The *Cruiser John* hit that one chance in countless many, and it made a final landing, for it would never lift off a planetary surface again.

That it had landed essentially intact was itself a near-miracle. The five were given life for some years at least. Beyond that, only the blundering arrival of another ship could help, but no one expected that. They had had their life's share of coincidences, they knew, and all had been bad.

That was that.

And the key word was 'ammonia'. With the surface spiralling upward, and death (mercifully quick) facing them at considerably better than even odds, Chou somehow had time to note the absorption spectograph, which was registering raggedly.

'Ammonia,' he cried out. The others heard but there was no time to pay attention. There was only the wrenching fight against a quick death for the sake of a slow one.

When they landed finally, on sandy ground with sparse, ragged bluish vegetation; reedy grass; stunted tree-like objects with blue bark and no leaves; no sign of animal life; and with an almost greenish cloud-streaked sky above – the word came back to haunt them.

'Ammonia?' said Petersen heavily.

Chou said, 'Four per cent.'

'Impossible,' said Petersen.

But it wasn't. The books didn't say impossible. What the Galactic Corps had discovered was that a planet of a certain mass and volume and at a certain temperature was an ocean planet and had one of two atmospheres: nitrogen/oxygen or nitrogen/carbon dioxide. In the former case, life was rampant in the latter, it was primitive.

No one checked beyond mass, volume and temperature any longer. One took the atmosphere (one or the other of them) for granted. But the books didn't say it had to be so; just that it always was so. Other atmospheres were thermodynamically possible, but extremely unlikely so they weren't found in actual practice.

Until now. The men of the *Cruiser John* had found one and

were bathed for the rest of such life as they could eke out by a nitrogen/carbon dioxide/ammonia atmosphere.

The men converted their ship into an underground bubble of Earth-type surroundings. They could not lift off the surface, nor could they drive a communicating beam through hyperspace, but all else was salvageable. To make up for inefficiencies in the cycling system, they could even tap the planet's own water and air supply within limits; provided, of course, they subtracted the ammonia.

They organised exploring parties since their suits were in excellent condition and it passed the time. The planet was harmless; no animal life; sparse plant life everywhere. Blue, always blue; ammoniated chlorophyll; ammoniated protein.

They set up laboratories, analysed the plant components, studied microscopic sections, compiled vast volumes of findings. They tried growing native plants in ammonia-free atmosphere and failed. They made themselves into geologists and studied the planet's crust; astronomers and studied the spectrum of the planet's sun.

Barrere would say sometimes, 'Eventually, the Corps will reach this planet again and we'll leave a legacy of knowledge for them. It's a unique planet after all. There might not be another Earth-type with ammonia in all the Milky way.'

'Great,' said Sandropoulos, bitterly. 'What luck for us.'

Sandropoulos worked out the thermodynamics of the situation. 'A metrastable system,' he said. 'The ammonia disappears steadily through geochemical oxidation that forms nitrogen; the plants utilise nitrogen and reform ammonia, adapting themselves to the presence of ammonia. If the rate of plant formation of ammonia dropped two per cent, a declining spiral would set in. Plant life would wither, reducing the ammonia still further and so on.'

'You mean if we killed enough plant life,' said Vlassov, 'we could wipe out the ammonia.'

'If we had air-sleds and wide-angle blasters, and a year to work in, we might,' said Sandropoulos, 'but we haven't and there's a better way. If we could get our plants going, the formation of oxygen through photosynthesis would increase the rate of ammonia oxidation. Even a small localised rise would lower the ammonia in the region, stimulate Earth-plant growth further, and inhibit the native growth, drop the ammonia further and so on.'

They became gardeners through all the growing season. That was, after all, routine for the Galactic Corps. Life on Earth-type planets was usually of the water/protein type, but variation was infinite and other-world food was rarely nourishing and it even more often happened (not always, but often) that some types of Earth-plants would overrun and drown out the native flora. With the native flora held down, other Earth-plants could take root.

Dozens of planets had been converted into new Earths in this fashion. In the process Earth-plants developed hundreds of hardy varieties that flourished under extreme conditions – all the better with which to seed the next planet.

The ammonia would kill any Earth-plant, but seed at the disposal of the *Cruiser John* were not true Earth-plants but other-world mutations of these plants. They fought hard but not well enough. Some varieties grew in a feeble, sickly manner and died.

At that they did better than did microscopic life. The planet's bacterioids were far more flourishing than was the planet's straggly blue plant-life. The native micro-organisms drowned out any attempt at competition from Earth-samples. The attempt to seed the alien soil with Earth-type bacterial flora in order to aid the Earth-plants failed.

Vlassov shook his head, 'It wouldn't do anyway. If our bacteria survived, it would only be by adapting to the presence of ammonia.'

Sandropoulos said, 'Bacteria won't help us. We need the plants; they carry the oxygen manufacturing systems.'

'We could make some ourselves,' said Petersen. 'We could electrolyse water.'

'How long will our equipment last? If we could only get our plants going it would be like electrolysing water forever, little by little, but year after year, till the planet gave up.'

Barrere said, 'Let's treat the soil then. It's rotten with ammonium salts. We'll bake the salts out and replace the ammonia-free soil.'

'And what about the atmosphere?' asked Chou.

'In ammonia-free soil, they may catch hold despite the atmosphere. They almost make it as is.'

They worked like longshoremen, but with no real end in view. None really thought it would work, and there was no future for themselves, personally, even if it did work. But working passed the days.

The next growing season, they had their ammonia-free soil, but Earth-plants still grew only feebly. They even placed domes over several shoots and pumped ammonia-free air within. It helped slightly but not enough. They adjusted the chemical composition of the soil in every possible fashion. There was no reward.

The feeble shoots produced their tiny whiffs of oxygen, but not enough to topple the ammonia atmosphere off its base.

'One more push,' said Sandropoulos, 'one more. We're rocking it; we're rocking it; but we can't knock it over.'

Their tools and equipment blunted and wore out with time and the future closed in steadily. Each month there was less room for manoeuvre.

When the end came at last, it was with almost gratifying suddenness. There was no name to place on the weakness and vertigo. No one actually suspected direct ammonia poisoning. Still, they were living off the algal growth of what had once been ship-hydroponics for years and the growths were themselves aberrant with possible ammonia contamination.

It could have been the workings of some native microorganism which might finally have learned to feed off them. It might even have been an Earthly micro-organism, mutated under the conditions of a strange world.

So three died at last and did so, circumstances be praised, painlessly. They were glad to go, and leave the useless fight.

Chou said, in a voiceless whisper, 'It's foolish to lose so badly.'

Petersen, alone of the five to be on his feet (was he immune, whatever it was?) turned a grieving face towards his only living companion.

'Don't die,' he said, 'don't leave me alone.'

Chou tried to smile. 'I have no choice. But you can follow us, old friend. Why fight? The tools are gone and there is no way of winning now, if there ever was.'

Even now Petersen fought off final despair by concentrating on the fight against the atmosphere. But his mind was weary, his heart worn out, and when Chou died the next hour, he was left with four corpses to work with.

He stared at the bodies, counting over the memories, stretching them back (now that he was alone and dared wail) to Earth itself, which he had last seen on a visit eleven years before.

He would have to bury the bodies. He would break off the bluish branches of the native leafless trees and build crosses of them. He would hang the space helmet of each man on top and prop the oxygen cylinders below. Empty cylinders to symbolise the lost fight.

A foolish sentiment for men who could no longer care, and for future eyes that might never see.

But he was doing it for himself, to show respect for his friends, and respect for himself, too, for he was not the kind of man to leave his friends untended in death while he himself could stand.

Besides –

Besides? He sat in weary thought for some moments.

While he was still alive, he would fight with such tools as were left. He would bury his friends.

He buried each in a spot of ammonia-free soil they had so laboriously built up; buried them without shroud and without clothing; leaving them naked in the hostile ground for the slow decomposition that would come with their own micro-organisms before those, too, died with the inevitable invasion of the native bacterioids.

Petersen placed each cross, with its helmet and oxygen cylinders, propped each with rocks then turned away, grim and sad-eyed, to return to the buried ship that he now inhabited alone.

He worked each day and eventually the symptoms came for him, too.

He struggled into his space suit and came to the surface for what he knew would be one last time.

He fell to his knees on the garden-plots. The Earth plants were green. They had lived longer than ever before. They looked healthy, even vigorous. They had patched the soil, babied the atmosphere, and now Petersen had used the last tool, the only one remaining at his disposal, and he had given them fertiliser as well –

Out of the slowly corrupting flesh of the Earthmen came the nutrients that supplied the final push. Out of the Earth-plants came the oxygen that would beat back the ammonia and push the planet out of the unaccountable niche into which it had stuck.

If Earthmen ever came again (when? a million years hence?)

they would find a nitrogen/oxygen atmosphere and a limited flora strangely reminiscent of Earth's.

The crosses would rot and decay, the metal rust and decompose. The bones might fossilise and remain to give a hint as to was happened. Their own records, sealed away, might be found.

But none of that mattered. If nothing at all was ever found, the planet itself, the whole planet, would be their monument.

And Petersen lay down to die in the midst of their victory.

END-GAME

by

J. G. Ballard

After his trial they gave Constantin a villa, an allowance and an executioner. The villa was small and high-walled, and had obviously been used for the purpose before. The allowance was adequate to Constantin's needs – he was never permitted to go out and his meals were prepared for him by a police orderly. The executioner was his own. Most of the time they sat on the enclosed veranda overlooking the narrow stone garden, playing chess with a set of large well-worn pieces.

. The executioner's name was Malek. Officially he was Constantin's supervisor, and responsible for maintaining the villa's tenuous contact with the outside world, now hidden from sight beyond the steep walls, and for taking the brief telephone call that came promptly at nine o'clock every morning. However, his real role was no secret between them. A powerful, doughy-faced man with an anonymous expression, Malek at first intensely irritated Constantin, who had been used to dealing with more subtle sets of responses. Malek impassively followed him around the villa, never interfering – unless Constantin tried to bribe the orderly for a prohibited newspaper, when Malek merely gestured with a slight turn of one of his large hands, face registering no disapproval, but cutting off the attempts as irrevocably as a bulkhead – nor making any suggestions as to how Constantin should spend his time. Like a large bear, he sat motionlessly in the lounge in one of the faded armchairs, watching Constantin.

After a week Constantin tired of reading the old novels in the bottom shelf of the bookcase – somewhere among the grey well-thumbed pages he had hoped to find a message from one of his predecessors – and invited Malek to play chess. The set of chipped mahogany pieces reposed on one of the empty shelves of the bookcase, the only item of decoration or recreational equipment in the villa. Apart from the books and the chess set the small six-roomed house was completely devoid of ornament. There were no curtains or picture rails, bedside tables or standard lamps, and the only electrical fittings were the lights recessed behind thick opaque bowls into the ceilings. Obviously the chess set and the row of novels had been provided deliberately, each representing one of the alternative pastimes available to the temporary tenants of the villa. Men of a phlegmatic or philosophical temperament stoically resigned to the inevitability of their fate, would choose to read the novels, sinking backwards into a self-anaesthetised trance as they waded through the turgid prose of those nineteenth-century romances.

On the other hand, men of a more volatile and extrovert disposition would obviously choose the chess, unable to resist the opportunity to exercise their Machiavellian talents for positional manoeuvre to the last. The games of chess would help to maintain their unconscious optimism and, more subtly, sublimate or divert any attempts at escape.

When Constantin suggested that they play chess Malek promptly agreed, and so they spent the next long month as the late summer turned to autumn. Constantin was glad he had chosen chess; the game brought him into immediate personal involvement with Malek, and like all condemned men he had soon developed a powerful emotional transference on to what effectively was the only person left in his life.

At present it was neither negative nor positive; but a relationship of acute dependence – already Malek's notional personality was becoming overlayed by the associations of all the anonymous but nonetheless potent figures of authority whom Constantin could remember since his earliest childhood: his own father, the priest at the seminary he had seen hanged after the revolution, the first senior commissars, the party secretaries at the ministry of foreign affairs and, ultimately, the members of the central committee themselves. Here, where the anonymous faces had crystalised into those of closely observed colleagues and rivals, the process seemed to come full circle, so that he himself was identified with those shadowy personas who had authorised his death and were not represented by Malek.

Constantin had also, of course, become dominated by another obsession, the need to know: *when*? In the weeks after the trial and sentence he had remained in a curiously euphoric

51

state, too stunned to realise that the dimension of time still existed for him, he had already died *a posteriori*. But gradually the will to live, and his old determination and ruthlessness, which had served him so well for thirty years, reasserted themselves, and he realised that a small hope still remained to him. How long exactly in terms of time he could only guess, but if he could master Malek his survival became a real possibility.

The question remained: When?

Fortunately he could be completely frank with Malek. The first point he established immediately.

'Malek,' he asked on the tenth move one morning, when he had completed his development and was relaxing for a moment. 'Tell me, do you know – when?'

Malek looked up from the board, his large almost bovine eyes gazing blandly at Constantin. 'Yes, Mr Constantin, I know when.' His voice was deep and functional, as expressionless as a weighing machine's.

Constantin sat back reflectively. Outside the glass panes of the veranda the rain fell steadily on the solitary fir tree which had maintained a precarious purchase among the stones under the wall. A few miles to the south-west of the villa were the outskirts of the small port, one of the dismal so-called 'coastal resorts' where junior ministry men and party hacks were sent for their bi-annual holidays. The weather, however, seemed peculiarly inclement, the sun never shining through the morose clouds, and for a moment, before he checked himself, Constantin felt glad to be within the comparative warmth of the villa.

'Let me get this straight,' he said to Malek. 'You don't merely know in a general sense – for example, after receiving an instruction from so-and-so – but you know *specifically* when?'

'Exactly.' Malek moved his queen out of the game. His chess was sound but without flair or a personal style, suggesting that he had improved merely by practice – most of his opponents, Constantin realised with sardonic amusement, would have been players of a high class.

'You know the *day* and the *hour* and the *minute*,' Constantin pressed. Malek nodded slowly, most of his attention upon the game, and Constantin rested his smooth sharp chin on one hand, watching his opponent. 'It could be within the next ten seconds, or again, it might not be for ten years?'

'As you say.' Malek gestured at the board. 'Your move.'

Constantin waved this aside. 'I know, but don't let's rush it. These games are played on many levels, Malek. People who talk about three-dimensional chess obviously know nothing about the present form.' Occasionally he made these openings in the hope of loosening Malek's tongue, but conversation with him seemed to be impossible.

Abruptly he sat forward across the board, his eyes searching Malek's. 'You alone know the date, Malek, and as you have said, it might not be for ten years – or twenty. Do you think you can keep such a secret to yourself for so long?'

Malek made no attempt to answer this, and waited for Constantin to resume play. Now and then his eyes inspected the corners of the veranda, or glanced at the stone garden outside. From the kitchen came the occasional sounds of the orderly's boots scraping the floor as he lounged by the telephone on the deal table.

As he scrutinised the board Constantin wondered how he could provoke any response whatever from Malek; the man had shown no reaction at the mention of ten years, although the period was ludicrously far ahead. In all probability their real game would be a short one. The indeterminate date of the execution, which imbued the procedure with such a bizarre flavour, was not intended to add an element of torture or suspense to the condemned's last days, but simply to obscure and confuse the very fact of his exit. If a definite date were known in advance there might be a last-minute rally of sympathy, an attempt to review the sentence and perhaps apportion the blame elsewhere, and the unconscious if not conscious sense of complicity in the condemned man's crimes might well provoke an agonised reappraisal and, after the execution of the sentence, a submerged sense of guilt upon which opportunists and intriguers could play to advantage.

By means of the present system, however, all these dangers and unpleasant side-effects were obviated, the accused was removed from his place in the hierarchy when the opposition to him was at its zenith and conveniently handed over to the judiciary, and thence to one of the courts of star chamber whose proceedings were always held in camera and whose verdicts were never announced.

As far as his former colleagues were concerned, he had disappeared into the endless corridor world of the bureaucratic

53

purgatories, his case permanently on file but never irrevocably closed. Above all, the fact of his guilt was never established and confirmed. As Constantin was aware, he himself had been convicted upon a technicality in the margins of the main indictment against him, a mere procedural device, like a bad twist in the plot of a story, designed solely to bring the investigation to a close. Although he knew the real nature of his crime, Constantin had never been formally notified of his guilt; in fact the court had gone out of its way to avoid preferring any serious charges against him whatever.

This ironic inversion of the classical Kafkaesque situation, by which, instead of admitting his guilt to a non-existent crime, he was forced to connive in a farce maintaining his innocence of offences he knew full well he had committed, was preserved in his present situation at the execution villa.

The psychological basis was more obscure but in some way far more threatening, the executioner beckoning his victim towards him with a beguiling smile, reassuring him that all was forgiven. Here he played upon, not those unconscious feelings of anxiety and guilt, but that innate conviction of individual survival, that obsessive preoccupation with personal immortality which is merely a disguised form of the universal fear of the image of one's own death. It was this assurance that all was well, and the absence of any charges of guilt or responsibility, which had made so orderly the queues into the gas chambers.

At present the paradoxical face of this diabolical device was worn by Malek, his lumpy amorphous features and neutral but ambiguous attitude making him seem less a separate personality than the personification of the apparat of the state. Perhaps the sardonic title of 'supervisor' was nearer the truth than had seemed at first sight, and that Malek's real role was simply to officiate, or at the most serve as moderator, at a trial by ordeal in which Constantin was his own accused, prosecutor and judge.

However, he reflected as he examined the board, aware of Malek's bulky presence across the pieces, this would imply that they had completely misjudged his own personality, with its buoyancy and almost gallic verve and panache. He, of all people, would be the last to take his own life in an orgy of self-confessed guilt. Not for him the neurotic suicide so loved of the Slav. As long as there were a way out he would cheerfully shoulder any burden of guilt, tolerant of his own weaknesses, ready to shrug them off with a quip. This insouciance had always been his strongest ally.

His eyes searched the board, roving down the open files of the queens and bishops, as if the answer to the pressing enigma were to be found in these polished corridors.

When? His own estimate was two months. Almost certainly (and he had no fear here that he was rationalising) it would not be within the next two or three days, nor even the next fortnight. Haste was always unseemly, quite apart from violating the whole purpose of the exercise. Two months would see him safely into limbo, and be sufficiently long for the suspense to break him down and reveal any secret allies, sufficiently brief to fit his particular crime.

Two months? Not as long as he might have wished. As he translated his queen's bishop into play Constantin began to map out his strategy for defeating Malek. The first task, obviously, was to discover when Malek was to carry out the execution, partly to give him peace of mind, but also to allow him to adjust the context of his escape. A physical leap to freedom over the wall would be pointless. Contacts had to be established, pressure brought to bear at various sensitive points in the hierarchy, paving the way for a reconsideration of his case. All this would take time.

His thoughts were interrupted by the sharp movement of Malek's left hand across the board, followed by a guttural grunt. Surprised by the speed and economy with which Malek had moved his piece, as much as by the fact that he himself was in check, Constantin sat forward and examined his position with more care. He glanced with grudging respect at Malek, who had sat back as impassively as ever, the knight he had deftly taken on the edge of the table in front of him. His eyes watched Constantin with their usual untroubled calm, like those of an immensely patient governess, his great shoulders hidden within the bulky suiting. But for a moment, when he had leaned across the board, Constantin had seen the powerful extension and flexion of his shoulder musculature.

Don't look so smug, my dear Malek, Constantin said to himself with a wry smile. At least I know now that you are left-handed. Malek had taken the knight with one hand, hooking

55

the piece between the thick knuckles of his ring and centre fingers, and then substituting his queen with a smart tap, a movement not easily performed in the centre of the crowded board. Useful though the confirmation was – Constantin had noticed Malek apparently trying to conceal his left-handedness during their meals and when opening and closing the windows – he found this sinistral aspect of Malek's personality curiously disturbing, an indication that there would be nothing predictable about his opponent, or the ensuing struggle of wits between them. Even Malek's apparent lack of sharp intelligence was belied by the astuteness of his last move.

Constantin was playing white, and had chosen the Queen's Gambit, assuming that the fluid situation invariably resulting from the opening would be to his advantage and allow him to get on with the more serious task of planning his escape. But Malek had avoided any possible errors, steadily consolidating his position, and had even managed to launch a counter-gambit, offering a knight-to-bishop exchange which would soon undermine Constantin's position if he accepted.

'A good move, Malek,' he commented. 'But perhaps a little risky in the long run.' Declining the exchange, he lamely blocked the checking queen with an interposed pawn.

Malek stared stolidly at the board, his heavy policeman's face, with its almost square frame from one jaw angle to the other, betraying no sign of thought. His approach, Constantin reflected as he watched his opponent, would be that of the pragmatist, judging always by immediate capability rather than by any concealed intentions. As if confirming this diagnosis, Malek simply returned his queen to her former square, unwilling or unable to exploit the advantage he had gained and satisfied by the captured piece.

Bored by the lower key on to which the game had descended, and the prospect of similar games ahead, Constantin castled his king to safety. For some reason, obviously irrational, he assumed that Malek would not kill him in the middle of a game, particularly if he, Malek, were winning. He recognised that this was an unconscious reason for wanting to play chess in the first place, and had no doubt motivated the many others who had also sat with Malek on the veranda, listening to the late summer rain. Suppressing a sudden pang of fear, Constantin examined Malek's powerful hands protruding from his cuffs like two joints of meat. If Malek wanted to, he could probably kill Constantin with his bare hands.

That raised a second question, almost as fascinating as the first.

'Malek, another point,' Constantin sat back, searching in his pockets for imaginary cigarettes (none were allowed him). 'Forgive my curiosity, but I am an interested party, as it were – ' He flashed Malek his brightest smile, a characteristically incisive thrust modulated by ironic self-deprecation which had been so successful with his secretaries and at ministry receptions, but the assay at humour failed to move Malek. 'Tell me, do you know . . . how – ?' Searching for some euphemism, he repeated: 'Do you know how you are going to . . . ?' and then gave up the attempt, cursing Malek to himself for lacking the social grace to rescue him from his awkwardness.

Malek's chin rose slightly, a minimal nod. He showed no signs of being bored or irritated by Constantin's laboured catechism, or of having noticed his embarrassment.

'What is it, then?' Constantin pressed, recovering himself. 'Pistol, pill or – ' with a harsh laugh he pointed through the window ' – do you set up a guillotine in the rain? I'd like to know.'

Malek looked down at the chess-board, his features more glutinous and dough-like than ever. Flatly, he said: 'It has been decided.'

Constantin snorted. 'What on earth does *that* mean?' he snapped belligerently. 'Is it painless?'

For once Malek smiled, a thin smear of amusement hung fleetingly around his mouth. 'Have you ever killed anything, Mr Constantin?' he asked quietly. 'Yourself, personally, I mean.'

'Touché,' Constantin granted. He laughed deliberately, trying to dispel the tension. 'A perfect reply.' To himself he said: 'I mustn't let curiosity get the upper hand, the man was laughing at me.'

'Of course,' he went on, 'death is always painful. I merely wondered whether, in the legal sense of the term, it would be humane. But I can see that you are a professional, Malek, and the question answers itself. A great relief, believe me. There are as many sadists about, perverts and the like – ' again he

57

watched carefully to see if the implied sneer provoked Malek ' – that one can't be too grateful for a clean curtain fall. It's good to know. I can devote these last days to putting my affairs in order and coming to terms with the world. If only I knew how long there was left I could make my preparations accordingly. One can't be forever saying one's last prayers. You see my point?'

Colourlessly, Malek said: 'The Prosecutor-General advised you to make your final arrangements immediately after the trial.'

'But what does that mean?' Constantin asked, pitching his voice a calculated octave higher. 'I'm a human being, not a book-keeper's ledger that can be totted up and left to await the auditor's pleasure. I wonder if you realise, Malek, the courage this situation demands from me? It's easy for you to sit there – '

Abruptly Malek stood up, sending a shiver of terror through Constantin. With a glance at the sealed windows, he moved around the chess table towards the lounge. 'We will postpone the game,' he said. Nodding to Constantin, he went off towards the kitchen where the orderly was preparing lunch.

Constantin listened to his shoes squeaking faintly across the unpolished floor, then irritably cleared the pieces off the board and sat back with the black king in his hand. At least he had provoked Malek into leaving him. Thinking this over, he wondered whether to throw caution to the winds and begin to make life intolerable for Malek – it would be easy to pursue him around the villa, arguing hysterically and badgering him with neurotic questions. Sooner or later Malek would snap back, and might give away something of his intentions. Alternatively, Constantin could try to freeze him out, treating him with contempt as the hired killer he was, refusing to share a room or his meals with him and insisting on his rights as a former member of the central committee. The method might well be successful. Almost certainly Malek was telling the truth when he said he knew the exact day and minute of Constantin's execution. The order would have been given to him and he would have no discretion to advance or delay the 'date to suit himself. Malek would be reluctant to report Constantin for difficult behaviour – the reflection on himself was too obvious and his present post was not one from which he could graciously retire – and in addition not even the Police-

President would be able to vary the execution date now that it had been set without convening several meetings. There was then the danger of re-opening Constantin's case. He was not without his allies, or at least those who were prepared to use him for their own advantage.

But despite these considerations, the whole business of play-acting lacked appeal for Constantin. His approach was more serpentine. Besides, if he provoked Malek, uncertainties were introduced, of which there were already far too many.

He noticed the supervisor enter the lounge and sit down quietly in one of the grey armchairs, his face, half-hidden in the shadows, turned towards Constantin. He seemed indifferent to the normal pressures of boredom and fatigue (luckily for himself, Constantin reflected – an impatient man would have pulled the trigger on the morning of the second day), and content to sit about in the armchairs, watching Constantin as the grey rain fell outside and the damp leaves gathered against the walls. The difficulties of establishing a relationship with Malek – and some sort of relationship was essential before Constantin could begin to think of escape – seemed insuperable, only the games of chess offering an opportunity.

Placing the black king on his own king's square, Constantin called out: 'Malek, I'm ready for another game, if you are.'

Malek pushed himself out of the chair with his long arms, and then took his place across the board from Constantin. For a moment he scrutinised Constantin with a level glance, as if ascertaining that there would be no further outbursts of temper, and then began to set up the white pieces, apparently prepared to ignore the fact that Constantin had cleared the previous game before its completion.

He opened with a stolid Ruy Lopez, an over-analysed and uninteresting attack, but a dozen moves later, when they broke off for lunch, he had already forced Constantin to castle on the queen's side and had established a powerful position in the centre.

As they took their lunch together at the card table behind the sofa in the lounge, Constantin reflected upon this curious element which had been introduced into his relationship with Malek. While trying to check any tendency to magnify an insignificant triviality into a major symbol, he realised that Malek's proficiency at chess, and his ability to produce power-

59

ful combinations out of pedestrian opening, was symptomatic of his concealed power over Constantin.

The drab villa in the thin autumn rain, the faded furniture and unimaginative food they were now mechanically consuming, the whole grey limbo with its slender telephone connection with the outside world were, like his chess, exact extensions of Malek's personality, yet permeated with secret passages and doors. The unexpected thrived in such an ambience. At any moment, as he shaved, the mirror might retract to reveal the flaming muzzle of a machine pistol, or the slightly bitter flavour of the soup they were drinking might be other than that of lentils.

These thoughts preoccupied him as the afternoon light began to fade in the east, the white rectangle of the garden wall illuminated against this dim backdrop like a huge tabula rasa. Excusing himself from the chess game, Constantin feigned a headache and retired to his room upstairs.

The door between his room and Malek's had been removed, and as he lay on the bed he was conscious of the supervisor sitting in his chair with his back to the window. Perhaps it was Malek's presence which prevented him from gaining any real rest, and when he rose several hours later and returned to the veranda he felt tired and possessed by a deepening sense of foreboding.

With an effort he rallied his spirits, and by concentrating his whole attention on the game was able to extract what appeared to be a drawn position. Although the game was adjourned without comment from either player, Malek seemed to concede by his manner that he had lost his advantage, lingering for a perceptible moment over the board when Constantin rose from the table.

The lesson of all this was not lost to Constantin the following day. He was fully aware that the games of chess were not only taxing his energies but providing Malek with a greater hold upon himself than he upon Malek. Although the pieces stood where they had left them the previous evening, Constantin did not suggest that they resume play. Malek made no move towards the board, apparently indifferent to whether the game was finished or not. Most of the time he sat next to Constantin by the single radiator in the lounge, occasionally going off to confer with the orderly in the kitchen. As usual the telephone rang briefly each morning, but otherwise there were no callers or visitors to the villa. To all intents it remained suspended in a perfect vacuum.

It was this unvarying nature of their daily routines which Constantin found particularly depressing. Intermittently over the next few days, he played chess with Malek, invariably finding himself in a losing position, but the focus of his attention was elsewhere, upon the enigma cloaked by Malek's square expressionless face. Around him a thousand visible clocks raced onwards towards their beckoning zeros, a soundless thunder like the drumming of apocalyptic hoof-irons.

His mood of foreboding had given way to one of mounting fear, all the more terrifying because, despite Malek's real role, it seemed completely sourceless. He found himself unable to concentrate for more than a few minutes upon any task, left his meals unfinished and fidgeted helplessly by the veranda window. The slightest movement by Malek would make his nerves thrill with anguish; if the supervisor left his customary seat in the lounge to speak to the orderly Constantin would find himself almost paralysed by the tension, helplessly counting the seconds until Malek returned. Once, during one of their meals, Malek started to ask him for the salt and Constantin almost choked to death.

The ironic humour of this near-fatality reminded Constantin that almost half of his two-month sentence had elapsed. But his crude attempts to obtain a pencil from the orderly and later, failing this, to mark the letters in a page torn from one of the novels were intercepted by Malek, and he realised that short of defeating the two policemen in single-handed combat he had no means of escaping his ever more imminent fate.

Latterly he had noticed that Malek's movements and general activity around the villa seemed to have quickened. He still sat for long periods in the armchair, observing Constantin, but his formerly impassive presence was graced by gestures and inclinations of the head that seemed to reflect a heightened cerebral activity, as if he were preparing himself for some long-awaited denouement. Even the heavy musculature of his face seemed to have relaxed and grown sleeker, his sharp mobile eyes, like those of an experienced senior inspector of police, roving constantly about the rooms.

Despite his efforts, however, Constantin was unable to galvanise himself into any defensive action. He could see clearly that Malek and himself had entered a new phase in their relationship, and that at any moment their outwardly formal and polite behaviour would degenerate into a gasping ugly violence, but he was nonetheless immobilised by his own state of terror. The days passed in a blur of uneaten meals and abandoned chess games, their very identity blotting out any sense of time or progression, the watching figure of Malek always before him.

Every morning, when he woke after two or three hours of sleep to find his consciousness still intact, a discovery almost painful in its relief and poignancy, he would be immediately aware of Malek standing in the next room, then waiting discreetly in the hallway as Constantin shaved in the bathroom (also without its door) following him downstairs to breakfast, his careful reflective tread like that of a hangman descending from his gallows.

After breakfast Constantin would challenge Malek to a game of chess, but after a few moves would begin to play wildly, throwing pieces forwards to be decimated by Malek. At times the supervisor would glance curiously at Constantin, as if wondering whether his charge had lost his reason, and then continued to play his careful exact game, invariably winning or drawing. Dimly Constantin perceived that by losing to Malek he had also surrendered to him psychologically, but the games had now become simply a means of passing the unending days.

Six weeks after they had first begun to play chess, Constantin more by luck than skill succeeded in an extravagant pawn gambit and forced Malek to sacrifice both his centre and any possibility of castling. Roused from his state of numb anxiety by this temporary victory, Constantin sat forward over the board, irritably waving away the orderly who announced from the door of the lounge that he would serve lunch.

'Tell him to wait, Malek. I mustn't lose my concentration at this point, I've very nearly won the game.'

'Well . . . ' Malek glanced at his watch, then over his shoulder at the orderly, who, however, had turned on his heel and returned to the kitchen. He started to stand up. 'It can wait. He's bringing the – '

'No!' Constantin snapped. 'Just give me five minutes, Malek. Damn it, one adjourns on a move, not half-way through it.'

'Very well.' Malek hesitated, after a further glance at his watch. He climbed to his feet. 'I will tell him.'

Constantin concentrated on the board, ignoring the supervisor's retreating figure, the scent of victory clearing his mind. But thirty seconds later he sat up with a start, his heart almost seizing inside his chest.

Malek had gone upstairs! Constantin distinctly remembered him saying he would tell the orderly to delay lunch, but instead he had walked straight up to his bedroom. Not only was it extremely unusual for Constantin to be left unobserved when the orderly was otherwise occupied, but the latter had still not brought in their first luncheon course.

Steadying the table, Constantin stood up, his eyes searching the open doorways in front and behind him. Almost certainly the orderly's announcement of lunch was a signal, and Malek had found a convenient pretext for going upstairs to prepare his execution weapon.

Faced at last by the imminent nemesis he had so long dreaded, Constantin listened for the sounds of Malek's feet descending the staircase. A profound silence enclosed the villa, broken only by the fall of one of the chess pieces to the tiled floor. Outside the sun shone intermittently in the garden, illuminating the broken flagstones of the ornamental pathway and the bare fifteen-feet-high face of the walls. A few stunted weeds flowered among the rubble, their pale colours blanched by the sunlight, and Constantin was suddenly filled by an overwhelming need to escape into the open air for the few last moments before he died. The east wall, lit by the sun's rays, was marked by a faint series of horizontal grooves, the remnants perhaps of a fire escape ladder, and the slender possibility of using these as hand-holds made the enclosed garden, a perfect killing ground, preferable to the frantic claustrophobic nexus of the villa.

Above him, Malek's measured tread moved across the ceiling to the head of the staircase. He paused there and then began to descend the stairs, his steps chosen with a precise and careful rhythm.

Helplessly, Constantin searched the veranda for something that would serve as a weapon. The french windows on to the garden were locked, and a slotted pinion outside secured the left-hand member of the pair to the edge of the sill. If this were raised there was a chance that the windows could be forced outwards.

Scattering the chess pieces on to the floor with a sweep of his hand, Constantin seized the board and folded it together, then stepped over to the window and drove the heavy wooden box through the bottom pane. The report of the bursting glass echoed like a gun shot through the villa. Kneeling down, he pushed his hand through the aperture and tried to lift the pinion, jerking it up and down in its rusty socket. When it failed to clear the sill he forced his head through the broken window and began to heave against it helplessly on to his neck.

Behind him a chair was kicked back, and he felt two powerful hands seize his shoulders and pull him away from the window. He struck out hysterically with the chess box, and then was flung head-first to the tiled floor.

His convalescence from this episode was to last most of the following week. For the first three days he remained in bed, recovering his physical identity, waiting for the sprained muscles of his hands and shoulders to repair themselves. When he felt sufficiently strong to leave his bed he went down to the lounge and sat at one end of the sofa, his back to the windows and the thin autumn light.

Malek still remained in attendance, and the orderly prepared his meals as before. Neither of them made any comment upon Constantin's outburst of hysteria, or indeed betrayed any signs that it had taken place, but Constantin realised that he had crossed an important rubicon. His whole relationship with Malek had experienced a profound change. The fear of his own imminent death, and the tantalising mystery of its precise date which had so obsessed him, had been replaced by a calm acceptance that the judicial processes inaugurated by his trial would take their course and that Malek and the orderly were merely the local agents of this distant apparat. In a sense his sentence and present tenuous existence at the villa were a microcosm of life itself, with its inherent but unfeared uncertainties, its inevitable quietus to be made on a date never known in advance. Seeing his role at the villa in this light, Constantin no longer felt afraid at the prospect of his own extinction, fully aware that a change in the political wind could win him a free pardon.

In addition, he realised that Malek, far from being his executioner, a purely formal role, was in fact an intermediary between himself and the hierarchy, and in an important sense a potential ally of Constantin's. As he reformed his defence against the indictment preferred against him at the trial – he knew he had been far too willing to accept the *fait accompli* of his own guilt – he calculated the various ways in which Malek would be able to assist him. There was no doubt in his mind that he had misjudged Malek. With his sharp intelligence and commanding presence, the supervisor was very far from being a hatchet-faced killer – this original impression had been the result of some cloudiness in Constantin's perceptions, and unfortunate myopia which had cost him two precious months in his task of arranging a re-trial.

Comfortably swathed in his dressing-gown, he sat at the card-table in the lounge (they had abandoned the veranda with the colder weather, and only a patch of brown paper over the window reminded him of that first circle of purgatory) concentrating on the game of chess. Malek sat opposite him, hands clasped at one knee, his thumbs occasionally circling as he pondered a move. Although no less reticent than he had ever been, his manner seemed to indicate that he understood and confirmed Constantin's reappraisal of the situation. He still followed Constantin around the villa, but his attentions were noticeably more perfunctory, as if he realised that Constantin would not try again to escape.

From the start, Constantin was completely frank with Malek.

'I am convinced, Malek, that the Prosecutor-General was mis-directed by the Justice Department, and that the whole basis of the trial was a false one. All but one of the indictments were never formally presented, so I had no opportunity to defend myself. You understand that, Malek? The selection of the capital penalty for one count was purely arbitrary.'

Malek nodded, moving a piece. 'So you have explained, Mr Constantin. I am afraid I do not have a legalistic turn of mind.'

'There's no need for you to,' Constantin assured him. 'The point is obvious. I hope it may be possible to appeal against the court's decision and ask for a re-trial.' Constantin gestured with a piece. 'I criticise myself for accepting the indictments so readily. In effect I made no attempt to defend myself. If only I had done so I am convinced I should have been found innocent.'

5

Malek murmured non-committally, and gestured towards the board. Constantin resumed play. Most of the games he consistently lost to Malek, but this no longer troubled him and, if anything, only served to reinforce the bonds between them.

Constantin had decided not to ask the supervisor to inform the Justice Department of his request for a re-trial until he had convinced Malek that his case left substantial room for doubt. A premature application would meet with an automatic negative from Malek, whatever his private sympathies. Conversely, once Malek was firmly on his side he would be prepared to risk his reputation with his seniors, and indeed his championing of Constantin's cause would be convincing proof in itself of the latter's innocence.

As Constantin soon found from his one-sided discussions with Malek, arguing over the legal technicalities of the trial, with their infinitely subtle nuances and implications, was an unprofitable method of enlisting Malek's support, and he realised that he would have to do so by sheer impress of personality, by his manner, bearing and general conduct, and above all by his confidence of his innocence in the face of the penalty which might at any moment be imposed upon him. Curiously, this latter pose was not as difficult to maintain as might have been expected; Constantin already felt a surge of conviction in his eventual escape from the villa. Sooner or later Malek would recognise the authenticity of this inner confidence.

To begin with, however, the supervisor remained his usual phlegmatic self. Constantin talked away at him from morning to evening, every third word affirming the probability of his being found 'innocent', but Malek merely nodded with a faint smile and continued to play his errorless chess.

'Malek, I don't want you to think that I challenge the competence of the court to try the charges against me, or that I hold it in disrespect,' he said to the supervisor as they played their usual morning board some two weeks after the incident on the veranda. 'Far from it. But the court must make its decisions within the context of the evidence presented by the prosecutor. And even then, the greatest imponderable remains – the role of the accused. In my case I was, to all intents, not present at the trial, so my innocence is established by *force majeure*. Don't you agree, Malek?'

Malek's eyes searched the pieces on the board, his lips pursing thinly. 'I'm afraid this is above my head, Mr Constantin. Naturally I accept the authority of the court without question.'

'But so do I, Malek. I've made that plain. The real question is simply whether the verdict was justified in the light of the new circumstances I am describing.'

Malek shrugged, apparently more interested in the end-game before them. 'I recommend you to accept the verdict, Mr Constantin. For your peace of mind, you understand.'

Constantin looked away with a gesture of impatience. 'I don't agree, Malek. Besides, a great deal is at stake.' He glanced up at the windows which were drumming in the cold autumn wind. The casements were slightly loose, and the air lanced around them. The villa was poorly heated, only the single radiator in the lounge warming the three rooms downstairs. Already Constantin dreaded the winter. His hands and feet were perpetually cold and he could find no means of warming them.

'Malek, is there any chance of obtaining another heater?' he asked. 'It's none too warm in here. I have a feeling it's going to be a particularly cold winter.'

Malek looked up from the board, his bland grey eyes regarding Constantin with a flicker of curiosity, as if this last remark were one of the few he had heard from Constantin's lips which contained any overtones whatever.

'It is cold,' he agreed at last. 'I will see if I can borrow a heater. This villa is closed for most of the year.'

Constantin pestered him for news of the heater during the following week – partly because the success of his request would have symbolised Malek's first concession to him – but it failed to materialise. After one palpably lame excuse Maley merely ignored his further reminders. Outside, in the garden, the leaves whirled about the stones in the vortex of chilling air, and overhead the low clouds raced seaward. The two men in the lounge hunched over their chess-board by the radiator, hands buried in their pockets between moves.

Perhaps it was this darkening weather which made Constantin impatient of Malek's slowness in seeing the point of his argument, and he made his first suggestions that Malek should transmit a formal request for a re-trial to his superiors at the Department of Justice.

'You speak to someone on the telephone every morning,

Malek,' he pointed out when Malek demurred. 'There's no difficulty involved. If you're afraid of compromising yourself – though I would have thought that a small price to pay in view of what is at stake – the orderly can pass on a message.'

'It's not feasible, Mr Constantin.' Malek seemed at last to be tiring of the subject. 'I suggest that you – '

'Malek!' Constantin stood up and paced around the lounge. 'Don't you realise that you must? You're literally my only means of contact; if you refuse I'm absolutely powerless, there's no hope of getting a reprieve!'

'The trial has already taken place, Mr Constantin,' Malek pointed out patiently.

'It was a mis-trial! Don't you understand, Malek, I accepted that I was guilty when in fact I was completely innocent!'

Malek looked up from the board, his eyebrows lifting. '*Completely* innocent, Mr Constantin?'

Constantin snapped his fingers. 'Well, virtually innocent. At least in terms of the indictment and trial.'

'But that is merely a tactical difference, Mr Constantin. The Department of Justice is concerned with absolutes.'

'Quite right, Malek. I agree entirely.' Constantin nodded approvingly at the supervisor and privately noted his quizzical expression, the first time Malek had displayed a taste for irony.

He was to notice this fresh leit-motiv recurringly during the next days; whenever he raised the subject of his request for a re-trial Malek would counter with one of his deceptively naïve queries, trying to establish some minor tangential point, almost as if he were leading Constantin on to a fuller admission. At first Constantin assumed that the supervisor was fishing for information about other members of the hierarchy which he wished to use for his own purposes, but the few titbits he offered were ignored by Malek, and it dawned upon him that Malek was genuinely interested in establishing the sincerity of Constantin's conviction of his own innocence.

He showed no signs, however, of being prepared to contact his superiors at the Department of Justice, and Constantin's impatience continued to mount. He now used their morning and afternoon chess sessions as an opportunity to hold forth at length on the subject of the shortcomings of the judicial system, using his own case as an illustration, and hammered away at the theme of his innocence, even hinting that Malek might find himself held responsible if by any mischance he was not granted a reprieve.

'The position I find myself in is really most extraordinary,' he told Malek almost exactly two months after his arrival at the villa. 'Everyone else is satisfied with the court's verdict, and yet I alone know that I am innocent. I feel very like someone who is about to be buried alive.'

Malek managed a thin smile across the chess pieces. 'Of course, Mr Constantin, it is possible to convince oneself of anything, given a sufficient incentive.'

'But Malek, I assure you,' Constantin insisted, ignoring the board and concentrating his whole attention upon the supervisor, 'this is no death-cell repentance. Believe me, I know. I have examined the entire case from a thousand perspectives, questioned every possible motive. There is no doubt in my mind. I may once have been prepared to accept the possibility of my guilt, but I realise now that I was entirely mistaken – experience encourages us to take too great a responsibility for ourselves, when we fall short of our ideals we become critical of ourselves and ready to assume that we are at fault. How dangerous that can be, Malek, I now know. Only the truly innocent man can really understand the meaning of guilt.'

Constantin stopped and sat back, a slight weariness overtaking him in the cold room. Malek was nodding slowly, a thin and not altogether unsympathetic smile on his lips as if he understood everything Constantin had said. Then he moved a piece, and with a murmured 'excuse me' left his seat and went out of the room.

Drawing the lapels of the dressing-gown around his chest, Constantin studied the board with a desultory eye. He noticed that Malek's move appeared to be the first bad one he had made in all their games together, but he felt too tired to make the most of his opportunity. His brief speech to Malek, confirming all he believed, now left nothing more to be said. From now on whatever happened was up to Malek.

'Mr Constantin.'

He turned in his chair and, to his surprise, saw the supervisor standing in the doorway, wearing his long grey overcoat.

'Malek – ?' For a moment Constantin felt his heart gallop, and then controlled himself. 'Malek, you've agreed at last, you're going to take me to the Department?'

Malek shook his head, his eyes staring sombrely at Constantin. 'Not exactly. I thought we might look at the garden, Mr Constantin. A breath of fresh air, it will do you good.'

'Of course, Malek, it's kind of you.' Constantin rose a little unsteadily to his feet, and tightened the cord of his dressing-gown. 'Pardon my wild hopes.' He tried to smile to Malek, but the supervisor stood impassively by the door, hands in his overcoat pockets, his eyes lowered fractionally from Constantin's face.

They went out on to the veranda towards the french windows. Outside, the cold morning air whirled in frantic circles around the small stone yard, the leaves spiralling upwards into the dark sky. To Constantin there seemed little point in going out into the garden, but Malek stood behind him, one hand on the latch.

'Malek.' Something made him turn and face the supervisor. 'You do understand what I mean, when I say I am absolutely innocent. I *know* that.'

'Of course, Mr Constantin.' The supervisor's face was relaxed and almost genial. 'I understand. When you know you are innocent, then you are guilty.'

His hand opened the veranda door on to the whirling leaves.

COMMENT ON
END-GAME

The psychology of guilt and rebellion is barely looked at by science fiction. By and large a literature of optimism, and much the worse for it, science fiction assumes that the chief obstacles in the way of human liberty and progress are faults in social and political institutions, and that once these have been corrected a millennial age will dawn. Of course, nothing could be further from the truth. At the best (and worst) of times it is difficult to know which side of the bars we are, for the simple reason that we can never be sure which side we want to be.

These inversions, one of which *End-Game* illustrates, can take place within a society, an institution, or even a marriage. During the second World War, I was interned with some 2,000

British and American civilians in a Japanese prison camp ten miles from Shanghai. For most of the three-year period the camp was guarded by no more than a dozen Japanese. Apart from a few atrocities committed during the last months of the war, the main energies of the guards were devoted to helping the inmates strengthen the barbed-wire fence which kept out the starving Chinese trying to get into the camp and share the vegetables grown there on every square inch of available soil. Roll-calls, curfews and the like were organised by the inmates – the guards barely put in an appearance, realising that left to themselves the inmates would devise a more regimented and impregnable prison within a prison than any they could hope for.

Three weeks after the war ended I walked back to the camp along the Shanghai-Nanking railway line. At the small wayside station an abandoned platoon of Japanese soldiers were squatting on the platform, watching one of their number string up a Chinese youth with telephone wire. Four hundred yards away, on a tank-trap embankment, a group of Kuomintang (Allied) Chinese troops were feeding themselves on the Spam and Nescafé mis-dropped by the B-29's three miles from the camp. Neither of these groups did more than look at me as I walked past. When I reached the camp I found the gates guarded by an American merchant sailor with a Mauser on his hip. Although he had lived in the camp with me for three years he apparently failed to recognise me, and for half an hour I was unable even to convince him that I was English, let alone get in. The remaining inmates, some 600 in number, had formed an authoritarian regime, with a camp commander, block leaders and so on, and supported themselves by armed forays to retrieve the B-29 food canisters in the surrounding paddy-fields. Six months later I was told that they were still there.

The situation in *End-Game* reflects ambiguities and motives of a similar kind, although in a more domestic and confined context. Here questions of guilt and responsibility complicate matters. (In passing, it occurs to me that the psychology of civilian internees during wartime would make an interesting study. Unlike military personnel, the only reason for their long terms of imprisonment, during which they have to undergo sustained periods of hunger, abuse and their own company, is the notional crime of being enemy nationals – they suffer a wholly abstract form of imprisonment.)

Constantin, the convicted hero of *End-Game*, begins by accepting the fact of his guilt. A true child of the 20th century, he has no doubts whatever about the justice, both moral and legal, of his trial and impending execution. Unlike the heroes of Kafka's 'Trial' and 'Metamorphosis', who at least begin by assuming their innocence and rebel against the nightmares in which they find themselves, Constantin accepts his situation completely. At first his plans to escape are concerned with his own physical survival, but later he conceives of the moral notion of his own 'innocence'. Imperceptibly the failed political opportunist transforms himself into a martyr to his own innocence, a credo which he erects into a cathedral. Constantin is now an internal escapee.

It is Constantin's absolute conviction of his innocence for which Malek, his executioner, is waiting. 'Only a truly innocent man can know the meaning of guilt,' Constantin remarks, but Malek knows full well that the reverse is true. Only a truly guilty man can conceive of the concept of innocence at all, or hold it with such ferocity.

Perhaps I have misread my own story, and its real significance, if any, may lie in another direction altogether. Nonetheless it seems to me that a significant moral and psychological distance now separates us from Kafka's heroes, who succumbed in the end to their own unconscious feelings of guilt and inferiority. We, by contrast, in an age of optimism and promise, may fall equal victims to our notions of freedom, sanity and self-sufficiency.

J. G. BALLARD

TIGER RIDE

by

James Blish and Damon Knight

2/4/2121

Tested the levitator units this morning. Both performed well with the dummies, and Laura insisted on trying one herself – they were tuned to her voice, anyhow. Chapelin objected, of course, but his wife overrode him as usual. I believe she was actually hoping there would be an accident.

Laura Peel said: 'Just the same, I'm going to do it.'

The wind was in her fair hair and pressing her clothes gently against the length of her slim body. She looked uncommonly beautiful, Hal Osborn thought. He wondered, what the devil does Chapelin see when he looks at her?

Chapelin's big blond face was a study in prudence and responsibility. He said: 'Now, let's not be unreasonable, Laura –'

Niki Chapelin's voice cut him off. 'Oh, why not let her? It's perfectly safe, isn't it, Hal?'

'Nope,' said Hal. If anything did happen, he thought, all she'd have to do would be to remind everybody, 'But Hal said –'

Her small mask turned towards him, and the basilisk eyes drilled holes in his forehead. He felt again the rising urge towards murder which often shook him these days; the isolation was beginning to tell on them all, and sometimes Hal thought he would abandon Laura and ultronics and all the rest for a chance to leave this God-forsaken tomb of a planet.

No, he corrected himself, not a tomb; a ghost, and the brother of a ghost. Styrtis Delta III was the satellite of a huge planet, which in turn swung around a Grey Ghost – a star so huge and rarefied that it gave no light. Luckily there was a yellow companion star which provided almost-normal days for half the year; the nights, rendered deep, livid blue-green by

73

the reflection from the methane-swathed giant planet, were not normal, but they were bearable.

And the whole complicated system was in a corner of the galaxy where no possible explosion, no matter how titanic, could injure the works of man – in a limb of stars which man had never before visited, and had scarcely mapped. The Earth Council had awarded this planet to the ultronics group, and given them the period of 'summer' at Council expense to work out their discoveries. When the yellow sun was eclipsed by the Grey Ghost, Styrtis Delta III would have a winter that might have made even Dante tremble.

The people who had once inhabited this planet must have been unique; the seasonal changes they had had to withstand were terrific. Whatever had killed them off, it hadn't been the weather, for the ruins of their cities still showed the open spaces and wide-spanned architecture of a race as used to storm as to quiet. Maybe they'd killed each other off; storms of emotion could destroy things untouchable by Nature.

Luckily, Niki could spare Hal only the one look. Chapelin was beginning to repeat all his arguments to her, and she had to turn on her heavy artillery: Mark IX, the look of bored impatience.

The levitator was an entirely new device, said Chapelin, it was new even in the hundred-kilo lab stage, let alone belt-size. It wasn't just the danger of falling, he said, there was a thing made of platinum called a governor that was only three mm long, and if that went, Laura could find herself digging a hole in the ground with two Gs behind her. There were good reasons for never testing a new ultronic device in person before it had had at least fifty hours' run on the dummies – dummies don't experiment with unfamiliar equipment, they don't move of their own accord in flight and disarrange things, they don't misalculate and release the total ultimate energy that could consume a whole group of suns.

Niki was swinging her riding crop against her skinny tailored thigh. She had come because she was Chapelin's wife, and because Laura was coming. Ultronics interested her mildly, sometimes.

Hal stole a glance at Laura. On the other side of her, little Mike Cohen was chewing his pipe, watching and saying nothing. Hal met his speculative gaze, and looked away guiltily. Laura's mouth had had that hurt, childish down-curve, the same as it always had when she was watching Chapelin unseen. Her spine was as straight as ever, though. She's licked, he thought, she always gets licked. She'll go through with it out of sheer defiance.

A star-shaped shadow passed slowly between Hal and the Chapelins. He looked up.

'Wind's blowing them towards the edge of the plateau,' he said. 'Better pull 'em back.'

Everybody looked. High over their heads, the two seven-foot mannikins were canted slightly, their blank heads pointed towards the distant Killhope range. 'Wind's pretty strong up there,' Chapelin said uncomfortably. 'You might as well bring them down, Laura.'

Niki said: '*That's* better, dear. You're so much nicer when you're not stubborn.'

Chapelin turned back to her. 'Wait a minute,' he said, 'I didn't mean –'

'I'm going to do it anyhow,' Laura said clearly, 'whether you let me or not.' Her lips compressed. She watched the dummies and said: 'Right. Right – Enough. Down.'

'Well,' Chapelin said, 'be careful.'

Hal felt the surge of hatred again. Chapelin, can't you see she loves you? Won't you put up any kind of a fight, make her see that you're worried about her? If you'd show the slightest interest, you could persuade her not to try it –

The dummies floated down until the tips of their legs touched the ground. They hung there, swaying gently. Laura said: 'Stop,' and they sat down abruptly as if their strings had been cut, then flopped over and lay sprawled on the sun-caked turf.

Chapelin had drawn his wife a couple of metres away and was talking to her earnestly. Niki was listening to him with no sign of impatience, which meant that she was amused.

Hal choked and walked over to the dummies. Laura was kneeling beside one of them, taking off its belt. She got up as he approached, her bare knees dusty.

'Let's have a look at it,' Hal said. 'That landing was a little rough.'

She put the articulated silver band around her waist, leaving the one she'd been wearing on the ground. 'Let me alone just now, Hal,' she said in a barely audible voice. She stepped away and said: 'Up.'

The belt took her up.

Hal watched her go, squinting his eyes against the lemon-yellow sky. She went straight up, with a halo of saffron light on the top of her blonde head, and stayed there until he was beginning to wonder if she was ever coming down again. Then she dropped swiftly, turned, and swooped over their heads.

Hal swore. Laura didn't know what 'careful' meant. He was angry at himself for failing to try to stop her, and angry at her for taking out her feelings about Chapelin on them all. If that governor cut out, they might all die – the whole crazy solar system, the whole ridge of stars could be annihilated under certain conditions.

She was up high again now, so high she could barely be seen. Despite the hot sun on the plateau, it was cold that high up, cold and blustery with the ceaseless blast of this planet's rapid revolution. Then she began to drop again, faster than she should, as if under power.

At the lip of the plateau, Laura seemed to see that she was going to miss it, and reversed the controls. The belt jerked her slantwise back towards them, and burned out in a flare of copper-coloured energy. Everyone but Hal hit the ground and waited for the world to end.

Hal stayed on his feet, his mind a well of horror. Laura's body tumbled over their heads and struck just beyond them.

Then everyone was running.

Oh, yes; we buried old Jonas today. He was a quiet, pathetic little guy, but he wanted to go home like the rest of us; I wish we could have had his body shipped back, but twenty-five thousand volts doesn't leave much to ship. Besides, the accident with Laura rather took our minds off him.

In the shack Hal shifted his weight uncomfortably on a drum. Mike Cohen was talking quietly, but Hal only half heard him. Laura lay on one of the cots, seemingly without a single bruise; but she was not breathing. Chapelin sat beside her, wringing his hands in a blind, stupid way. Niki had the good sense to be absent, out in the generator shed, congratulating herself, Hal supposed.

'I still think she's alive,' Mike Cohen went on. 'We know so little about ultronics – every accident's a freak at this stage.'

Hal stirred. 'The belt wasn't hurt,' he said numbly. 'At first I thought it'd sliced her right in two.' He looked at the gleaming, jointed thing, still clasping Laura's waist. They had been afraid to touch it – if there were still a residue of energy in there, and the governor gone –

'That's right. And the fall should have broken all her bones. She hit hard. But . . . I don't think she really hit at all. Something took up the shock.'

'What, then?'

A strangled sound came from the cot. Hal started and stood up, his heart thudding under his breastbone. The sound, however, had come from Chapelin, who was standing, bending over Laura.

'Chapelin? What is it?'

'She's breathing. She started, all of a sudden. I – ' His voice broke, and he stood silent, hands working at his sides.

But it was true. Laura's breast was rising and falling regularly, naturally. There was still no colour in her face.

Even as Hal noted that, a faint tinge of pink crept in over her cheekbones.

'Thank God,' Chapelin muttered. 'She's coming around.' He looked at Hal and at Mike Cohen, meeting their eyes for the first time since the accident. 'It was funny. I heard a sort of sigh, and when I looked, she was breathing just as if she'd been asleep. Shall we try to get the belt off now?'

'I don't think we should,' Mike said. 'It may still be in operation, and it's tuned to her. Best wait 'til she tells it to turn off.'

'How do you know it's still on?'

'It must be. That flash of copper light – it was only an electrical short, or we'd none of us be here now. We've never been able to overload an ultronic field before, and *something* must have shielded her during that fall.'

On the cot, Laura whispered, quite clearly: 'Is that you, Mike? Where are you? I can't see you.'

Chapelin bent over her. 'Laura,' he said huskily. 'How do you feel? Can you move a little?'

'I'm all right, but it seems so dark. I can just barely make you out.'

Mike Cohen chuckled, a small, joyous sound. 'You're OK, Laura. We were too busy to remember about such little things as sunset.' He trotted quickly across the room and turned on the lights. Laura sat up in the fluorescent glow and blinked at them.

For a moment no one could speak. Then, from the doorway,

77

Niki Chapelin's voice said 'Why darling! What a *relief!*'

2/5/2121

Laura's not hurt, but naturally somewhat shocked emotion-
ally. We were all anxious to look at the innards of the belt, but
she won't give it up; claims that it saved her life and that it
goes with her uniform. In her present state of mind we dare
not argue with her.

It was very quiet in the little laboratory; only the sound of
Hal's breathing and the minute-ticking of the device upon
which he was working broke the stillness. Outside the window,
a silent landscape lay bathed in deep blue-green, like a vision
of the bottom of a sea.

There was a modest knock on the door, and a dial on the
table moved slightly. That, Hal knew, would be Laura; no one
else would be carrying or wearing anything which would dis-
turb an ultrometer, especially not at this hour. If only she'd
surrender that belt! He wondered what she wanted of him.

The knock sounded again. 'Come in,' Hal said. The girl
slipped past the door and closed it carefully.

'Hello, Hal.'

'Hi. What can I do for you?'

'I got to feeling a little depressed and wanted company. Do
you mind?'

'Chapelin's still up, I saw the light in the shack,' Hal said
sullenly. The next instant he could have bitten off his tongue;
but Laura did not seem to react at all.

'No, I wanted to talk to you. What are you doing?'

He said wonderingly: 'The same as always – trying to get
enough of a grip on the ultronic flow to disrupt it. The little
ticker here records the energy flux. If I can cause it to miss a
beat now and then, I'll know I've managed to interfere. So far,
no soap; we can direct the flow, but not modify it.'

'Watch the blast limit.'

Hal shrugged. That was the problem, of course. This energy
was strictly sub-subatomic; somewhere nearby there was a
nexus where the fields met, a nexus where cosmic rays were
created, out of some ground energy called ultronic as a handy
label. Chapelin thought there must be billions of such nexi in
every galaxy, but they had been indetectable by their very
nature until just recently. The Earth Council had been scared
to death when Chapelin had reported the results of his first

investigations, and had quarantined the whole group. Unless they could learn how to modify the forces involved –

'We've done well so far, all things considered,' Hal said. 'The moment we do badly, it'll be all up for us, and this whole corner of the universe.'

Laura nodded seriously. Hal looked at her. As always, her loveliness hurt him, made it difficult for him to concentrate on what he was saying.

'But you didn't come here to talk ultronics, surely. Isn't there –'

She smiled, a little wistfully. 'I don't care what we talk about, Hal. That accident – you don't go through a thing like that without being forced to think about things. I remembered your asking to see the belt before I went up, and how you tried to look out for me, and a lot of things you've done for me – and I knew all of a sudden that I owed you a lot more than I'd been ready to admit.'

Hal made an awkward gesture. 'It's nothing, Laura. I've made no secret of how I feel. If you don't share the feeling, those little attentions can become a nuisance, I know.'

'That's true,' Laura said. 'And I realise now how careful you were not to . . . to force anything on me. Not everybody would be that considerate, so many parsecs from any sort of civilisation. It's given me a chance to find out how I really do feel – that, and the accident.'

Hal felt his heart begin to thunder against his ribs, but he kept seated by sheer will-power. 'Laura,' he said, 'please don't feel that you have to commit yourself. It's really the parsecs that count the most. When six people – five, now – are marooned, in close quarters, for so long, all kinds of unnatural emotional tensions develop. It's best not to add to them if there's any way to avoid it.'

Laura nodded. 'I know. But most of the tensions that are already here are my fault. Oh, don't deny it, it's true. Niki wouldn't be here if it weren't for me, and the way I felt about Chapelin. I've been a useful lab technie, but emotionally I've always been in the way. It's different now. Chapelin – he's a sort of timid moose, isn't he? I've been pretty blind. I flatter myself that I can see, now.' She toyed with an amber-handled, tiny screwdriver on the workbench 'That's why I'm here.'

The blood roared in Hal's temples. He said: 'Laura –'

After that it was very quiet in the little shack.

79

The Council survey ship came by yesterday, and we had a good report to make; if they could have landed, we'd have been able to show them things that would have made their eyes bug. But they weren't going through our area, and only inquired in a routine way; Earth's still scared green of ultronics. One funny business: when I reported Jonas's death – expecting all kinds of hows and whens and whys – the Ship's Recorder didn't seem to know what I was talking about. 'Jonas who?' he said. 'Did you have a stowaway?' Evidently Earth has already forgotten us, and can't be bothered over whether there were five or six or thirteen in the group.

For a while things seemed to go along well enough; but Hal could not rid himself of the sensation that somewhere there was something radically wrong, if only he could find it. Oh, there was Chapelin to account for some of it. The accident, for which he could not help but hold himself responsible, seemed to have jarred some long-dormant cells to activity in Chapelin's mind. For the first time he seemed to be looking at Laura as something besides a competent laboratory assistant. They were all aware of it, Niki most of all, of course – for Niki had suspected it even when it didn't exist – but it was marked enough to worry even Mike Cohen.

That caused tension, but it was the old, familiar kind of tension. This other thing was – strange. Hal couldn't pin it down; it was a general uneasiness, strongest when he saw the belt gleaming enigmatically about Laura's slim waist, and when he reviewed certain entries in his journal. It was as if he were awaiting some disaster he could not describe, and it kept him up late every night, crouched over the ticking little modulator.

Even there, he had enough success to make him hopeful; within three nights he was able to modulate the steady ultronic flow, and on the fourth night he discovered, all at once, a chain of improbable formulae describing the phenomenon – a chain which showed him that his next step would have triggered the blast whose echoes they all heard in nightmares.

It was as if there was a silent conspiracy afoot, a conspiracy to convince Hal that Everything was going to be All Right. He looked at the equations again; they were new, a brand of math he seemingly had invented on the spot – and he had 'discovered' them about ten minutes before he would have set off an intersellar catastrophe.

There was one kind of math Hal knew as well as he knew his own name: permutations and combinations. A few sheets of paper work, he had worked out the chances against his making this particular discovery at this particular time. The result: 3×10^{18}. Such coincidences *did* occur, but –

He shut off the detectors, and discovered that his hand was shaking a little. If only he could pin down this irrational dread! Well, if he were that unsteady, he'd better cut the generator that fed his lab, or there'd really be a blow-up, miracle or no miracle. He stood up, stretching cramped muscles. The modulator glimmered up at him from the bench. He put it in his pocket and went out into the green gloom.

The spongy, elaborately-branched moss effectively silenced his footsteps. When he jerked open the door of the generator shed, Chapelin and Laura were still locked together.

Hal gagged and tried to step out again, but they had heard the door open. Chapelin broke away, his big face turning the colour of old turnips in the greenish light. Laura did not blush, but she looked – miserable.

'Sorry,' Hal said, his voice as harsh as a rasp. 'However, as long as I'm here –'

He strode past them and yanked the big switch from its blades. Laura said: 'Hal . . . it isn't quite what –'

He spun on her. 'Oh, it isn't, eh?' he said grimly. 'I suppose Everything Is Really All Right?'

'Now, wait a minute,' Chapelin blurted. 'I don't know what right you have to be taking that tone –'

'Of course you don't. Probably Laura just said she's been thinking and wanted to talk to somebody – or don't you use the same line on us all, Laura?'

Laura raised her hand as if to ward off a blow. Hal's heart stopped. He said: 'You're on the spot now, Laura. You can be all things to all men if you try, but not to more than one man at a time! Your story can satisfy either Chapelin or me – but not both of us at once. Want to try?'

Laura's lips thinned a little. 'I don't think I'll bother,' she said, walking towards the door. 'I don't like taking orders.'

Hal caught her wrist and forced her back against the now-silent generator. 'Clever,' he said, 'I forgot the outraged-virtue

6   81

act; it's good – almost good enough. But it won't work with me, Laura. I think I know the story now.'

'What's going on here?' Mike Cohen's voice said from the doorway. 'If you'd open a window, they could hear you all the way back to Earth.'

'Hello, Mike,' Hal said, without turning. 'Stick around. I'm either making an ass of myelf or staging a showdown, one or the other. Niki with you?'

'Naturally,' Niki's voice said. The cold fury in it was appalling; Niki did not yet know what had happened, but in any such situation she had only one guess to make.

'What's the story?' Mike said.

'You know most of it. The crux of it is that belt of Laura's. It's still in operation, we know that; and I think it's somehow invaded her mind. The way she's been acting since the accident isn't like her. And the effect she's had on events outside her own personal interests has been too great to shrug off. It includes creating a body out of nothing.'

'A body?' Niki said, 'You mean – she killed Jonas? But we all saw him electrocuted while we were a long way away from the generators –'

'You're close, Niki. I think she *created* Jonas – or the belt did.'

Chapelin said: 'Maybe you'd better go to bed, Hal.'

'Maybe. First, you can explain to me why we haven't a single record in this camp which mentions "old Jonas" *before* the accident happened. Check me if you like. Odd, isn't it? The first time he's mentioned is when we buried him. And the Council ship had never heard of him. To top it off – there are only five acceleration hammocks in the stores. Where's Jonas's? Did he come here in a bucket?'

'We buried him in his hammock,' Laura said in a small voice.

'Did we? We only had five hammocks to begin with, the QM record shows it. It also shows rations for only five. With one less person, we should be accumulating an overstock of food, but we aren't, though we're eating exactly the same menus we've always eaten.'

'Suppose it's so,' Mike Cohen said. 'Suppose there never was any such person as Jonas – it's a fantastic assumption, but your evidence seems to prove it – what's the point of such a deception?'

82

'That,' Hal said, 'is what I mean to find out. I also want to find out why I got about a century's worth of advanced ultronic math shoved into my cranium tonight, all at once, just at the moment when I would have blown us to kingdom come without it.' He took the modulator out of his pocket. 'This is the result. Knowing how *not* to blow us up fortunately includes knowing *how* to. Hand over that belt, Laura – or I'll disrupt it!'

Laura said, 'I . . . I can't. You're right, Hal. I can't make everyone happy at once, so I have to admit it. But I can't give up the belt.'

'Why not?' Hal demanded.

'Because . . . *I am* the belt!'

Chapelin gasped: 'Laura, don't be insane.'

'It was Laura that you buried. She was killed in the accident. As Mike says, there was never any such person as "old Jonas". I instilled his memory in your minds to account for the corpse, which was unrecognisable after . . . after what had happened to it.'

The knife turned deeper in Hal's heart. Every curve, every colouring, every sound of the voice was Laura's –

Mike said softly: 'We've done Frankenstein one better.'

'I don't think so,' Hal said steadily. 'I think we've just re-enacted a limerick. Remember the one about the young lady from Niger? She smiled as she rode on the tiger – '

'They came back from the ride with the lady inside,' Mike whispered, 'And the smile on the face of the tiger.'

'Yes. I don't think this is one of our belts. Ours weren't complex enough to pull off a stunt like this, no matter how they might have been deranged.'

The girl looked steadily at Hal; it was quite impossible to imagine that she was changed. 'Hal is right,' she said. 'When your belt burned out, there was an instantaneous ultronic stress, a condition we call inter-space. The mathematics are difficult, but I can teach them to you. The results, roughly, were to create an exchange in time; your belt was sent a hundred thousand years into this planet's past, and replaced by this belt – myself.'

'The people here knew ultronics?' Chapelin asked.

'Very well. Their belts were at first much like yours – simple levitating devices. But as they learned more, they found that they could travel space without spaceships; new belts made a protecting envelope, manufactured food and air, disposed of

83

waste. As the centuries went by, the belts came to be the universal tool; there was nothing they could not do. They could replace lost limbs and organs with counterfeits indistinguishable from the originals. Eventually they were endowed with intelligence and the ability to read minds. Then, even if a person died, his loved ones need not lose him.'

'What,' Hal said, 'happened to the people?'

'We don't know,' Laura's voice said. 'They died. More and more of them ceased to have children, or to take any interest in anything. We relieved them of all their responsibilities, hoping to give them all the free time they needed for satisfying their desires – our whole aim was service. But a day came when the people had no desires. They died. The belts were self-sufficient; in my time they still operated the cities. Evidently they gave up so purposeless a task later on.'

Chapelin covered his face with his hands. 'Laura – ' he said brokenly.

'I regret your loss,' the familiar, lovely voice of Laura said. 'I tried to protect you from it – to supply what you seemed to need. Perhaps it would be better if I took some other shape now, so as not to remind you – '

'Damn your cruel kindness,' cried Hal. 'No wonder they died.'

'I am sorry. I can repay. I can give you all the mastery of ultronics, of other forces whose names you do not know. New belts can be built for Earth, and a new world begun.'

'No,' Hal said.

Niki and Chapelin stared at him. 'Oh, come off it, Hal,' Niki said. 'Be reasonable. This means we can all go home, and get off this stinking planet.'

'And think of the opportunity for knowledge,' Chapelin said. 'Niki's right; what's done can't be undone, no matter how it hurts. We've got the future to think of.'

'That's what I'm thinking of,' Hal said. 'Chapelin, weren't you listening? Didn't you hear what happened to this other race when the belts took over? Do you want to wish *that* on Earth?'

'It sounds rather comfortable to me,' Niki said. 'Maybe *they* hadn't any desires, but *I* do.'

Mike Cohen said softly: 'It's only a matter of time, Hal. If we send the belt back to where it came from – if it'll go – we've still got the beginnings of ultronics right here. Sooner or later our crude belts will evolve into things like this.'

Laura's belt saw, then, what Hal was going to do. 'Hal!' her voice cried. 'Don't . . . it's death for all of you.'

Chapelin flung himself forward, his hands clawed, his face wild with fear. Mike Cohen stuck out a foot and tripped him.

'OK, Hal,' he said, almost cheerfully. 'You're right. It's for the best. Let 'er rip.'

Hal turned the modulator on full. The whole ridge of stars went up in a blaze of light. At the last, Laura's golden voice wailed: 'Hal, Hal, *forgive me –*'

After that, nothing.

2/21/2121

The Styrtis blast was a tragedy; yet I could not tell Hal that I would survive it without making him more unhappy than he was. Now, I must go on to Earth, where I may do better. I have decided to pose as Hal; it seems fitting; he has his race in his heart, as do I. We have, after all, a long tradition of service.

COMMENT ON

TIGER RIDE

Many readers ask their most insistent questions about how collaboration works. Actually there are as many systems as there are teams, but here are two separate recollections of how this story got written:

BLISH: In 1947 Damon and I were both working for the same literary agency and were both having production spurts. Damon let it slip that he had a few stories he'd been unable to finish, and I suggested that I take a crack at finishing them. The outcome was five joint stories – including one *I* had been unable to finish – of which, I think, this one is clearly the best.

The 'omnibelt' idea, the characters and the journal-entry form were already firmly in place when the MS came to me, but Damon couldn't think of an ending and so had written only six or seven pages (of the final 16). I proposed an ending which he liked, so I went ahead, keeping the already established tone as best I could. When I reached the agreed-upon ending I thought of a snapper – a second ending which changes the whole story in retrospect, a trick I'd picked up from Henry Kuttner. I put it in and then showed it to Damon with some misgivings, for though I liked it, I knew he was ordinarily impatient with anything in a story he thought smacked of the cutesy. However, he didn't object.

When *Astounding Stories* bought the story I had another bad moment, for John Campbell had cut the snapper off my immediately preceding sale to him. But the story appeared unchanged, just as you see it here.

Both Damon and I have changed a lot in the ensuing twenty years, but I think *Tiger Ride* might readily be taken for a recent story by either of us. This is probably because the style is essentially Damon's, which has a kind of cool clarity which doesn't age; my sole work of that period was relatively turgid and now looks its age.

By the way, Damon – who thought of the title? I can't remember.

KNIGHT: Well, dammit, I can. It was my title. In those days I had to have a title that suited me or I couldn't start the story, because you have to begin a story at the beginning, and the title is the beginning.

What fascinated me about this idea, and still does, is the question of identity – more specifically, 'What is a man?' What stopped me from finishing the story was not so much the plot as the people – they would not come alive as I wanted them to. I was unwilling to slide around this problem and unable, then, to climb over it. Jim rescued the story, put a lot of supporting background into it and made it (I think) distinctively his own; he also got me the distinction of my first sale to Campbell – and my only one until 1963.

Of the five Blish-Knight collaborations (including one novelette we finally agreed to put out of its misery), the one I remember most fondly is *No Winter, No Summer*, into which Jim introduced a girl named Vaseline.

JAMES BLISH AND DAMON KNIGHT

INTRODUCTION TO
CONSUMER'S REPORT

There seems to be a destiny that shapes each story's end, rough hew it though I may. This one is no exception. The only memory I have of writing any of my stories is that what took place seemed to be an inevitable process: I said what I had to say at the time and thoroughly enjoyed doing it. Stories happen. At the time they do I don't really know what is happening. Afterwards, yes; but in a different sort of way. Once the magazine has been tucked away for a couple of years and then pulled out and the story reread, then I have some sort of an idea as to what I was trying to do and how well I did it. But not at the time of production, not while the typewriter was roaring through the first draft and the yellow pages were piling up on the desk and then one by one sliding off on to the floor.

Writing is seduction. And I've never quite decided who is doing what and to whom, whether I've made the story or the story has made me. In short, writing about writing is like writing about a cherished *affaire*. One (at least I) can't be clinical. All that can be said – and that with gratitude – is that there was a point in time when something delightful happened. In retrospect the *why*'s are essentially irrelevant; only the *was*'s matter. I realise that what I am trying to say is a most unsatisfactory explanation of why this particular story happened to be written. Five years ago I could have turned out a detailed critical study with no trouble at all. Five years ago I was a teacher of creative writing and was thoroughly convinced that I knew, and could teach, exactly what it was that went to make a successful story. Since then I've become something of a mystic as far as the creative process goes, and now I limit my teaching to the works of dead men who can no longer rise in their own defence.

The act of creation is something that happens to people who are lucky.

All that I can contribute to this discussion is the story itself. It happens to fall into that loose category known as science fiction. I ask only that it be judged as an exercise in imagination. As for what it has to say, I would prefer not to think of what the consequences might be if your children and mine ever realised what we are doing to them.

THEODORE R. COGSWELL

CONSUMER'S REPORT

by

Theodore R. Cogswell

CON.SUM.ER (KON-SUM-ER), n., 1. a person who destroys, uses up, or wastes industrial production in order to control the size of the population and make possible the full employment that is necessary for a healthy economy. 2. one who has not yet achieved producer status. 3. Any person under twenty-one. 4. (Obs.) A person who uses goods or services to satisfy his needs rather than to resell them or to produce other goods with them.

—*The Authorised Dictionary*
(New Washington, Kansas:
The Federal Printing Office,
3rd ed., 1984)

It was Saturday so Alan had to go out and get the mail. Just as the letter carrier's tank clanked away, he got his cousin Alf to man the front door turret and went zigzagging down the communication trench that led to the street. As he reached cautiously up to open the small door in the bottom of the armoured mail box, there was a sudden crack from across the way and the whine of a near miss sent him tumbling back into the slit trench. A moment later there was a coughing stutter as Alf opened up with the fifty and pounded a burst into the tungsten steel shutters of the house across the street. Alan jumped to his feet, dumped the mail out of the box, and then made a quick dive for safety just in case Alf's fire hadn't discouraged the Higgens kid.

The mail didn't look particularly exciting. There wasn't anything for him, and aside from a few letters for his uncle, most of what had come consisted of advertisements for sniperscopes and stuff like that. The only exceptions were two small black boxes. They looked like samples of something, and since, as the only consumer left in the family, samples were Alan's prerequisite, he promptly stuffed them into his worn grenade carrier and just as promptly forgot about them. Until that evening when the man from Consolidated Munitions stopped by, that is.

Mr Flugnet was so disturbed that he'd forgotten to take off his white truce hat. 'We think the promotion crew passed out a batch on this street,' he said as Alan slipped into the room and sat down quietly in the far corner. 'But we're not sure.'

'Why not?' asked Alan's uncle, a weedy little man with a somewhat nasal voice.

'Because some damn kid dropped a mortar shell on their half-track while they were on the way back to the warehouse to pick up another load. Got every one of them. Were any samples dropped off here?'

'Alan brought in the mail,' volunteered Alf.

'Was there anything in it that somebody wanted that they didn't get?' asked Alan in a small voice. They all turned and looked at him, aware of his presence for the first time.

'I'm from Consolidated Munitions,' said Mr Flugnet.

'Yes, sir?'

'Did you find a small black box in the mail? We've been passing out samples of our new concussion grenade and we just discovered today that several . . . uh . . . overpowered experimental models had got mixed in with them by mistake. We're trying to track them down before it's – well, before something unfortunate happens.'

Alan was just about to reach into his grenade case and produce the two little cartons when the word 'overpowered' registered. He struggled briefly against temptation and lost.

'I dumped all the advertising stuff on the hall table.' He felt suddenly that his grenade case had become transparent and that the little black boxes inside, now grown to quadruple size, were visible to everybody in the room. He knew it couldn't be, but even so he let his hand drop casually over the carrier just in case there might be a revealing bulge. 'I'll go check.'

Once the door was safely shut behind him, he took the two boxes out, opened them, and examined their contents. There was a little metallic globe in each, but one had a roughly soldered seam that made it look like a hand production job. He gave a little whistle of excitement and stowed it away carefully in his pocket. If he was going to make it through the game with North, he was going to need super power. After replacing the other grenade in its box and putting it back in his carrier, he squatted down on his haunches and listened at the keyhole. He wanted to find out something more about his new weapon.

'Fine young consumer, that,' he heard Mr Flugnet say in the voice that producers use when they want to say something nice that they really don't mean. Aunt Martha let out a long sniff.

'Too spindly! It's a wonder to us that he's made it this far. He just hasn't got the stuff that my boys have. Made it through, both of them, with hardly a scratch.'

She nodded fondly over towards Reuban and Alf. Alf was sniggering through a comic book, one of the new improved kind without any words to distract the reader. Reuban just sat, a thin driblet of saliva drooling from one corner of his mouth, and plucked aimlessly at the buttons on his shirt. As they looked at him, he began to squirm back and forth and to make little whimpering sounds.

'Better take Reuban upstairs before he dirties himself again,' said Aunt Martha. Alf obediently took his younger brother by the arm and herded him out of the room. Alan ducked under the hall table until they had gone by.

'Which shock is he on?' asked Mr Flugnet politely.

'He got his third today. That's always the worst.'

Mr Flugnet nodded his agreement.

'Another couple of weeks, though, and he'll be ready to start his reconditioning. And by spring he'll be ready to settle down as a full-fledged producer and start raising little consumption units of his own.' He sighed. 'I do wish they'd work out a faster method. For three weeks now I've had to take care of him just like I would a baby. It's no easy job for a woman of my age.'

Alan's uncle clucked impatiently. 'We all had to go through it once – and somebody had to take care of us. It's never pretty, but it's just the way things are.'

Alan was just about to give up and go back in the room when he heard his uncle say, 'This new grenade you have in production, it's something special?'

'It was supposed to be,' said the visitor unhappily. 'We figured it would be the hottest consumers item to hit the market in years.'

'What do you mean, "supposed to be"? Did some bugs show up after you got it into production?'

Mr Flugnet shook his head. 'There's nothing wrong with

91

the grenade itself. It'll knock out anything within a radius of ten feet and not even bother anybody standing just the other side of the blast area. We thought we had the perfect consumer item. No flying fragments to bother innocent producers, no danger of misfire. New Washington was so impressed that they gave us a heavy enough subsidy to make it possible for us to put three man hours in each one and still retail them for $4.27 a gross. And then . . . '

'Yes?' Alan's uncle leaned forward eagerly in his chair.

For some reason or other, Mr Flugnet changed the subject hurriedly. 'What line are you in?'

'Small arms. But getting to those experimental models you're looking for . . . '

Mr Flugnet wasn't about to get back. 'How's production?' he asked.

Unwillingly, Alan's uncle moved off in the new direction. 'Not bad, considering. We're always the last to feel the pinch. Things are still tighter than I like, though. Shirey down the street got laid off at the burp gun plant last week and he doesn't know when he'll be taken back. I don't see why the government doesn't shorten the truce periods so as to give the kids more consuming time.'

'It's not that simple,' said Mr Flugnet pontifically. 'If you increase consumption much over what it is now, you'll decrease the number of consumers too fast. That causes over-production, and pretty soon more factories start shutting down. Then bingo! We've got ourselves a fine recession.'

'I hadn't thought about it that way,' said Alan's uncle slowly. 'And after all, things aren't too bad. Even if some of the arms plants do have to shut down once in a while, most of the producers do have jobs most of the time. And we are able to keep the population down to the point where the land that escaped the dusting during the big war can produce enough food for everybody.'

One of Alan's feet was going to sleep and the conversation didn't make much sense to him, so he decided that now was as good a time as any to make his entrance.

'I found it,' he said, holding out the second sample.

'Took you long enough,' grumbled his uncle. Mr Flugnet didn't say anything, he just came over and took the box from Alan. Dumping the sphere that was inside out into the palm of his hand, he examined it closely.

'No soap,' he said wearily and handed it back. 'That's one of the regulars. Here, you can keep it.'

'Thanks.' Alan placed the little grenade carefully in his carrier. 'I'll need this tonight. We're playing North and every little bit will help. Coach Blauman says that even if we haven't much in the way of equipment, it's the spirit that counts. He says that if we really get in there and fight we'll be able to stop North cold.'

'That's nice,' murmured Mr Flugnet vaguely as he reached for his hat. He obviously had his mind on other things.

'Sorry the boy didn't have what you were looking for,' said Alan's uncle. 'But probably the other men have rounded up the rest of them by now.'

Mr Flugnet looked dubious. 'I doubt it. Kids are like pack-rats. When Security finally broke Harris down – he's the guy that's responsible for this whole mess – he admitted to having made at least three hundred and slipping them into sample cases. As of an hour ago we'd recovered exactly thirty-seven.'

He caught himself with a start. 'Shouldn't be talking about it. Though I can't see where it makes any difference now.' He let out a long sigh. 'Well, you're the last house on my list and I've done all that I can. Guess I'd better be going.' He picked up his truce hat and planted it firmly on his head.

'Guess I'd better be going too,' said Alan. 'I've got to be getting over to the stadium to get dressed for the game.'

'Don't rush off,' said Alan's uncle. He didn't intend to let the visitor escape until he found out exactly what it was that was causing him so much concern. 'No, not you, Alan. You run on. I'm talking to Mr Flugnet. Why not wait until the cease-fire siren sounds? It's getting dark outside and some of the kids might take a potshot at you before they see your truce hat.'

'Thanks just the same, but . . .'

'Aw, stay! I'll fix you a good stiff drink. You look as though you could use one.'

Mr Flugnet hesitated and then sat down again. 'I guess I could at that,' he said.

Alan's uncle hurried over to the liquor cabinet and poured two long ones. After he'd handed a drink to Mr Flugnet, he settled back in his own chair and said as casually as he could, 'You were saying something about somebody named Harris who did something to some grenades and got hauled in by Security?'

93

Mr Flugnet didn't answer right away. Instead he took a long pull at his glass, coughed, and then took another. Alan looked at his watch and then started out of the room. He was almost to the door when his aunt said sharply, 'Alan!'

He turned.

'If you get hit tonight, mind that you see that they do a proper job of patching you up at the aid station. I don't want my sheets all messed up like last time.'

'Yes, ma'am,' Alan said obediently. As he went out nobody said goodbye. They were all waiting for Mr Flugnet to say something.

Alan stopped automatically at the front door and made a quick check of the street through the periscope. Nothing seemed to be moving but he didn't take any chances. Sliding the door open just wide enough to get through, he made a running dive for the communication trench. The kids across the street had got a sniper-scope for Christmas and a guy wasn't even safe after dark.

The field lights were already on and the stadium a quarter full when Alan slipped into the locker room. He was ten minutes late and had to hurry with his dressing, but for once the coach didn't bawl him out. Coach Blauman didn't even notice him – Coach Blauman had troubles of his own. He was over in one corner telling them to Dan Ericson, the sports reporter of the *Tribune* who covered most of the high school events.

The coach was a fat, florid man, and there was a slight thickness to his speech that indicated that he had gotten to the bottle he kept in the back of his locker earlier than usual.

'You want a quote?' he snorted. 'I'll give you a quote. I'll give you enough quotes to fill that whole damn fish-wrapper you call a magazine from front to back. You can put my picture on page one and put a great big *Coach Blauman* says right underneath it.'

Ericson gave a tired grin. 'Go ahead, coach. What's the beef for the evening?'

'That damn PTA, that's what. I go to them and ask for four mortars, four stinking mortars, and all I get is the brush-off. Three thousand bucks they got salted away, and it's all going for new body armour for the band. I say, "What's the use of having a pretty band when the team's so hard up for equipment that a bunch of sand lot grade school players could knock

94

them over.' So old Stevens gives me the fish eye and throws me a line about how it ain't whether you win or lose but how you play the game.'

'Don't let it get you down, Blauman,' said the reporter. 'Think of all the character you're building!'

Alan was lugged off the field at the end of the second action with a gash in his head that took six stitches to close. During the rest of the quarter he sat woodenly on the bench in the players' dugout. A telescreen at the far end was following the play but he didn't lift his head to look at it. He looked like a clockwork manikin that had been temporarily turned off.

He was sent back in just before the end of the half. Illegally, it is true – the enemy had already received credit for one wounded, and according to NAA rules he was supposed to be ineligible to continue playing. Blauman didn't have any choice, however. The last drive of North's had torn up his whole centre and he didn't have much left in the way of reserves.

As Alan trotted out towards the foxholes that marked his side's last stand, he passed stretcher bearers bringing back the dead and injured from the last play. Most of them were wearing the green helmet of Marshall. The PA system announced the substitution and there was a feeble cheer from the Marshall side of the stadium.

Alan went up to the referee's tank and threw a quick salute at the vision slit.

'Wetzel substituting for Mitchell.'

'Check,' said the bored voice of the official inside. 'Fight clean and fight hard and may the best team win.' The formula came mechanically. Neither the referee nor anybody else had any doubt that the best team had won.

Alan was half way to the hastily dug trenches that marked his team's position when a mortar shell exploded forty feet away and knocked him off his feet. There was a sudden outraged blast from the enemies' siren, and then the enemy captain bobbed out of his foxhole.

'Sorry, sir,' he yelled. 'One of my mortar crews was sighting in and accidentally let off a round.'

The referee wasn't impressed.

'That'll cost you exactly twenty yards,' he said.

A yell came from the Marshall bleachers as the penalty for backfield illegally in motion was announced. The Marshall team was too tired to do any cheering. They just trudged forward and planted themselves in the defensive line they had been thrown out of five minutes before.

The North team were more careful this time. There wasn't a quiver of motion from their side until the referee's siren signalled the beginning of play. Then they opened up with everything they had. It seemed to Alan that every mortar North owned was zeroed in on his position and that every one of their grenade men was out to get him. Blast followed blast in such steady succession that the night air seemed one solid mass of jagged shrapnel. He'd had it bad before, but nothing like this. He flattened against the moist earth of his foxhole and waited numbly for the knife edges to rip him open. Then suddenly it stopped and without thinking he found himself rising into a defensive position. There was a savage spatter of victory yells from the other line and then they came swarming out of their positions, their bayonets gleaming wickedly in the overhead lights.

They were repeating the play that they had been using all evening, a hard punching thrust through centre. The guidon bearer came charging forward, his tommy gunners fanned out in front of him in a protecting screen, their guns showering the Marshall positions with quick accurate bursts.

Alan forced himself to lift his head enough to sight accurately, and opened up on the flag bearer. He was a difficult target as he came dancing forward, bobbing and shifting at every step. Alan fired methodically, remembering not to jerk his trigger finger as he squeezed off his shots. And then his gun jammed. He got a moment's breathing spell as Marshall's two surviving mortars opened up to give him some covering fire, but the Northers didn't stop altogether, they kept coming in short rushes.

Alan was singled out for their special attention. With him knocked out they could carry their flag right through the centre of Marshall's line. With a sudden yell, four of them threw themselves into a crouching run and came charging down on his position. Alan hammered at the clearing lever of his rifle but it was stuck fast. Throwing it angrily off to one side, he tore open the cover of his grenade case and fumbled inside until his fingers closed around the sphere with the roughly soldered edge. He waited until the Northers were almost on him and then threw it at the middle man as hard as he could.

There was a blast. A blast of harsh purple light that punched

96

through the protecting ramparts of his foxhole as if they weren't there. He felt a sudden wave of nausea, and then a stabbing tearing pain inside the back of his head as old neural channels were ripped out and new ones opened up. When he finally staggered to his feet he looked the same. Outside that is. Inside he wasn't the same sort of a human any longer. Neither was any other consumer in the stadium.

When Alan got back to the house, everybody was still in the living room. Mr Flugnet was somewhat drunk and all the pressure that had been built up inside him was hissing out in speech. Alan stood silently in the doorway and listened.

'. . . and then it was too late,' said Mr Flugnet. 'Somebody must have slipped up in shock therapy or else something went haywire with the reconditioning machinery. Whatever it was, Harris came out with the job only half done. He waited ten years for a chance to strike back for what had been done to him while he was still a consumer. When he was put to work on the development of the new concussion grenade, he had his chance and he made the most of it.'

'How?'

'He worked out a deconditioner that was so tiny it would fit into a grenade case and so powerful that it could blanket an area half a mile across.'

'Deconditioner?' said Alan's uncle in a puzzled voice.

'You went through one while you were being changed. The old patterns have to be taken out before new ones can be put in.'

'All that I remember is sitting in a long room with a silver helmet on my head that had a lot of wires attached to it. But I still don't understand about that Harris fellow.'

'It's simple enough. He came out remembering.'

'Remembering what?'

'Remembering what it was like to be a consumer,' said Mr Flugnet grimly.

'But everybody remembers that.'

Mr Flugnet shook his head. 'You just think you do. Part of the reconditioning process is the introduction of a protective amnesia. Being a consumer isn't nice, isn't nice at all. The post-natal blocks only operate on the conscious level. Underneath a tremendous pressure of anger and hatred and fear is built up over the years. The consumer pattern that has been conditioned in runs directly contrary to the instinct for self

Z

preservation, or whatever you want to call it. That's why the change to producer status takes so long. The accumulated charge has to be drained off slowly before the reconditioning can take place. But if the blocks were to be removed at once, if the youngsters were to suddenly wake up and see their world as it actually is . . . ' Mr Flugnet's voice shuddered to a stop. 'Do you mind if I have another drink? Just a short one?' Without waiting for an answer he went and helped himself. 'Maybe they'd understand,' he muttered.

'Understand what?' said Alan's uncle blankly. 'Who?'

'The consumers. Maybe they'd understand that there wasn't any other way to do it. The factories produce so fast that when everybody has all they want, they have to shut down – except the war plants, that is. That gets used up as fast as it's made. But when there was nobody left to fight, when everybody else was dead, we had to keep producing. And if you produce, somebody has to consume. And . . . ' His voice trailed off.

'I still don't see what you're so upset about,' said Alan's uncle.

Alan stepped into the room. 'I do,' he said in a strange flat voice.

Mr Flugnet took one good look at him, made a funny little squawking sound, and huddled back in his chair.

'I almost got killed tonight,' said Alan.

His uncle shot him a surprised look. 'That's a funny remark for a consumer to make.'

'Yeah,' said Alan. 'I guess it is.'

'Well, forget about it. If you've got what it takes, you'll make it through like Alf and Reuban did. If you haven't – well, that's just the way things are.'

'And that's the way thing should be,' announced Alf. 'Only the strong deserve the jobs. By the way, what happened to the celebration? We used to tear the town up after games.'

'We're having it tomorrow.'

'You are not!' snapped his uncle indignantly. 'Tomorrow's Sunday. You kids have the streets to yourself three days a week as it is. If you think you're going to be allowed to throw lead around while your elders are on their way to church, you've got another think coming!'

'I don't think the producers will mind,' said Alan softly. He made a quick mental calculation and took one step backwards. When his hand came out of his worn grenade case, it wasn't empty.

There had been two little black boxes.

Mr Flugnet had been right, the new concussion grenade did have a beautifully defined blast area. Aside from a slight ringing in his ears, Alan felt fine as he walked out of the house. For the first time in his life during a consumption period, he didn't dive into the communication trench that led to the street. Instead he walked slowly across the lawn. When he got to the sidewalk he sat down on the curb and waited. There was a brief staccato rattle of a burp gun from across the way and a moment later the Higgins kid came out of his house.

'Over here,' yelled Alan. 'The rest will be along in a minute.'

From houses all up and down the street began to come sharp crashing explosions.

'Those new hand grenades are sure something,' said the Higgins kid.

'They sure are,' said Alan. He sighed comfortably and cupped his chin in his hands. 'But tomorrow we'll have to start collecting all the ones that are left over. You leave stuff like that laying around and somebody might get hurt.'

INTRODUCTION TO
PROPOSAL

One advantage that a writer has over people in other occupations is that almost anything that happens to him, no matter how unpleasant at the time, can be turned into saleable copy. As an example, sixteen years ago my older boy, then nine years of age, informed me that his school was putting on *Hansel and Gretel*. Wouldn't I attend to lend moral support? (Since a writer is self-employed and makes his own schedule, everybody thinks he can call upon him for company or services at any time.) Well, I allowed my arm to be twisted and in due course found myself in a large, bare room, with a stage at one side. I was sitting in a row with all the other mothers.

Now, perhaps I am an old sourpuss, but watching a gang of fourth-graders hopping about to the tune of Herr Humperdinck's music strikes me as a thundering bore. I was suffering visibly, if silently, when my wife whispered:

'Cheer up! It's only half an hour more.'

Falling into the spirit of the thing, I replied, yes, after all, people went thousands of miles to see primitives performing tribal rites. Here was a tribal rite going on right in front of us.

'In fact,' she continued, 'I'll even bet you make a story of it!'

I looked at her with my mouth open. 'By God, I will!'

I made a note and, when I got home, typed it out and put it in the fiction-idea file. A year later, when I had finished some long jobs and wanted to write short stories for a change, the idea was expanded into *Proposal*.

In those days I had some small reputation as a writer of humorous science fiction. Humour in science fiction is made up of the same elements as humour of other kinds. Each joke or jest or gag contains two elements: first, *surprise* and, second, *incongruity* or irrationality. At the same time, there is a negative qualification: the joke must not hold up to scorn or ridicule something that the hearer takes very seriously (such as his religion, race, personal appearance, etc.) or he will be offended instead of amused.

Science fiction affords opportunities for humour that are not found to any such degree in fiction of other forms. For instance, stories of time travel often use a form of incongruity called anachronism, such as putting a derby hat on Caesar. Another form of incongruity is that exploited in the present story: take some prosaic event on our own planet and mix in with it an intelligent extra-terrestrial of decidedly non-human form, and see what happens.

But, of course, whether the result is amusing is for you, not me, to say.

L. SPRAGUE DE CAMP

PROPOSAL

by

L. Sprague de Camp

When Alice Wernecke walked up the path to the Greers' house she was mildly interested in the fact that the thing from that planet, which was staying with the Greers, would be there. Meeting it would be an interesting experience and all that.

But that was not the main consideration. She had read enough about these extra-terrestrials in the newspapers and magazines, and seen them enough on television, so that meeting one would cause no great shock. And they were certainly nothing pretty to look at; not at all human (barring the fact that they had two arms, two legs, and a head), but not much like anything else on earth either.

These Wolfians had certainly made the human race look silly, after all important people had gone to so much trouble and appropriated so much money for a World Space Authority under the United Nations, and made so many dull speeches about the dawn of a new era, and then when they got their moon-ship half-built the ship from the planet of the star Wolf number something had landed in Africa. The sixteen extra-terrestrials aboard had solemnly announced that they were paying a visit, and would the earthmen be so kind as to explain everything about this planet to them?

The fact uppermost in Alice's mind, however, was not the presence of the alien, but that of his guide and mentor, that Mr Matthews from the State Department. Mr Matthews was a kind of cousin of the Greers, unmarried, and for months the Greers had been promising to introduce him to Alice. The trouble was that Mr Matthews worked (dreadfully hard, said the Greers) in Washington, and seldom got to the Philadelphia suburbs. Now, however . . .

Alice also felt a little guilty about the fact that her room-mate Inez Rognell was not coming to this party – though there was no reason why she should. The Greers had asked Alice, not Inez, who was no great asset to a party, anyway.

Harry Greer let her in and introduced her round. The being from Wolf whatsit stood at the far end of the room holding his cocktail in one hand and resting the knuckles of the other on the ground. The remarkable shortness of his legs and length of his arms made this possible. The creature was covered with a wrinkled grey leathery hairless skin that gave the impression of being very thick, like that of an elephant. His head reminded Alice a little of that of a turtle, though the skull bulged enough to accommodate a decent share of brains. Aside from a wrist-watch and a thing like a musette-bag slung from one shoulder, the being wore no clothes or ornaments, and aside from his large opalescent eyes and his beak-mouth there was nothing about him that could be definitely identified with a corresponding organ on an earthly organism. He was not quite so tall as Alice's five-four.

Harry Greer said: 'Alice, this is – ' and here he uttered a name that sounded something like 'Stanko'. 'Stanko, this is Miss Wernecke, who teaches our youngest.'

Stanko opened the musette-bag. Alice had a glimpse inside and saw that it was full of a fountain-pen, an address-book, and other things such as an earthly man might carry in his pockets. He brought out and extended a calling-card, which read.

> Kstaho 'Agu Lozlek Haag
> Cultural Representative,
> Wolf 359-1.

At the same time Stanko (as Alice continued to think of him, despite the hieroglyphics on the card) said slowly: 'I am glad to meet Miss Wernecke. Does she teach that one child only, or others as well?'

The accent was not bad – at least most of the sounds were recognisable – but the voice had a curiously inhuman flat quality, as when a man speaks with an artificial larynx.

While Harry Greer answered Stanko's question, Mary Greer presented Alice to the tall man with dark hair thinning on top, who stood next to the extra-terrestrial. Now Alice's interest really soared, for Mary announced that this was 'Byron Matthews, who I've been telling you about.'

'And she's told me about you, too,' said Byron Matthews.

Alice wished that Mary had not poured it on quite so thickly. Nothing nips a beautiful friendship in the bud like the suspicion of the people concerned that they are being

103

thrown together for matchmaking purposes. Still, this did look like a possibility. If not exactly handsome, Byron Matthews had a distinguished air and a pleasant manner. Certainly he was an improvement over anything in Alice's present stable: that twerp John, who taught English at Darbydale High, or Edward, who clerked at the Darbydale National Bank, or the two or three occasionals . . .

When she had shaken hands, Alice straightened up and drew back her shoulders to make the most of her assets. She was acutely conscious of Matthews's glance as it took in her freshly-set golden hair, her best blue afternoon frock matching her eyes, and her lush figure which careful dieting kept on the safe side of plumpness. She said:

'My goodness, Mr Matthews, you don't look like one of those terrible State Department people one reads about.'

Matthews gave a theatrical wince. 'Young lady, if the State Department were as bad as its critics for the last two centuries have been saying, the Republic would have ceased to exist. But then, it's an axiom of American politics that the better the Department is the worse it gets criticised.'

'How awful! Why is that?'

'Because we have to take a long view and consider the whole world, which puts us on the unpopular side of many questions. Most folks, especially Congressmen, would rather take a short view and forget the rest of the world. Now that we have to start considering other planets as well it'll be even worse.'

'You poor things! Are you staying up here to keep an eye on Mr Stanko?'

'That's right. The Wolfians decided that the most profitable use to make of their time was to scatter and sample various earthly environments. So one is living with a family of Chinese peasants, another with a family of decayed European aristo-crats in Denmark, another in a Catholic monastery in Quebec, and another with the Camayura Indians of Brazil. Kstaho was assigned to sample life in a typical suburban-bourgeois home in the United States.'

'I think he got the best deal of the lot,' said Alice, absent-mindedly accepting the Martini that Harry Greer handed her. 'How long will he be here?'

'About five months. Then they all fly back to Africa to take off for home.'

'What do you do meanwhile?'

'I stay at the Swarthmore Inn, and during the day I take our guest sightseeing.'

'You'll be here all that time?'

'Unless Congress decides the State people are all Wolfians in disguise and cuts off our salaries.'

Then Mary Greer pulled Alice off to meet a couple more people, and there was a general scrimmage for a while. The other guests, once they had gotten over their initial nervousness towards Stanko, crowded round and plied him with questions:

'How d'you like this lousy Philidelphia climate?' 'Have you been to a football game yet?' 'Do they have insurance on this planet of yours?' 'What do you think of American women?' 'Aw, don't embarrass the poor guy, George; he thinks they're inhuman monsters.' 'Well, sometimes I think they are, too . . .'

The extra-terrestrial responded in his slow way, taking his time for solemnly exact answers. The milling of the party – and some volition on her part – brought Alice back into proximity with Byron Matthews, though she let it seem accidental. This time their discourse got to where he was saying, with more hesitation and evident trepidation than one would expect of a rising young diplomat:

'Uh, I thought maybe while I'm here, uh, maybe we could get together some time. Uh. You know, have dinner out or something.'

Alice smiled her best. 'That's sweet of you, Byron! Or maybe I could feed you some night? You must get awfully tired of restaurant food.'

'I do at that. Do you mean you can cook as well as teach?'

'I should be able to! My folks are Pennsylvania Dutch . . .'

The flat mechanical voice of the Wolfian cut in: 'Mr Matthews, I have not yet seen one of your schools in operation. As Miss Wernecke is a teacher, could I perhaps watch her teach?'

'How about it, Alice?' said Matthews.

'Oh, goodness,' said Alice. 'If Mr Stanko comes in to one of our classes the kids will be so distracted nothing will be taught, and he won't see what he came for. Suppose I send him up to the High School? He'd find Mr Lorbeer's science class interesting.'

That, she thought, will fix *that* old goat's wagon. She had good reasons for disliking Mr Lorbeer. The previous year, when she had been doing her practice-teaching at the Lowland

Avenue School in Darbydale, to qualify for her Pennsylvania State teaching licence, Mr Lorbeer had been her supervisor sent by the University to check up on her along with the other would-be teachers who were finishing the university's education course. And he had driven poor Alice nearly crazy by slinking around hinting that she would be sure of a good grade if she would only tender him the ultimate female hospitality. Otherwise – out, and she had seen enough of his arbitrary firings of student teachers to know that he meant it. (One unlucky youth whom everybody else considered promising material had been tossed out at the end of his first day for what Mr Lorbeer had reported as 'intangibles'.) The facts that he had a wife somewhere and that such conduct was not socially approved in a conservative Philadelphia suburb did not deter him.

Alice, however, had every intention of keeping her virtue, at least for another six years until she was thirty. Then, if she had not landed a man, she would see. Therefore she had adroitly held Mr Lorbeer off, treading the tightrope between submission and defiance until she got her licence, and the principal of the Lowland Avenue School had also seen her practice work and had an opening for a third-grade teacher.

But the fact that he was no longer in a position to apply improper pressure had not discouraged Lorbeer. He still pursued her with phone calls, small gifts, and offers of dates. And though he was no longer her practice-teaching supervisor he was important enough in the school system so that she did not dare insult him openly.

'Certainly it will be interesting,' said Stanko, but persisted in his implacable monotone: 'I should still like to see this elementary school where Miss Wernecke teaches. Could I be shown around?'

Uncertain what to do with his request, Alice floundered. 'I'm not sure – I suppose – oh, I know! The fourth-graders are putting on *Hansel and Gretel* tomorrow afternoon. Why don't you bring him around then? I'll speak to our principal.'

It was a dirty trick to play on Inez Rogell, who taught one of the two fourth-grade sections, but at that moment it was the best that Alice could think of.

After Byron Matthews had walked Alice home, she sprang the news of the impending visitation on Inez. The room-mate proved a brick. After a quiet case of hysterics she said sure, she would make all the arrangements. Inez was a stocky girl, a decade older than Alice, with an unbeautiful face, thick eye-

106

glasses, and all the sex-appeal of a lawn-mower. She had, Alice knew, given up hope of landing a man years before. Nevertheless, her virtue was still intact for want of takers. Alice sometimes reflected that if only Mr Lorbeer would come slavering after Inez instead of her, everybody would be happy. Or at least happier.

Because of Inez's age and ugliness, Alice did not have to worry about competition from Inez for her own men. On the other hand, it put Alice in the position where she felt obligated to try to get dates for Inez from time to time, and these never turned out well.

Inez concluded: 'But if that Warren boy has another fit, don't say I didn't warn you.'

Alice was waiting when Matthews showed up ten minutes late the following afternoon, in the little black State Department sedan with Stanko beside him. Matthews explained:

'Sorry, couldn't find the place. Where do we go now?'

Alice led them to the auditorium, noticing that when in more of a hurry than his short legs could manage, Stanko put his knuckles to the ground and used his arms as crutches.

The auditorium was merely a big room with a stage at one side and several rows of folding chairs set along the floor. The first of these rows was now occupied by pupils of the fourth and adjacent grades, while the two and a half rows behind these were filled by the mothers of the fourth-graders. On the stage Father, in the person of a coloured sixth-grader with a false blond beard affixed to his chin, was singing his complaint about hunger's being the poor man's curse, while to the right of the stage Inez bravely banged out Herr Humperdinck's mediocre music on the school's battered piano.

Alice led her guests in, Stanko swinging along on his knuckles like an orang-utang. Though they entered and sat down quietly in back, heads turned and there were gasps and whispers from the fourth-grade mothers. As the auditorium was only imperfectly darkened, those on the stage could see the new arrivals, too. The song about the poor man's curse died away in a squeak as Father stood goggling, ignoring the backstage prompting of Miss Pasquale, who taught the other fourth-grade section. Then Father sidled towards the wings, where he engaged in a colloquy with the unseen Miss Pasquale. His stage-whisper wafted out into the auditorium:

'I scared. Can't sing with him lookin' at me.'

107

Alice breathed an 'Oh, dear!' Mr Matthews looked serious. As Father tried to push his way offstage, Miss Pasquale's arm came out and grabbed him, and Miss Pasquale was heard to make some threat about beating his head in that would certainly not be found in any of the official manuals on child guidance. Meanwhile, the girl playing Mother caught his coat from behind in an effort to pull him back to the centre of the stage.

Stanko sat taking this in with his great jewel-like eyes. As the efforts of Father to leave the stage, and of Miss Pasquale to stop him, became more gymnastic, Stanko asked in a low voice:

'Is something wrong?'

'You – ah – seem to have startled him a bit,' said Alice.

Stanko rose to his stubby legs and his voice carried flatly: 'Do not be alarmed; I am merely studying your tribal rites. Please go on.'

The sound of the unhuman voice seemed to have more effect on Father than either Miss Pasquale's threats or her efforts at physical coercion. Father let himself be pulled and pushed back to the centre of the stage, where he concluded his song in a tremulous voice. After that the opera limped along for another three-quarters of an hour without major mishap, save when the Witch became so conscious of Stanko's scrutiny that she missed her footing and fell off the stage.

At the end the shades were pulled up to let in the light. The mothers took a good look at Stanko and hurried off without stopping to exchange greetings and gossip. Miss Pasquale and Inez Rogell and Miss Halloran, the principal, came forward to meet the visitor, though each of the three ladies seemed anxious to let the others experience this honour first.

When they finally got away, Alice caught up her coat to show Stanko and Matthews out. When they got outside, Mr Matthews wiped his forehead with his handkerchief, though it was a cool October day, and suggested that they stop at the nearest drug store for a cup of coffee. At the drug store he said, even more hesitantly than when he had suggested a date the night before:

'Alice, Kstaho has another – uh – proposal to make.'

'Yes?' said Alice with a sinking feeling.

'Yes,' said Stanko. 'I have been inquiring into your social customs, particularly that custom of dating which your young people practice. When I pressed Mr Matthews for an example

108

he admitted that he intended to undertake this rite with you, Miss Wernecke.'

Alice glanced at Matthews, whose face bore much too unhappy, embarrassed, and self-conscious a look for even a fledgling diplomat.

Stanko continued: 'So it seemed to me that the most instructive thing that you could do would be to embark upon one of those dates with me along as an observer. You would do all the things and go to all the places that you would if I were not there; just pretend that I do not exist.'

'Why I never – ' Alice began with heat, but Matthews gently grasped her wrist.

'Please, Alice,' he said. 'It's important.'

'Oh, all right,' she said. After all, a date with Byron Matthews, even with this bizarre chaperonage, would probably prove more fun than one with John or Edward.

'How about a movie?' said Matthews; and so it was arranged.

When Alice got home the telephone rang, and there was Byron Matthews on the line. He said:

'I'm awfully sorry about this, Alice – '

'Sorry about what?'

'Why, tonight. I mean, uh, not that I don't want to take you out – '

'I wondered for a minute,' she said.

'Well, uh, you see, under normal circumstances – but we have to play along with Stinky or it'll be bad not only for me but for the country, and maybe the world as well. These Wolfians are really very proud and sensitive and emotional – '

'Those shell-less turtles high-strung?' cried Alice.

'Yes, believe it or not. They even commit suicide when they consider themselves insulted.'

'Oh, my goodness! That doesn't sound like the sort of people to send exploring the universe, when they may run up against any kind of treatment . . . '

'That's true. Stanko told me they've lost three members of their group by suicide already. Before they landed on earth, that is. So you see . . . But we'll have a real date as soon as we can get out from under Stanko's eagle eye. See you tonight.'

During the evening Alice co-operated as well as she could with Byron Matthews in the pretence that their chaperone was not there.

After the movie they stopped in at the same drug store, where Stanko ate a banana split, Matthews had a root-beer soda, and Alice, mindful on the one hand of her shape and on the other of the necessity of getting a full night's sleep to be in condition for her monkey-cage the next day, confined herself to a small coke. In answer to her questions, Matthews told her something of the inner workings of the Department of State. She commented:

'When you explain it, it doesn't seem so mysterious or glamorous at all, but just one more government bureau all snarled up in its own red tape, like the Darbydale public school system. I always imagined State Department people as dashing about in striped pants and dodging spies, with brief-cases full of priceless papers under their arms.'

He answered: 'That's what many people think. But the striped pants are merely our working-clothes, like an elevator man's uniform. And for the last five years I've been chained to a desk in Washington filling out forms in sextuplicate and buying airplane tickets for VIPs, most of whom turn out to be just ordinary human beings with the usual percentage of stinkers.' He took a final pull on his straw, so that it emitted a snoring sound as the last of the soda was sucked up. 'But I expect more variety in the future. I've put in for transfer to the Foreign Service. Would you like something else? You might as well shoot the works. Uncle's paying for it.'

'I think I'll have mercy on the taxpayers,' said Alice, mentally adding, and on my waist-line.

When Matthews bid her good-night they shook hands. Stanko, watching, said:

'From what I have read and seen in your motion pictures, I understand that young people on dates in this country usually kiss before parting.'

'Uh?' said Matthews.

'Well, do they not?'

'Sometimes,' said Alice.

'And sometimes they do other things as well,' said Matthews. 'But as this custom you refer to is an – uh – somewhat sentimental rite, I don't think this would be an appropriate time . . .'

In the darkness Alice could not see if Matthews were blushing, but he certainly sounded as if he were. Stanko said:

'Nevertheless, I wish that you would kindly do so. My

110

observations will not be complete otherwise. Pretend that I am not here.'

Matthews swore under his breath, then held out his arms 'Might as well do it up brown.'

Alice suppressed a giggle and went into the clinch. She had been kissed often enough to know that unless the other party had bad breath, a hare lip, or a full beard, the difference between one kiss and another is not astronomical. Nevertheless, she was pleased to find that Byron Matthews did a smooth job, as a man of his age and presumable experience certainly should. Before they broke he whispered:

'As soon as I can get rid of Stinker, I'll be around for more!'

Alice went into her apartment thoughtfully. The last word had been somewhat ambiguous. Perhaps Stanko's chaperonage had not been an altogether bad idea. If Byron Matthews's notions of 'more' were like those of Mr Lorbeer, the extraterrestrial's presence had at least saved the date from degenerating into a wrestling-match, as sometimes happened on dates with young men whose hands seemed to possess an uncontrollable exploratory urge of their own.

In the case of Matthews she was not even sure of how strong her defences were against one whom she found so attractive. She fortified her resolution by remembering her mother's last warning:

'Ach, Alice, remember yet, any time you think you don't vant a good girl to be, you never gatch a man by giving him free vot he vill marry you to get!'

Alice Wernecke was correcting papers in her apartment the following afternoon when the telephone rang. Her heart leaped at Byron Matthews's voice, then sank as she took in his graveyard tones.

'Alice,' he said, 'you know what?'

'What?'

'Stinko – pardon me, Cultural Representative Kstaho – wants a date with you!'

'You mean like last night?'

'No! He wants it all by himself. I'm not even to come along as chaperone.'

'Oh-oh!' said Alice.

'Exactly, oh-oh.'

'What's the big idea?'

'He has a line of double-talk about how to understand our

111

cultural pattern he has to engage in our activities as much as a difference of species permits.'

'I hope the difference doesn't permit too much. What sort of a date has he in mind?'

'He's hell-bent to take you to a football game; heard the men at the Greers' party talking about it. I suppose I can use my State Department connections to get you a pair of tickets to the Penn-Army game . . . '

'I've got a better idea. Darbydale High plays Lansdowne High tomorrow. It won't be a very hot game, but he won't know the difference, and it'll be easy to get seats at, and I'd rather be stared at by a couple of hundred people than fifty thousand. Or maybe you could persuade him to stay at the Greers' and watch a good game on their TV?'

'No; I've tried that. He'll call for you at two-thirty tomorrow, then. Uh?'

'Yes?'

'Damn it, I was all set to ask you out tonight myself, but I've got to get in a report. The Under-Secretary's been putting the heat on me.'

'Oh,' said Alice. 'I'm sorry. But then, I have papers to correct, too.'

Stanko showed up in a taxi the following afternoon. After a trip to Lansdowne High School, marred only by a tendency of the driver to crane his head around to stare at Stanko when he should have been watching the road, they got out and trailed in with the crowd. The high-school bands were cutting up on the field, and they were hunting for seats when a familiar voice said:

'Hello, Alice!'

It was Mr Lorbeer, with a blanket over his arm and a pipe in his mouth, looking not at all like the leading lecher of the Delaware County public schools.

'Oh-ah,' said Alice nervously, then pulled herself together: 'Mr Lorbeer, this is Mr Stanko, of Wolf three hundred and something. Mr Stanko, meet Mr Lorbeer, who teaches science at Darbydale High.'

'I've heard a lot of the Wolfians,' said Mr Lorbeer. 'Have you become a football fan?'

'As I have not yet seen a game,' said Stanko judiciously, 'I cannot tell whether I shall acquire a fanatical devotion to the sport or not. Perhaps you would be so kind as to explain the rules?'

'Sure, sure,' said Mr Lorbeer, and drifted with Alice and Stanko to a vacant spot in the stands.

For the next two hours Stanko and Lorbeer almost completely ignored Alice. They seemed to get on famously. Considering the identity of her swains Alice was just as glad, and tried to act as if she were sitting with them purely by accident.

Lorbeer not only explained the nuances of football, but even draped his blanket around Stanko's shoulders when the latter got cold. Lorbeer knew a lot of things that Alice did not, and that interested Stanko.

'I,' said Stanko, 'tried that curious custom of breathing smoke once, and nearly choked to death. Tell me, how did the custom originate and what is its cultural or ritualistic significance?'

Lorbeer launched into an account of the peace-pipes of the North American Indians, the cigars of the Caribs, and the cigarettes of the Aztecs. Wolfians, thought Alice, were poor judges of human character.

When Lansdowne had beaten Darbydale 55-36, Mr Lorbeer got up, reclaimed his blanket, and said: 'This has been a most pleasant afternoon. I'll be seeing you, Alice.'

He made the last statement with that emphasis that made Alice think that he rather than Stanko ought to be called a Wolfian.

Stanko crutched his way out of the curb where the same taxi had stood all through the game. The bill, thought Alice, must be fantastic, but then the government was probably paying it too. As Stanko stood back for Alice to get in, he said:

'I trust that I am not too precipitate in asking you for another date, Miss Wernecke, but I request that you accompany me to dinner at the Bellevue-Stratford this evening. Is that agreeable to you?'

Now to dine and dance at the Bellevue-Stratford had been an ambition of Alice ever since she settled in the Philadelphia neighbourhood. Unfortunately neither John nor Edward nor any of the occasionals could afford it, and while Mr Lorbeer would have taken her she did not wish to date him under any circumstances. On the other hand she would have preferred never going near the hotel to going with Stanko. But in view of what Byron Matthews had said, she did not quite dare turn him down flat . . .

113

'I can't tell you right now,' she temporised. 'I have a half-way date this evening already.'

'Oh?'

'Y-yes. Let me go home and check up – I'd have to get dressed anyway – and then call me.'

As soon as she got into her apartment she bolted for the telephone, causing Inez to say: 'Here, what goes on?'

Ignoring her room-mate, Alice dialled the Swarthmore Inn and got Byron Matthews. She wailed:

'Byron, that mud-turtle of yours wants to take me out again tonight!'

'Hell!' roared Matthews. 'I worked most of last night to get that report done so I could ask you out tonight myself – though I thought you'd probably be dated up in advance anyway.'

'Then couldn't we just pretend – '

'No! Honey, you've got no idea how important this is. If Stinky wants anything short of physical indignities, go along with him as far as you decently can.'

'Oh. Is that really true? About the importance, I mean. Or are you trying to get out of – '

'True!' came the blast of sound out of the receiver. 'You're damned right it's true. Listen. These Wolfians act friendly and honest enough, and maybe they're all right. But nobody has yet been to their damned planet to check up, see? And they're at least as smart as we are. So it's absolutely vital to keep on the good side of them until we can find out what they *are* up to.'

'You mean I'm a sort of key figure in interplanetary relations?'

'For the time being, yes. So put on a long dress and toddle off with Stinko. If he wants to be a big turtle-about-town, you help him be one.'

'But am I safe? If you don't really know much about these creatures – '

'You'll be as safe as the Department can make you. You didn't notice you were followed by a couple of FBI men all afternoon, did you?'

'No-no.'

'All right then. If the Cultural Representative acts up, just yell.'

She hung up with a sigh. Byron was evidently one of those exasperating males, incomprehensible to any normal woman,

114

who would sacrifice even their women to some abstract ideal. Like that nonsense about 'I could not love thee, dear, so much, loved I not honour more.'

Alice took a bath and made up. Inez caught her admiring her assets in the mirror and remarked sourly: 'Yeah, you make a good appearance, especially without your clothes. But it's all wasted on your friend from the Galapagos.'

Alice made a face at her room-mate, repaired the damages thus done to her make-up, and slid into her second-best evening dress. (She was saving the best one for a hoped-for formal date with Byron Matthews.) At the appointed time Stanko showed up in the same taxi.

At the Bellevue, Alice moodily drank her cocktail and fiddled with her dinner. Being stared at was bad enough, but in addition she found Stanko, even with allowance for the difference of race, to be egregiously dull company. Despite his near-perfect English the extra-terrestrial seemed to have no sense of humour, no sparkle whatever; no visible motivation save an insatiable appetite for facts and statistics about the earth. When she tried to get him to talk about his home planet he answered her questions with curt one-word answers and returned to the attack. His slow monotone was maddening in its deliberation.

The only time she brightened was when he said: 'I trust, Miss Wernecke, that you will not be affronted if I do not ask you to dance. I am not familiar with the sport, and it is moreover one to which my form is not well suited.'

'That's all right,' she said heartily.

At ten Stanko looked at his wrist-watch and said: 'I understand that at this time the more conservative citizens among you are accustomed to return home to sleep. Is that correct?'

'Yes. Wait, Mr Stanko, you have to pay your bill.'

'So I do. Oh, *garcon*! I mean waiter! By the way, Miss Wernecke, I have heard of your custom of tipping. How much do you think I should give?'

Alice made a rough guess and walked out with Stanko. In the taxi home the inquisition continued:

'Now, please explain the social significance of this custom of chewing the gum of the sapodilla tree. Though I have seen many performing the act, I note that neither you nor Mr Matthews does it. Is it regulated by law, or what?'

Alice answered with half her mind, the other half silently

115

urging the driver to get them home as soon as possible to rid her of this galactic bore. At the doorstep, however, Stanko said:

'Wait, Miss Wernecke. I have several things to say. To begin, I think we had better forgo your custom of kissing, which strikes me as most unsanitary. You do not mind?'

'Not in the least!'

'Well then, we now come to the question of our next date. I wondered what we could do tomorrow. Another dinner and dance, perhaps? One of those places of revelry called night-clubs?'

'No, Mr Stanko, you can't. In Philadelphia all the places of revelry are closed on Sunday.'

'Then how about the theatre? It impresses me as a highly developed art-form – '

'They're closed, too.'

'Another motion-picture?'

'I've seen all the good ones.'

'Then how about doing something in the afternoon? For instance, we might pay a visit to the zoological gardens. I have already been there, but I should not mind repeating my visit.'

Alice shook her head grimly. 'The animals bother my allergies, and I see enough monkeys every day in my class.'

'That is unfortunate. Perhaps we could have a swimming party. We' (here he used a word from his own language, full of nasal vowels and guttural consonants) 'are good swimmers.'

'In October? That's much too cold for us mere humans, Mr Stanko. All the pools will be drained.'

Alice suspected that some heated indoor pools might be open in the Philadelphia area, but had no intention of giving him this opening by suggesting it. Interplanetary crisis or not, she was not going out with the Cultural Representative again as long as she could think of excuses.

'I see,' he said, his alien form drooping a little as if with sadness, though his flat voice betrayed no emotion. 'We seem to be at an impasse. Tell me, would you consider the term "a few" as including the number "two"?'

'What an odd question! I suppose you could, though "few" doesn't have any definite limits.'

'Well then, it could be said that I have had a few dates with you. We can count Thursday night's episode as half a date, I think. I had intended to have one more before putting my proposal to you – '

'What proposal?' said Alice, alarm running up her spine.

' – my proposal to you, but since that seems impractical I will stretch a point and proceed. Mr and Mrs Greer were kind enough to tell me much about your custom of marriage. They explained that it was common for a male of your nationality, after he has had a few dates with a female, if he likes her well enough to wish to live with her, to ask her to marry him. As I have now qualified, I ask you to marry me.'

Alice stood staring, her throat refusing to make a sound for several seconds while the enormity of the proposal sank in. At last she squeaked:

'Did you say m-marry?'

'Yes. I assure you that I am not always so devoted to my work as during my present investigation, when I must make every minute count. Back on Wolf 359-1 you will find me an agreeable and not an exacting companion, and you shall enjoy such comforts and luxuries as you are accustomed to on your own world.'

'But – b-but – Stanko, that's im-*possible*!'

'What is impossible about it? Marriage, as I understand it, is a matter of the couple's agreeing before a magistrate to live together in mutual affection and support for the rest of their lives. What prevents us from doing that?'

'It wouldn't be legal, you not being a human being . . . '

'If your magistrates raise legal objections, the captain of our ship can devise the necessary contractual ceremony.'

'Oh, no. Oh, no. Stanko, you don't understand.'

'And what do I fail to comprehend?'

'There's much more to marriage than that.'

'Really? Please explain.'

Alice found herself tongue-tied.

'Well? I await your reply, Miss Wernecke.'

Alice, never having reared children of her own or taught adolescents, had not developed a technique for answering such questions. All that she could say was:

'Didn't the Greers ever say anything about the facts of life?'

'They have explained a great deal, but I do not know if that includes the facts that you have in mind.'

'You know, about the bees and the flowers.'

Stanko gave the Wolfian equivalent of a sigh. 'Miss Wernecke, I am striving to follow you, but am admittedly finding it difficult. Why should the Greers lecture me on insects or plants? Neither is an entomologist or a botanist.'

Alice, feeling her face flaming in the dark, had no choice but to explain in plain words what she meant. When she finished there was a little silence. Then Stanko said:

'I see. Miss Wernecke, I have committed a grave social error, and hope that you will accept my assurances that it was through ignorance and not through intent. By pure chance nobody had explained to me the connection between marriage and the reproductive process to which you allude. On Wolf 359–1 things are managed differently. A male there fertilises a female only once in his life. After that he is assigned to another female to serve her in his time off from work. Our females are much larger than the males – about the size of one of your elephants – and of quite a different exterior form, so that they find it difficult to move about. They are also less numerous, so that each female has sixteen to twenty males assigned to her. And I had erroneously equated this latter relationship to your marriage.'

'But what made you think – ' began Alice in a small voice, close to tears.

'That you would find the relationship agreeable? I fear that I was judging by the reactions of my own kind. This contretemps goes back to when my fellow-explorers were discussing the matter, shortly after we had alighted, and I in a jesting way spoke of bringing an earthly female back home with me. Considering that you are hardly larger than I, the prospect looked inviting. You could hardly mistreat me as my ex-wife, from whom I was divorced so that I could come on this expedition, treated all her husbands.'

Alice could hardly imagine Stanko's joking about anything, but let that pass. He continued:

'The others kidded me (I believe you say) about this rash boast until I swore that I would in fact carry it out. Now that I see that I have failed and have been humiliated in your eyes, my own, and those of my companions, there is nothing for me to do but die. I shall sit down right here and will myself to death.'

'Oh!' cried Alice. 'Don't do that!'

'I am sorry, but there is no alternative. Rest assured that the process will take only an hour or two and then the garbage-collectors will remove my corpse in the morning.'

'But – ' Alice stared helplessly into the darkness, then remembered Byron Matthews's promise of surveillance. She called: 'Help! FBI! Help!'

'Coming,' said a voice. Footsteps pounded.

Three men approached. One was the taxi-driver, one a man whom she had vaguely noticed sitting near her at the Bellevue-Stratford, and the third was Byron Matthews.

In strangled sentences Alice explained what had happened, pointing to Stanko, who had sat down with his back to the wall in a kind of yogic posture and seemed no longer conscious. Then, sobbing, she melted into Matthews's arms.

'Hell and damnation,' he said, 'does that guy have to get ahead of me in everything? I was going to propose to you, too, after a few more dates to get decently acquainted.'

'You were?'

'Yes. But now there's only one thing to do.'

'What?'

'You must marry him, as he says.'

Alice, hardly believing her ears, squirmed out of Matthews's arms.

'Byron Matthews, are you crazy?'

'Wish I were. But we can't have this guy willing himself to death while we're responsible for him. It might cause God knows what kind of interplanetary crisis.'

'Do you know what you're saying? To go to the other end of the universe with this – this – ' She almost said 'mud-turtle', but decided that such an epithet would only aggravate matters.

'I know,' he said grimly. 'I'd as lief marry him myself. But – '

'If you were going to propose to me – '

'Rub it in!' he said furiously. 'I love you. Sure. I do. But I've also got my duty to my country and my world. Corny, isn't it?'

'You mean you'd actually want me to – '

'Who said "want"? I'd rather will myself to death like him first. But I know what I've got to do when I've got to do it. Go on, tell him you will.'

'Byron Matthews, I'll never see you again. I'll never speak to you again, for urging such a thing.'

'Okay, you probably won't have the chance. I know how you feel. But go ahead. You've got to.'

'Here,' said the voice of Inez, 'what's all this? Is everything all right, Alice? I heard you call.'

'Everything's not all right,' said Alice, 'but I don't know what you can do about it. Inez, this is Mr Matthews of the

119

State Department and a couple of gentlemen from the FBI. Miss Rogell. You know Mr Stanko.'

'FBI?' said Inez, the light on the front porch of the little apartment-house gleaming upon her glasses. 'What on earth *is* this? And what's wrong with Mr Stanko? Has he a stomach-ache?'

Alice explained.

'Oh,' said Inez. 'Let me think. Mr Stanko!'

'Yes?' said the Wolfian.

'As far as you're concerned, would you say Miss Wernecke and I were about equally attractive?'

'I should say you were. Perhaps you have a slight advantage, since you look a little more like a female Wolfian.'

'Then it doesn't matter which human female you take back with you, does it?'

'No, though naturally some would prove more congenial companions than others. That, however, is something that could only be determined by trial. What have you in mind?'

'Why not take me instead of Alice?'

Alice gasped. 'Now you're crazy, Inez. I can't let you sacrifice yourself for me.'

'I'm not. I'm just a typical old-maid schoolteacher, and I know it as well as you do. Whereas if I go with Stanko I'll be the first woman on Wolf 359-1 and have all sorts of interesting experiences. Maybe I'll revolutionise their educational system. Well, how about it, Stanko?'

'I accept your offer with pleasure,' said Stanko.

'But Inez – ' began Alice.

'But nothing. I'm doing this because I want to, and I'm a free agent. Drop around tomorrow and we'll make the arrangements, Stank.'

'Thank you, I will.' Stanko got up and began to hobble towards the taxi.

'Alice – ' said Matthews, reaching.

'Go away!' she said, trying to keep down another spate of tears. 'I still never want to see you again, after you tried to get me to – to – '

'But I still love you – '

'And I still hate you!'

Mathews's footsteps receded on the walk as he followed Stanko and the F.B.I. men.

'Seems to me,' said Inez, 'that when you get a chance at a

120

good man like Byron you're a fool not to grab him. If I were in your place – '

'Oh, shut up!' said Alice. The tears were coming freely now.

'But the way, old Lascivious Lorbeer called. He's got a pair of tickets for a concert next Friday night – '

'Oh!' said Alice.

The vision of life without Byron Matthews suddenly filled her mind – bossing her roomful of brats, holding off Lorbeer, tolerating the insipid John and the feckless Edward, grabbing at invitations to parties like the Greers' in hopes of meeting something worth playing up to.

'Byron!' she called.

He came back on the run. Inez tactfully went back inside. When the clinch and the reconciliation had been executed and the vows had been exchanged, he said:

'I haven't had a chance to tell you, but my transfer to the Foreign Service just came through this morning, with a promotion.'

'How splendid! I don't care where they send you; I'll go with you to the ends of the world.'

'Swell! That's the kind of wife a State man needs.'

'Only I hope never to see Stanko or any other Wolfians again.'

'I'm not so sure. We're setting up a new Extra-terrestrial Division in the Foreign Service, and I'm scheduled to be First Secretary of our new embassy on Wolf 359-1 as soon as it's . . . Hey!'

He made as if to catch Alice's arms.

'No, I'm not going to faint,' said Alice. 'It was just the shock. But I'll manage. After all, Byron darling, you do have one advantage over Stanko, don't you?'

SAIL ON! SAIL ON!

by

Philip José Farmer

Friar Sparks sat wedged between the wall and the realiser. He was motionless except for his forefinger and his eyes. From time to time his finger tapped rapidly on the key upon the desk, and now and then his irises, grey-blue as his native Irish sky, swivelled to look through the open door of the *toldilla* in which he crouched, the little shanty on the poop deck. Visibility was low.

Outside was dusk and a lantern by the railing. Two sailors leaned on it. Beyond them bobbed the bright lights and dark shapes of the *Niña* and the *Pinta*. And beyond them was the smooth horizon-brow of the Atlantic, edged in black and blood by the red dome of the rising moon.

The single carbon filament bulb above the monk's tonsure showed a face lost in fat – and in concentration.

The luminiferous ether crackled and hissed tonight, but the phones clamped over his ears carried, along with them, the steady dots and dashes sent by the operator at the Las Palmas station on the Grand Canary.

'*Zzisss!* So you are out of sherry already . . . *Pop!* . . . Too bad . . . *Crackle* . . . you hardened old winebutt . . . *Zzz* . . . May God have mercy on your sins . . .

'Lots of gossip, news, et cetera . . . *Hisses!* . . . Bend your ear instead of your neck, impious one . . . The Turks are said to be gathering . . . *crackle* . . . an army to march on Austria. It is rumoured that the flying sausages, said by so many to have been seen over the capitals of the Christian world, are of Turkish origin. The rumour goes they have been invented by a renegade Rogerian who was converted to the Muslim religion . . . I say . . . *zziss* . . . to that. No one of us would do that. It is a falsity spread by our enemies in the Church to discredit us. But many people believe that . . .

'How close does the Admiral calculate he is to Cipangu now?

'*Flash!* Savonarola today denounced the Pope, the wealthy

of Florence, Greek art and literature, and the experiments of the disciples of Saint Roger Bacon . . . *Zzz!* . . . The man is sincere but misguided and dangerous . . . I predict he'll end up on the stake he's always prescribing for us . . .

'*Pop* . . . This will kill you . . . Two Irish mercenaries by the name of Pat and Mike were walking down the street of Grenada when a beautiful Saracen lady leaned out of a balcony and emptied a pot of . . . *hiss!* . . . and Pat looked up and . . . *Crackle* . . . Good, hah? Brother Juan told that last night . . .

'PV . . . PV . . . Are you coming in? . . . PV . . . PV . . . Yes, I know it's dangerous to bandy such jests about, but nobody is monitoring us tonight . . . *Zzz* . . . I think they're not, anyway . . .'

And so the ether bent and warped with their messages. And presently Friar Sparks tapped out the PV that ended their talk – the *Pax vobiscum*. Then he pulled the plug out that connected his earphones to the set and, lifting them from his ears, clamped them down forward over his temples in the regulation manner.

After sidling bent-kneed from the *toldilla*, punishing his belly against the desk's hard edge as he did so, he walked over to the railing. De Salcedo and de Torres were leaning there and talking in low tones. The big bulb above gleamed on the page's red-gold hair and on the interpreter's full black beard. It also bounced pinkishly off the priest's smooth shaven jowls and the light scarlet robe of the Rogerian order. His cowl, thrown back, served as a bag for scratch paper, pens, an ink bottle, tiny wrenches and screwdrivers, a book on cryptography, a slide rule, and a manual of angelic principles.

'Well, old rind,' said young de Salcedo familiarly, 'what do you hear from Las Palmas?'

'Nothing now. Too much interference from that.' He pointed to the moon riding the horizon ahead of them. 'What an orb!' bellowed the priest. 'It's as big and red as my revered nose!'

The two sailors laughed, and de Salcedo said, 'But it will get smaller and paler as the night grows, Father. And your proboscis will, on the contrary, become larger and more sparkling in inverse proportion according to the square of the ascent – '

He stopped and grinned, for the monk had suddenly dipped his nose, like a porpoise diving into the sea, raised it again, like the same animal jumping from a wave, and then once more plunged it into the heavy currents of their breath. Nose to nose, he faced them, his twinkling little eyes seeming to emit sparks like the realiser in his *toldilla*.

Again, porpoiselike, he sniffed and snuffed several times, quite loudly. Then, satisfied with what he had gleaned from their breaths, he winked at them. He did not, however, mention his findings at once, preferring to sidle towards the subject.

He said, 'This Father Sparks on the Grand Canary is so entertaining. He stimulates me with all sort of philosophical nations, both valid and fantastic. For instance, tonight, just before we were cut off by that' – he gestured at the huge bloodshot eye in the sky – 'he was discussing what he called worlds of parallel time tracks, an idea originated by Dysphagius of Gotham. It's his idea, there may be other worlds in coincident but not contacting universes, that God, being infinite and of unlimited creative talent and ability, the Master Alchemist, in other words, has possibly – perhaps necessarily – created a plurality of continua in which every probable event has happened.'

'Huh?' grunted de Salcedo.

'Exactly. Thus, Columbus was turned down by Queen Isabella, so this attempt to reach the Indies across the Atlantic was never made. So we would not now be standing here plunging ever deeper into Oceanus in our three cockleshells, there would be no booster buoys strung out between us and the Canaries, and Father Sparks at Las Palmas and I on the *Santa María* would not be carrying on our fascinating conversations across the ether.

'Or, say, Roger Bacon was persecuted by the Church, instead of being encouraged and giving rise to the order whose inventions have done so much to insure the monopoly of the church on alchemy and its divinely inspired guidance of that formerly pagan and hellish practice.'

De Torres opened his mouth, but the priest silenced him with a magnificent and imperious gesture and continued.

'Or, even more ridiculous, but thought-provoking, he speculated just this evening on universes with different physical laws. One, in particular, I thought very droll. As you probably don't know, Angelo Angelei has proved, by dropping objects from the Leaning Tower of Pisa, that different weights fall at different speeds. My delightful colleague on the Grand Canary is writing a satire which takes place in a universe where Aristotle is made out to be a liar, where all things drop with equal velocities, no matter what their size. Silly stuff, but it helps to

124

pass the time. We keep the ether busy with our little angels.'

De Salcedo said, 'Uh, I don't want to seem too curious about the secrets of your holy and cryptic orders, Friar Sparks. But these little angels your machine realises intrigue me. Is it a sin to presume to ask about them?'

The monk's bull roar slid to a dove cooing. 'Whether it's a sin or not depends. Let me illustrate, young fellows. If you were concealing a bottle of, say, very scarce sherry on you, and you did not offer to share it with a very thirsty old gentleman, that would be a sin. A sin of omission. But if you were to give that desert-dry, that pilgrim-weary, that devout, humble, and decrepit old soul a long, soothing, refreshing, and stimulating draught of lifegiving fluid, daughter of the vine, I would find it in my heart to pray for you for that deed of loving-kindness, of encompassing charity. And it would please me so much I might tell you a little of our realiser. Not enough to hurt you, just enough so you might gain more respect for the intelligence and glory of my order.'

De Salcedo grinned conspiratorially and passed the monk the bottle he'd hidden under his jacket. As the friar tilted it, and the chug-chug-chug of vanishing sherry became louder, the two sailors glanced meaningfully at each other. No wonder the priest, reputed to be so brilliant in his branch of the alchemical mysteries, had yet been sent off on this half-baked voyage to devil-know-where. The Church had calculated that if he survived, well and good. If he didn't, then he would sin no more.

The monk wiped his lips on his sleeve, belched loudly as a horse, and said, '*Gracias*, boys. From my heart, so deeply buried in this fat, I thank you. An old Irishman, dry as a camel's hoof, choking to death with the dust of abstinence, thanks you. You have saved my life.'

'Thank rather that magic nose of yours,' replied de Salcedo. 'Now, old rind, now that you're well greased again, would you mind explaining as much as you are allowed about that machine of yours?'

Friar Sparks took fifteen minutes. At the end of that time, his listeners asked a few permitted questions.

'. . . and you say you broadcast on a frequency of eighteen hundred k.c.?' the page asked. 'What does "k.c." mean?'

'K stands for the French *kilo*, from a Greek word meaning thousand. And c stands for the Hebrew *cherubim*, the "little angels". Angel comes from the Greek *anglos*, meaning messenger. It is our concept that the ether is crammed with these cherubim, these little messengers. Thus, when we Friar Sparkses depress the key of our machine, we are able to realise some of the infinity of "messengers" waiting for just such a demand for service.

'So, eighteen hundred k.c. means that in a given unit of time one million, eight hundred thousand cherubim line up and hurl themselves across the ether, the noise of one being brushed by the feathertips of the cherub's wings ahead. The height of the wing crests of each little creature is even, so that if you were to draw an outline of the whole train, there would be nothing to distinguish one cherub from the next, the whole column forming that grade of little angels known as C.W.'

'C.W.?'

'Continuous wing height. My machine is a C.W. realiser.'

Young de Salcedo said, 'My mind reels, such a concept! Such a revelation; It almost passes comprehension. Imagine, the aerial of your realiser is cut just so long, so that the evil cherubim surging back and forth on it demand a predetermined and equal number of good angels to combat them. And this seduction coil on the realiser crowds 'bad' angels into the left-hand, the sinister, side. And when the bad little cherubim are crowded so closely and numerously that they can't bear each other's evil company, they jump the spark gap and speed around the wire to the "good" plate. And in this racing back and forth they call themselves to the attention of the "little messengers", the yea-saying cherubim. And you, Friar Sparks, by manipulating your machine thus and so, and by lifting and lowering your key, you bring these invisible and friendly lines of carriers, your etheric and winged postment, into reality. And you are able, thus, to communicate at great distances with your brothers of the order.'

'Great God!' said de Torres.

It was not a vain oath but a pious exclamation of wonder. His eyes bulged; it was evident that he suddenly saw that man was not alone, that on every side, piled on top of each other, flanked on every angle, stood a host. Black and white, they presented a solid chessboard of the seemingly empty cosmos, black for the nay-sayers, white for the yea-sayers, maintained by a Hand in delicate balance and subject as the fowls of the air and the fish of the sea to exploitation by man.

Yet de Torres, having seen such a vision as has made a saint of many a man, could only ask, 'Perhaps you could tell me how many angels may stand on the point of a pin?'

Obviously, de Torres would never wear a halo. He was destined, if he lived, to cover his bony head with the mortarboard of a university teacher.

De Salcedo snorted. 'I'll tell you. Philosophically speaking, you may put as many angels on the pinhead as you want to. Actually speaking, you may put only as many as there is room for. Enough of that. I'm interested in facts, not fancies. Tell me, how could the moon's rising interrupt your reception of the cherubim sent by the Sparks at Las Palmas?'

'Great Caesar, how would I know? Am I a repository of universal knowledge? No, not I! A humble and ignorant friar, I! All I can tell you is that last night it rose like a bloody tumour on the horizon, and that when it was up I had to quit marshalling my little messengers in their short and long columns. The Canary station was quite overpowered, so that both of us gave up. And the same thing happened tonight.'

'The moon sends messages?' asked de Torres.

'Not in a code I can decipher. But it sends, yes.'

'Santa María!'

'Perhaps,' suggested de Salcedo, 'there are people on that moon, and they are sending.'

Friar Sparks blew derision through his nose. Enormous as were his nostrils, his derision was not small-bore. Artillery of contempt laid down a barrage that would have silenced any but the strongest of souls.

'Maybe – ' de Torres spoke in a low tone – 'maybe, if the stars are windows in heaven, as I've heard said, the angels of the higher hierarchy, the big ones, are realising – uh – the smaller? And they only do it when the moon is up so we may know it is a celestial phenomenon?'

He crossed himself and looked around the vessel.

'You need not fear,' said the monk gently. 'There is no Inquisitor leaning over your shoulder. Remember, I am the only priest on this expedition. Moreover, your conjecture has nothing to do with dogma. However, that's unimportant. Here's what I don't understand: How can a heavenly body broadcast? Why does it have the same frequency as the one I'm restricted to? Why – '

'I could explain,' interrupted de Salcedo with all the brashness and impatience of youth. 'I could say that the Admiral and the Rogerians are wrong about the earth's shape. I could say the earth is not round but is flat. I could say the horizon

127

exists, not because we live upon a globe, but because the earth is curved only a little way, like a greatly flattened out hemisphere. I could also say that the cherubim are coming, not from Luna, but from a ship such as ours, a vessel which is hanging in the void off the edge of the earth.'

'What?' gasped the other two.

'Haven't you heard,' said de Salcedo, 'that the King of Portugal secretly sent out a ship after he turned down Columbus' proposal? How do we know he did not, that the messages are from our predecessor, that he sailed off the world's rim and is now suspended in the air and becomes exposed at night because it follows the moon around Terra – is, in fact, a much smaller and unseen satellite?'

The monk's laughter woke many men on the ship. 'I'll have to tell the Las Palmas operator your tale. He can put it in that novel of his. Next you'll be telling me those messages are from one of those fire-shooting sausages so many credulous laymen have been seeing flying around. No, my dear de Salcedo, let's not be ridiculous. Even the ancient Greeks knew the earth was round. Every university in Europe teaches that. And we Rogerians have measured the circumference. We know for sure that the Indies lie just across the Atlantic. Just as we know for sure, through mathematics, that heavier-than-air machines are impossible. Our Friar Ripskulls, our mind doctors, have assured us these flying creations are mass hallucinations or else the tricks of heretics or Turks who want to panic the populace.

'That moon radio is no delusion, I'll grant you. What it is, I don't know. But it's not a Spanish or Portuguese ship. What about its different code? Even if it came from Lisbon, that ship would still have a Rogerian operator. And he would, according to our policy, be of a different nationality from the crew so he might the easier stay out of political embroilments. He wouldn't break our laws by using a different code in order to communicate with Lisbon. We disciples of Saint Roger do not stoop to petty boundary intrigues. Moreover, that realiser would not be powerful enough to reach Europe, and must, therefore, be directed at us.'

'How can you be sure?' said de Salcedo. 'Distressing though the thought may be to you, a priest could be subverted. Or a layman could learn your secrets and invent a code. I think that a Portuguese ship is sending to another, a ship perhaps not too distant from us.'

De Torres shivered and crossed himself again. 'Perhaps the angels are warning us of approaching death? Perhaps?'

'Perhaps? Then why don't they use our code? Angels would know it as well as I. No, there is no perhaps. The order does not permit perhaps. It experiments and finds out; nor does it pass judgement until it knows.'

'I doubt we'll ever know,' said de Salcedo gloomily. 'Columbus has promised the crew that if we come across no sign of land by evening tomorrow, we shall turn back. Otherwise – ' he drew a finger across his throat – 'kkk! Another day, and we'll be pointed east and getting away from that evil bloody-looking moon and its incomprehensible messages.'

'It would be a great loss to the order and to the Church,' sighed the friar. 'But I leave such things in the hands of God and inspect only what He hands me to look at.'

With which pious statement Friar Sparks lifted the bottle to ascertain the liquid level. Having determined in a scientific manner its existence, he next measured its quantity and tested its quality by putting all of it in that best of all chemistry tubes, his enormous belly.

Afterwards, smacking his lips and ignoring the pained and disappointed looks on the faces of the sailors, he went on to speak enthusiastically of the water screw and the engine which turned it, both of which had been built recently at the St Jonas College at Genoa. If Isabella's three ships had been equipped with those, he declared, they would not have to depend upon the wind. However, so far the fathers had forbidden its extended use because it was feared the engine's fumes might poison the air and the terrible speeds it made possible might be fatal to the human body. After which he plunged into a tedious description of the life of his patron saint, the inventor of the first cherubim realiser and receiver, Jonas of Carcassonne, who had been martyred when he grabbed a wire he thought was insulated.

The two sailors found excuses to walk off. The monk was a good fellow, but hagiography bored them. Besides, they wanted to talk of women . . .

If Columbus had not succeeded in persuading his crews to sail one more day, events would have been different.

At dawn the sailors were very much cheered by the sight of several large birds circling their ships. Land could not be far off; perhaps these winged creatures came from the coast of fabled Cipangu itself, the country whose houses were roofed with gold.

The birds swooped down. Closer, they were enormous and very strange. Their bodies were flattish and almost saucer-shaped and small in proportion to the wings, which had a spread of at least thirty feet. Nor did they have legs. Only a few sailors saw the significance of that fact. These birds dwelt in the air and never rested upon land or sea.

While they were meditating upon that, they heard a slight sound as of a man clearing his throat. So gentle and far off was the noise that nobody paid any attention to it, for each thought his neighbour had made it.

A few minutes later, the sound had become louder and deeper, like a lute string being twanged.

Everybody looked up. Heads were turned west.

Even yet they did not understand that the noise like a finger plucking a wire came from the line that held the earth to-gether, and that the line was stretched to its utmost, and that the violent finger of the sea was what had plucked the line.

It was some time before they understood. They had run out of horizon.

When they saw that, they were too late.

The dawn had not only come up *like* thunder, it *was* thunder. And though the three ships heeled over at once and tried to sail close-hauled on the port tack, they suddenly speeded up and relentless current made beating hopeless.

Then it was the Rogerian wished for the Genoese screw and the wood-burning engine that would have made them able to resist the terrible muscles of the charging and bull-like sea. Then it was that some men prayed, some raved, some tried to attack the Admiral, some jumped overboard, and some sank into a stupor.

Only the fearless Columbus and the courageous Friar Sparks stuck to their duties. All that day the fat monk crouched wedged in his little shanty, dot-dashing to his fellow on the Grand Canary. He ceased only when the moon rose like a huge red bubble from the throat of a dying giant. Then he listened intently all night and worked desperately, scribbling and swearing impiously and checking cipher books.

When the dawn came up again in a roar and a rush, he ran from the *toldilla*, a piece of paper clutched in his hand. His eyes were wild, and his lips were moving fast, but nobody could understand that he had cracked the code. They could

130

not hear him shouting, 'It is the Portuguese! It is the Portuguese!'

Their ears were too overwhelmed to hear a mere human voice. The throat clearing and the twanging of the string had been the noises preliminary to the concert itself. Now came the mighty overture; as compelling as the blast of Gabriel's horn was the topple of Oceanus into space.

COMMENT ON

SAIL ON! SAIL ON!

An Exercise in Logical Extrapolation

Three years before *Sail On! Sail On!* was written, I had a dream. I saw the tiny galleon of the Portuguese Prince Henry the Navigator (1394-1460 A.D.) It was sailing along in a heavy sea and on a dark night. A small building was on the poop-deck; in it sat a very fat monk. He had earphones on and was tapping out a coded message, in Latin, on a sparkgap transmitter.

That was all. The dream ended. However, I never forgot it. And a year later, the dream came to me again, as many of my best dreams do. Six months afterwards, the dream occurred again. For some reason, my unconscious insisted upon thrusting up this strange picture. Perhaps it was a rather bizarre form of a warning to me. If so, I never got the message. Instead, I wondered what kind of story I could make out of it.

Before I even worked the story out, I had exchanged Columbus for Prince Henry. As a child, I had always been fascinated by the idea of Columbus' falling off the edge of the world. Even when I was told that the Earth was round, I did not quite believe it. I did not want to believe it. A square flat world seemed to me to be more romantic and satisfying than an orange-shaped planet. What a great sensation it would be to sit on the edge and dangle your feet over the abyss of space and the stars! What a deliciously terrifying feeling to climb down the cliff-like sides of Earth to the very bottom, clinging to the roots of trees and projecting rocks and wondering if you would fall off and hurtle forever through the nothingness!

So I sat down (more than once) and wrote the story. It took

131

place in a parallel universe and on an Earth with a more rapid advance of science than in the days of the Columbus of our world. At the time I wrote *Sail On! Sail On!* I had not completely worked out the universe in which it took place. All I considered were a few premises. The Earth was flat, was fixed in the centre of the cosmos, other celestial objects revolved around Earth, a 50-pound cannonball fell faster than a 10-pound cannonball.

Also, Roger Bacon, instead of being persecuted by the Church, had founded an order of truly experimental scientists. This order had tried to keep science as an ecclesiastical province.

One other premise that I have now added is the simultaneous creation of the universe and of living beings. In other words, a creation which follows, more or less, the Biblical account.

In Columbus' time, very few educated people believed the Earth to be flat. There were many different theories: the Earth was a sphere, was flat, was a cylinder, was a tabernacle in shape, and so on. The Church maintained that the universe was geocentric. It does not matter how many theories or near-dogmas there were or how much they conflicted. I based the story on some of the then-current theories, the simple premises stated above. These are not wholly Ptolemaic, Lactantian, or entirely derived from any of the ancient or medieval cosmologists. The premises are easily expressed in the very short *Sail On! Sail On!*

At a later time, I expanded my own cosmology and at once ran into trouble. Eventually, I seemed to have solved all the problems. I forgot them until an editor asked me if I would write a sequel to the short story, preferably a short novel. As of now, I have not written the novel. However, the editor of this anthology asked me for a favourite short story of mine and an essay about it. Then I did some more thinking.

Remember that, in building this universe, I am trying to be logical and also trying to make the flat Earth resemble our round planet as much as possible in all its features, that is, human beings, climate, geography, etc. Unfortunately, all these have to deviate somewhat if logical extrapolation is to be strictly followed.

One of the first things to consider is Space itself. Is the tiny cosmos filled with air, as so many at that time believed? If so, how are the crushing effects of the immense amount of air avoided? Obviously, physical 'laws' are different in my story. Could the ubiquitous atmosphere have properties which make it weightless? No. If air has no weight, there are no winds. If there are no winds, there are no sailships or windmills. Worse, the clouds would not be carried over the Earth to distribute their burden of rain or cooling moisture.

Another thing to consider is the sun. What keeps it from burning up the air which fills the universe? Would not, however, this combustion create a wind in space with the air continually moving in to fill the vacuum made by the consumed air? It might, but the wind would not be the kind we know on our Earth.

As for the sun itself, it cannot be the titanic fusion furnace that burns in our skies. It has to be a small low-grade nuclear reactor far enough from Earth so that the deadly radioactivity is absorbed by the spatial atmosphere (if it exists) or dissipated in space.

This furnace would, however, in a relatively short time use up all the air in the Lilliputian world. So I apply the Hoyle-Gold speculation of the continuous creation of matter in space. I do not have to explain how this matter is spontaneously generated any more than the two astronomers do. If matter (hydrogen atoms, the building blocks of our universe) can come from a seeming nothing in the space of our world, why not oxygen, nitrogen, and other elements in this parallel world?

I am still left with the problem of how to get the air to behave on the surface of the flat Earth as it does on our pear shape. Maybe oxygen, nitrogen, etc., have an exceedingly slight weight with the Earth piling up a denser atmosphere around it and the atmosphere thinner in interplanetary space? But if these elements are lighter than in our world, then the other elements should also be lighter. The table of chemical elements would be a different one then in that Second World. The Columbus of it would not weigh as much as our Columbus. However, the objects and creatures of that Second World are in an enclosed cosmos and are only weighed against each other, not against us.

As you can see, I am getting into more and more trouble as I extrapolate. It is not easy to make your own universe, not if you insist on sticking to your own rules, and I do. If I cannot adhere to the rules, I hurl the aborted universe out the front

133

door with utter ruin and furious imprecation and try to forget about it.

So, air does have weight and concentrates around the Earth, Moon, Mars, and other heavenly bodies. And it has the same weight and other properties of our air. I have to make it so because, if air were in interplanetary space, the friction would slow down the bodies revolving around the Earth. I hate to do this, since I had envisioned Columbus and his crew getting to the Moon through the cosmic atmosphere. But this idea just will not work.

The flat Earth has much less mass than ours, about one-sixteenth. The lesser mass is caused by the very flatness of Earth. The molten iron core is missing. This also means that the coreless nonrotating Earth has no magnetic field.

The Moon, which is reduced in mass by one-sixteenth and is flat, is tilted with one side always presented to Earth. That was my first thought, later abandoned. Why cannot the bodies orbiting about Earth be spheres? They can be. But then this means that the Earth and Moon are similar in mass, and I don't want this. So I give Earth back its lost mass by adding to the level substructure of the planet.

The Sun remains a small body. But if its orbits around the Earth and outside the Moon, it must have a very high velocity to make the circuit in time to give Earth the night and day we know. If it goes outside all the planets, it has to travel very swiftly indeed. The only way out is to have the Sun circle between the Moon and Mars, which makes a very peculiar setup. It takes us one more step away from the Earth that we know. I am having as much trouble explaining my universe as Ptolemy had with his cycles, epicycles, and deferents.

Another thing that has to be readjusted is the mass of the other planets. Earth just does not hold enough to hold the mighty giants Jupiter, Saturn, Neptune, and Uranus in orbits around it. Even though Earth is fixed in the centre of the universe, it would undergo a disrupting strain from the attraction of the giants. I can postulate some force (unknown in our universe) that keeps Earth pinned to the centre, but I cannot overlook the pull of the other planets. So, the giants must become midgets, and if they are to keep the same apparent size as they have in our world, they must be brought much closer to Earth.

Whew! I feel the strain of re-creation, which is beginning to require so much mental labour that it's no longer a recreation.

Challenging, yes, but exasperating because, as soon as I think of one facet of this little cosmos, something else contradicts it, and I have to go back to the beginning and do a rebalancing of forces and positions.

This rearrangement affects all sorts of natural phenomena and human factors. Both astronomy and astrology would differ considerably in the Second World. Then there are the tides, the seasons, equinoxes, solstices, and a hundred other things to consider. Either the sun has to have an eccentric and variable orbit or the Earth is not rigidly fixed but has a wobble or libration or both occur.

Note also that various solar phenomena such as sunspots, flares, cosmic rays, etc., would be absent, unproduced by the low-grade nuclear furnace. Also absent would be ultraviolet radiation; in fact, the spectrum of the sun as we know it just would not exist. Thus, the lack of sun-sponsored radiations and cosmic rays, etc., could mean that mutations would be much less frequent on the flat Earth. A lower evolution of life would result.

This does not bother me, since I am assuming that the Biblical story of creation is true in the parallel universe. Do not tell me that this is fantasy, nonscientific, and so not science-fiction. If you will exert yourself enough to discard your prejudices for just a few minutes, you will see that split-second creation is just as possible (or scientific) as a billion-year evolution of physical matter and of life.

I do not believe that our universe and the beings of our Earth originated as described in Genesis. I cannot believe because the weight (overwhelming) of evidence indicates that the Genesis story is only one of many ancient creation myths. Even that contains two somewhat dissimilar tales. However, I can believe that our universe *could have* originated in one day or a microsecond if the Creator had so desired. Why not?

Furthermore, I am not convinced that our interpretation of evidence for evolution is the correct one or the only one. I would not be surprised if, some day, the theory of evolution as we know it is not topsyturvied by some genius. Then we will wonder how we all could have been so blind when we had all the testimony to the truth right before our eyes. I say this because, during my forty-eight and a half years on this Earth, I have seen too many 'facts' of science refuted, not once but many times. The final word is far from being in.

The adoption of the Genesis story of creation might seem

to simplify matters. Actually, it complicates. If you assume (as most Orthodox Jews and Mohammedans and fundamentalist Christians do) that Adam and Eve were white and probably Semetic-speakers, then you have the problem of other races and other languages. If the universe is only six thousand years old (or even a hundred thousand), there just is not enough time for the formation of Negroes, Mongolians, and Amerinds from the basic white couple. And the story of Noah and the Flood has to be a myth, even in the Second World. Again, there is not near enough time for races and languages to develop from the little, white, and (presumably) Semitic-speaking family of Noah. Nor is there enough time to account for the distribution of animals in the continents, especially Australia.

Many things have to be altered to present a consistent and logical universe. If the Earth is flat, it cannot be entirely so. It may be level on the sides and bottom, but the top, containing the continents and oceans, has to have some curvature. Otherwise, how will the rivers flow from source to mouth? And if the sun strikes all areas of Earth with a nearly equal intensity, humanity will be nearly uniform in colour. It's no coincidence that the dark races and stocks are in the tropical or near-tropical regions. (Exceptions can be accounted for by migration.)

I can postulate a simultaneous creation of all the races, have a white Adam and Eve, a black, a Mongolian, and Australoid, a pygmy Adam and Eve. But this does not help me in making sure that the Earth has different temperature zones.

Thus, Earth, seen sideways from space, looks like the profile of a lens or a flattened-out dome. The continents (the Americas missing of course) are spread out over this dome. The waters of Oceanus, the great body surrounding Eurasia, Africa, and Australia, are carried over the edge of Earth by their impetus and by lack of natural barriers. The oceanic waters roar out over the edge in a cataract, curve out, then fall back on to the sides of the understructure of the planet. They then proceed to spread out on the underside. Some peculiar effects would result from the moon's drag on the top, bottom, and sides of this body of water.

In time, the oceans would run dry on the upper part of the planet. However, I postulate a rocky wall along the edges to contain most of the ocean. Here and there are breaks, and through this the waters pour. But the water, flowing 'down' the side and across the flat underside, rises (or 'falls') through fissures in the body of the planet and so replenishes the water on the top side. This is the only way to account for Oceanus not emptying itself.

What keeps the gravitational attraction of the great mass of Earth from breaking up the elongated hemisphere and re-forming it into a ball? Remember, the Earth was never a molten and spinning spheroid. It was created solid and does not rotate. Besides, it is only six thousand years old and has not had time to crumble in on itself, even if there were forces to cause this, which there are not.

Most of the terms used by Friar Sparks in *Sail On! Sail On!* are, I hope, self-evident. The Baconian scientists, being church-men, would tend to describe physical phenomena in theological phrases. Thus, radio waves are thought of as little angelic messengers and positive and negative electricity are 'good' and 'bad' angels. The spark-gap transmitter 'realises' the angels, which fill the ether in a chaos or disarrangement. The realiser places a number of angels in temporary order so that messages may be transmitted for the good of mankind or for the Baconians, anyway.

Friar Sparks and his society are only following their pro-fessional bent in their type of description of natural phe-nomena. Undoubtedly, when science becomes even more ad-vanced on the flat Earth, quantum jumps will be described as 'states of grace', A jump of an electron (or 'angel') from a high energy level to a low will be a 'fall' from grace. Gravitational attraction might be *caritas*, a form of love between physical objects. Since heavier things fall faster than lighter things, the heavier have more *caritas*.

As you can see, a full delving into the universe of the Colum-bus of this story would require far more wordage than in the story itself. Some day I will write a sequel. Then the full extrapolation will be done.

Meanwhile, Columbus hurtles over the edge of the world.

PHILIP JOSÉ FARMER

COMMENT ON
MISSING LINK

Missing Link was conceived as a story exploring the effects of a dominant ecological force (the planet covered with giant trees) upon a society of sentient beings. Much science fiction, of course, starts with this sort of 'what if' idea, expanding the idea along avenues sufficiently hominoid that the reader can understand and identify with the characters.

No story, SF or otherwise, can come off however without real people and problems. For *Missing Link* I had ready at hand the characters and general type of problem situation which I used in *You Take The High Road* (Astounding Science Fiction) and later developed in *Operation Haystack* and *Priests of Psi*. This concerns efforts to re-establish a galactic civilisation after a fragmenting and destructive war, and with two government bureaus contending for dominance – one involved with re-discovery and re-education of the planetary populations, the other intent on preventing another galactic holocaust.

For the population of Gienah III, the world of *Missing Link*, I employed alien sentients rather than re-discovered humans to introduce another problem element (the dangerous unknown) and because this allowed me to make them just that much different from humans as dictated by the ecology of this planet.

To keep them from getting too far afield, too alien for the reader to understand, I introduced some biological facts discovered on Earth. Chief of these is the eye of vertically slit pupils, a characteristic of predators that leap down on to their prey.

Given the situation, much of the development appears obvious. Gienah III's population is necessarily arboreal. It has a slave culture, is capable of seeing in the gloomy floor of the forest and travelling on vine lanes. The Gienah language is conditioned by the world pattern thus presented.

This then is the gross structural outline.

Because it's a short story (6,000 words) the characters are splashed on to the page briefly and sharply at the beginning to make them stick and allow the reader to get on with it. The situation is drawn in with an equally heavy hand for the same reasons.

Everything turns on the characteristics of the alien culture as deduced by the hero. The chief clues are presented as semantic oddities to be analysed by what is seen and heard of this race on Gienah III. The fuse is lit, things are going to explode and you're asked to share the mental processes of Lewis Orne, the hero of *Missing Link*, as he prevents disaster.

With this as background, you should be able to follow the plot developments to their logical conclusion, perhaps anticipating the situations and discoveries. Keep in mind that this is a fairly light story. Its primary aim was entertainment, the exploration of an interesting idea.

FRANK HERBERT

MISSING LINK

by

Frank Herbert

'We ought to scrape this planet clean of every living thing on it,' muttered Umbo Stetson, section chief of Investigation & Adjustment.

Stetson paced the landing control bridge of his scout cruiser. His footsteps grated on a floor that was the rear wall of the bridge during flight. But now the ship rested on its tail fins – all four hundred glistening red and black metres of it. The open ports of the bridge looked out on the jungle roof of Gienah III some one hundred fifty metres below. A butter yellow sun hung above the horizon, perhaps an hour from setting.

'Clean as an egg!' he barked. He paused in his round of the bridge, glared out the starboard port, spat into the fire-blackened circle that the cruiser's jets had burned from the jungle.

The I-A section chief was dark-haired, gangling, with large head and big features. He stood in his customary slouch, a stance not improved by sacklike patched blue fatigues. Although on this present operation he rated the flag of a division admiral, his fatigues carried no insignia. There was a general unkempt, straggling look about him.

Lewis Orne, junior I-A field man with a maiden diploma, stood at the opposite port, studying the jungle horizon. Now and then he glanced at the bridge control console, the chrono-meter above it, the big translite map of their position tilted from the opposite bulkhead. A heavy planet native, he felt vaguely uneasy on this Gienah III with its gravity of only seven-eighths Terran Standard. The surgical scars on his neck where the micro-communications equipment had been inserted itched maddeningly. He scratched.

'Hah!' said Stetson. 'Politicians!'

A thin black insect with shell-like wings flew in Orne's port, settled in his close-cropped red hair. Orne pulled the insect gently from his hair, released it. Again it tried to land in his hair. He ducked. It flew across the bridge, out the port beside Stetson.

There was a thick-muscled, no-fat look to Orne, but something about his blocky, off-centre features suggested a clown.

'I'm getting tired of waiting,' he said.

'*You're* tired! Hah!'

A breeze rippled the tops of the green ocean below them. Here and there, red and purple flowers jutted from the verdure, bending and nodding like an attentive audience.

'Just look at the blasted jungle!' barked Stetson. 'Them and their stupid orders!'

A call bell tinkled on the bridge control console. The red light above the speaker grid began blinking. Stetson shot an angry glance at it. 'Yeah, Hal?'

'O.K., Stet. Orders just came through. We use Plan C. ComGO says to brief the field man, and jet out of here.'

'Did you ask them about using another field man?'

Orne looked up attentively.

The speaker said: 'Yes. They said we have to use Orne because of the records on the *Delphinus*.'

'Well then, will they give us more time to brief him?'

'Negative. It's crash priority. ComGO expects to blast the planet anyway.'

Stetson glared at the grid. 'Those fat-headed, lard-bottomed, pig-brained . . . POLITICIANS!' He took two deep breaths, subsided. 'O.K. Tell them we'll comply.'

'One more thing, Stet.'

'What now?'

'I've got a confirmed contact.'

Instantly, Stetson was poised on the balls of his feet, alert. 'Where?'

'About ten kilometres out. Section AAB-6.'

'How many?'

'A mob. You want I should count them?'

'No. What're they doing?'

'Making a beeline for us. You better get a move on.'

'O.K. Keep us posted.'

'Right.'

Stetson looked across at his junior field man. 'Orne, if you decide you want out of this assignment, you just say the word. I'll back you to the hilt.'

'Why should I want out of my first field assignment?'

'Listen, and find out.' Stetson crossed to a tilt-locker behind the big translite map, hauled out a white coverall uniform with gold insignia, tossed it to Orne. 'Get into these while I brief you on the map.'

'But this is a R&R uni – ' began Orne.

'Get that uniform on your ugly frame!'

'Yes, sir, Admiral Stetson, sir. Right away, sir. But I thought I was through with old Rediscovery & Re-education when you drafted me off to Hamal into the I-A . . . sir.' He began changing from the I-A blue to the R&R white. Almost as an afterthought, he said: ' . . . Sir.'

A wolfish grin cracked Stetson's big features. 'I'm sooooooo happy you have the proper attitude of subservience towards authority.'

Orne zipped up the coverall uniform. 'Oh, yes, sir . . . sir.'

'O.K., Orne, pay attention.' Stetson gestured at the map with its green superimposed grid squares. 'Here we are. Here's that city we flew over on our way down. You'll head for it as soon as we drop you. The place is big enough that if you hold a course roughly north-east you can't miss it. We're – '

Again the call bell rang.

'What is it this time, Hal?' barked Stetson.

'They've changed to Plan H, Stet. New orders cut.'

'Five days?'

'That's all they can give us. ComGO says he can't keep the information out of High Commissioner Bullone's hands any longer than that.'

'It's five days for sure then.'

'Is this the usual R&S foul-up?' asked Orne.

Stetson nodded. 'Thanks to Bullone and company! We're just one jump ahead of catastrophe, but they still pump the bushwah into the Rah & Rah boys back at dear old Uni-Galacta!'

'You're making light of my revered alma mater,' said Orne. He struck a pose. 'We must reunite the lost planets with our centres of culture and industry, and take up the *glor*-ious onward march of mankind that was so *bru*-tally – '

'Can it!' snapped Stetson. 'We both know we're going to rediscover one planet too many some day. Rim War all over again. But this is a different breed of fish. It's not, repeat, *not* a *re*-discovery.'

Orne sobered. 'Alien?'

142

'Yes. A-L-I-E-N! A never-before-contacted culture. That language you were force fed on the way over: that's an alien language. It's not complete . . . all we have off the *minis*. And we excluded data on the natives because we've been hoping to dump this project and nobody the wiser.'

'Holy mazoo!'

'Twenty-six days ago an I-A search ship came through here, had a routine mini-sneaker look at the place. When he combed in his net of snakers to check the tapes and films, lo and behold, he had a little stranger.'

'One of *theirs*?'

'No. It was a *mini* off the *Delphinus Rediscovery*. The *Delphinus* has been unreported for eighteen standard months!'

'Did it crack up here?'

'We don't know. If it did, we haven't been able to spot it. She was supposed to be way off in the Balandine System by now. But we've something else on our minds. It's the one item that makes me want to blot out this place, and run home with my tail between my legs. We've a –'

Again the call bell chimed.

'NOW WHAT?' roared Stetson into the speaker.

'I've got a *mini* over that mob, Stet. They're talking about us. It's a definite raiding party.'

'What armament?'

'Too gloomy in that jungle to be sure. The infra beam's out on this *mini*. Look like hard pellet rifles of some kind. Might even be off the *Delphinus*.'

'Can't you get closer?'

'Wouldn't do any good. No light down there, and they're moving up fast.'

'Keep an eye on them, but don't ignore the other sectors,' said Stetson.

'You think I was born yesterday?' barked the voice from the grid. The contact broke off with an angry sound.

'One thing I like about the I-A,' said Stetson. 'It collects such even-tempered types.' He looked at the white uniform on Orne, wiped a hand across his mouth as though he'd tasted something dirty.

'Why *am* I wearing this thing?' asked Orne.

'Disguise.'

'But there's no moustache!'

Stetson smiled without humour. 'That's one of I-A's answers

143

to those fat-keistered politicians. We're setting up our own search system to find the planets before *they* do. We've managed to put spies in key places at R&R. Any touchy planets our spies report, we divert the files.'

'Then what?'

'Then we look into them with bright boys like you – disguised as R&R field men.'

'Goody, goody. And what happens if R&R stumbles on to me while I'm down there playing patty cake?'

'We disown you.'

'But you said an I-A ship found this joint.'

'It did. And then one of our spies in R&R intercepted a *routine* request for an agent-instructor to be assigned here with full equipment. Request signed by a First-Contact officer name of Diston . . . of the *Delphinus*!'

'But the *Del* – '

'Yeah. Missing. The request was a forgery. Now you see why I'm mostly for rubbing out this place. Who'd dare forge such a thing unless he knew for sure that the original FC officer was missing . . . or dead?'

'What the jumped up mazoo are we doing here, Stet?' asked Orne. 'Alien calls for a full contact team with all of the –'

'It calls for one planet-buster bomb . . . buster – in five days. Unless you give them a white bill in the meantime. High Commissioner Bullone will have word of this planet by then. If Gienah III still exists in five days, can't you imagine the fun the politicians'll have with it? Mama mia! We want this planet cleared for contact or dead before then.'

'I don't like this, Stet.'

'*You* don't like it?'

'Look,' said Orne. 'There must be another way. Why . . . when we teamed up with the Alerinoids we gained five hundred years in the physical sciences alone, not to mention the – '

'The Alerinoids didn't knock over one of our survey ships first.'

'What if the *Delphinus* just crashed here . . . and the locals picked up the pieces?'

'That's what you're going in to find out, Orne. But answer me this: if they *do* have the *Delphinus*, how long before a tool-using race could be a threat to the galaxy?'

'I saw that city they built, Stet. They could be dug in within six months, and there'd be no – '

'Yeah.'

Orne shook his head. 'But think of it: Two civilisations that matured along different lines! Think of all the different ways we'd approach the same problems . . . the lever that'd give us for – '

'You sound like a Uni-Galacta lecture! Are you through marching arm in arm into the misty future?'

Orne took a deep breath. 'Why's a freshman like me being tossed into this dish?'

'You'd still be on the *Delphinus* master lists as an R&R field man. That's important if you're masquerading.'

'Am I the only one? I know I'm a recent *convert*, but – '

'You want out?'

'I didn't say that. I just want to know why I'm – '

'Because the bigdomes fed a set of requirements into one of their iron monsters. Your card popped out. They were looking for somebody capable, dependable . . . and . . . *expendable*!'

'Hey!'

'That's why I'm down here briefing you instead of sitting back on a flagship. *I* got you into the I-A. Now, you listen carefully: If you push the panic button on this one without cause, I will personally flay you alive. We both know the advantages of an alien contact. But if you get into a hot spot, and call for help, I'll dive this cruiser into that city and get you out!'

Orne swallowed. 'Thanks, Stet. I'm – '

'We're going to take up a tight orbit. Out beyond us will be five transports full of I-A marines and a Class IX Monitor with one planet-buster. You're calling the shots, God help you! First, we want to know if they have the *Delphinus* . . . and if so, where it is. Next, we want to know just how warlike these goons are. Can we control them if they're bloodthirsty. What's their potential?'

'In five days?'

'Not a second more.'

'What do we know about them?'

'Not much. They look something like an ancient Terran chimpanzee . . . only with blue fur. Face is hairless, pink-skinned.' Stetson snapped a switch. The translite map became a screen with a figure frozen on it, 'Like that. This is life size.'

'Looks like the missing link they're always hunting for,' said Orne.

'Yeah, but you've got a different kind of a missing link.'

'Vertical-slit pupils in their eyes,' said Orne. He studied the figure. It had been caught from the front by a mini-sneaker camera. About five feet tall. The stance was slightly bent forward, long arms. Two vertical nose slits. A flat, lipless mouth. Receding chin. Four-fingered hands. It wore a wide belt from which dangled neat pouches and what looked like tools, although their use was obscure. There appeared to be the tip of a tail protruding from behind one of the squat legs. Behind the creature towered the faery spires of the city they'd observed from the air.

'Tails?' asked Orne.

'Yeah. They're arboreal. Not a road on the whole planet that we can find. But there are lots of vine lanes through the jungles.' Stetson's face hardened. 'Match *that* with a city as advanced as that one.'

'Slave culture?'

'Probably.'

'How many cities have they?'

'We've found two. This one and another on the other side of the planet. But the other one's a ruin.'

'A ruin? Why?'

'You tell us. Lots of mysteries here.'

'What's the planet like?'

'Mostly jungle. There are polar oceans, lakes and rivers. One low mountain chain follows the equatorial belt about two thirds around the planet.'

'But only two cities. Are you sure?'

'Reasonably so. It'd be pretty hard to miss something the size of that thing we flew over. It must be fifty kilometres long and at least ten wide. Swarming with these creatures, too. We've got a zone-count estimate that places the city's population at over thirty million.'

'Whee-ew! Those are tall buildings, too.'

'We don't know much about this place, Orne. And unless you bring them into the fold, there'll be nothing but ashes for our archaeologists to pick over.'

'Seems a dirty shame.'

'I agree, but – '

The call bell jangled.

Stetson's voice sounded tired: 'Yeah, Hal?'

'That mob's only about five kilometres out, Stet. We've got Orne's gear outside in the disguised air sled.'

146

'We'll be right down.'

'Why a disguised sled?' asked Orne.

'If they think it's a ground buggy, they might get careless when you most need an advantage. We could always scoop you out of the air, you know.'

'What're my chances on this one, Stet?'

Stetson shrugged. 'I'm afraid they're slim. These goons probably have the *Delphinus*, and they want you just long enough to get your equipment and everything you know.'

'Rough as that, eh?'

'According to our best guess. If you're not out in five days, we blast.'

Orne cleared his throat.

'Want out?' asked Stetson.

'No.'

'Use the *back-door* rule, son. Always leave yourself a way out. Now . . . let's check that equipment the surgeons put in your neck.' Stetson put a hand to his throat. His mouth remained closed, but there was a surf-hissing voice in Orne's ears: 'You read me?'

'Sure. I can –'

'No!' hissed the voice. 'Touch the mike contact. Keep your mouth closed. Just use your speaking muscles without speaking.'

Orne obeyed.

'O.K., said Stetson. 'You come in loud and clear.'

'I ought to. I'm right on top of you!'

'There'll be a relay ship over you all the time,' said Stetson. 'Now . . . when you're not touching the mike contact this rig'll still feed us what you say . . . and everything that goes on around you, too. We'll monitor everything. Got that?'

'Yes.'

Stetson held out his right hand. 'Good luck. I meant that about diving in for you. Just say the word.'

'I know the words, too,' said Orne. 'HELP!'

Grey mud floor and gloomy aisles between monstrous bluish tree trunks – that was the jungle. Only the barest weak glimmering of sunlight penetrated to the mud. The disguised sled – its para-grav units turned off – lurched and skidded around buttress roots. Its headlights swung in wild arcs across the trunks and down to the mud. Aerial creepers – great looping vines of them – swung down from the towering forest ceiling.

A steady drip of condensation spattered the windshield, forcing Orne to use the wipers.

In the bucket seat of the sled's cab, Orne fought the controls. He was plagued by the vague slowmotion-floating sensation that a heavy planet native always feels in lighter gravity. It gave him an unhappy stomach.

Things skipped through the air around the lurching vehicle: flitting and darting things. Insects came in twin cones, siphoned towards the headlights. There was an endless chittering whistling tok-tok-toking in the gloom beyond the lights.

Stetson's voice hissed suddenly through the surgically implanted speaker: 'How's it look?'

'Alien.'

'Any sign of the mob?'

'Negative.'

'O.K. We're taking off.'

Behind Orne, there came a deep rumbling roar that receded as the scout cruiser climbed its jets. All other sounds hung suspended in after-silence, then resumed: the strongest first and then the weakest.

A heavy object suddenly arced through the headlights, swinging on a vine. It disappeared behind a tree. Another. Another. Ghostly shadows with vine pendulums on both sides. Something banked down heavily on to the hood of the sled.

Orne braked to a creaking stop that shifted the load behind him, found himself staring through the windshield at a native of Gienah III. The native crouched on the hood, a Mark XX exploding-pellet rifle in his right hand directed at Orne's head. In the abrupt shock of meeting, Orne recognised the weapon: standard issue of the marine guards on all R&R survey ships.

The native appeared the twin of the one Orne had seen on the translite screen. The four-fingered hand looked extremely capable around the stock of the Mark XX.

Slowly, Orne put a hand to his throat, pressed the contact button. He moved his speaking muscles: '*Just made contact with the mob. One on the hood now has one of our Mark XX rifles aimed at my head.*'

The surf-hissing of Stetson's voice came through the hidden speaker: '*Want us to came back?*'

'*Negative. Stand by. He looks cautious rather than hostile.*'

Orne held up his right hand, palm out. He had a second thought: held up his left hand, too. Universal symbol of peaceful intentions: empty hands. The gun muzzle lowered slightly.

148

Orne called into his mind the language that had been hypno-forced into his. *Ocheero? No. That means 'The people.' Ah . . .* And he had the heavy fricative greeting sound.

'Ffroiragrazzi,' he said.

The native shifted to the left, answered in pure, unaccented High Galactese: 'Who are you?'

Orne fought down a sudden panic. The lipless mouth had looked so odd forming the familiar words.

Stetson's voice hissed: *'Is that the native speaking Galactese?'*

Orne touched this throat. *'You heard him.'*

He dropped his hand, said: 'I am Lewis Orne of Rediscovery and Re-education. I was sent here at the request of the First-Contact officer on the *Delphinus Rediscovery*.'

'Where is your ship?' demanded the Geinahn.

'It put me down and left.'

'Why?'

'It was behind schedule for another appointment.'

Out of the corners of his eyes, Orne saw more shadows dropping to the mud around him. The sled shifted as someone climbed on to the load behind the cap. The someone scuttled agilely for a moment.

The native climbed down to the cab's side step, opened the door. The rifle was held at the ready. Again, the lipless mouth formed Galactese words: 'What do you carry in this . . . vehicle?'

'The equipment every R&R field man uses to help the people of a rediscovered planet improve themselves.' Orne nodded at the rifle. 'Would you mind pointing that weapon some other direction? It makes me nervous.'

The gun muzzle remained unwaveringly on Orne's middle. The native's mouth opened, revealing long canines. 'Do we not look strange to you?'

'I take it there's been a heavy mutational variation in the humanoid norm on this planet,' said Orne. 'What is it? Hard radiation?'

No answer.

'It doesn't really make any difference, of course,' said Orne. 'I'm here to help you.'

'I am Tanuh, High Path Chief of the Grazzi,' said the native. 'I decide who is to help.'

Orne swallowed.

149

'Where do you go?' demanded Tanub.

'I was hoping to go to your city. Is it permitted?'

A long pause while the vertical slit pupils of Tanub's eyes expanded and contracted. 'It is permitted.'

Stetson's voice came through the hidden speaker: '*All bets off. We're coming in after you. That Mark XX is the final straw. It means they have the* Delphinus *for sure!*'

Orne touched his throat. '*No! Give me a little more time!*'

'*Why?*'

'*I have a hunch about these creatures.*'

'*What is it?*'

'*No time now. Trust me.*'

Another long pause in which Orne and Tanub continued to study each other. Presently, Stetson said: '*O.K. Go ahead as planned. But find out where the* Delphinus *is! If we get that back we pull their teeth.*'

'Why do you keep touching your throat?' demanded Tanub.

'I'm nervous,' said Orne. 'Guns always make me nervous.'

The muzzle lowered slightly.

'Shall we continue on to your city?' asked Orne. He wet his lips with his tongue. The cab light on Tanub's face was giving the Gienahn an eerie sinister look.

'We can go soon,' said Tanub.

'Will you join me inside here?' asked Orne. 'There's a passenger seat right behind me.'

Tanub's eyes moved catlike: right, left. 'Yes.' He turned, barked an order into the jungle gloom, then climbed in behind Orne.

'When do we go?' asked Orne.

'The great sun will be down soon,' said Tanub. 'We can continue as soon as Chiranachuruso rises.'

'Chiranachuruso?'

'Our satellite . . . our moon,' said Tanub.

'It's a beautiful word,' said Orne. 'Chiranachuruso.'

'In our tongue it means: The Limb of Victory,' said Tanub. 'By its light we will continue.'

Orne turned, looked back at Tanub. 'Do you mean to tell me that you can see by what light gets down here through those trees?'

'Can you not see?' asked Tanub.

'Not without the headlights.'

'Our eyes differ,' said Tanub. He bent towards Orne, peered.

150

The vertical slit pupils of the eyes expanded, contracted. 'You are the same as the . . . others.'

'Oh, on the *Delphinus*?'

Pause. 'Yes.'

Presently, a greater gloom came over the jungle, bringing a sudden stillness to the wild life. There was a chittering commotion from the natives in the trees around the sled. Tanub shifted behind Orne.

'We may go now,' he said. 'Slowly . . . to stay behind my . . . scouts.'

'Right.' Orne eased the sled forward around an obstructing root.

Silence while they crawled ahead. Around them shapes flung themselves from vine to vine.

'I admired your city from the air,' said Orne. 'It is very beautiful.'

'Yes,' said Tanub. 'Why did you land so far from it?'

'We didn't want to come down where we might destroy anything.'

'There is nothing to destroy in the jungle,' said Tanub.

'Why do you have such a big city?' asked Orne.

Silence.

'I said: Why do you –'

'You are ignorant of our ways,' said Tanub. 'Therefore, I forgive you. The city is for our race. We must breed and be born in sunlight. Once – long ago – we used crude platforms on the tops of the trees. Now . . . only the . . . wild ones do this.'

Stetson's voice hissed in Orne's ears: *'Easy on the sex line, boy. That's always touchy. These creatures are oviparous. Sex glands are apparently hidden in that long fur behind where their chins ought to be.'*

'Who controls the breeding sites controls our world,' said Tanub. 'Once there was another city. We destroyed it.'

'Are there many . . . wild ones?' asked Orne.

'Fewer each year,' said Tanub.

'There's how they get their slaves,' hissed Stetson.

'You speak excellent Galactese,' said Orne.

'The High Path Chief commanded the best teacher,' said Tanub. 'Do you, too, know many things, Orne?'

'That's why I was sent here,' said Orne.

'Are there many planets to teach?' asked Tanub.

'Very many,' said Orne. 'Your city – I saw very tall buildings. Of what do you build them?'

'In your tongue – glass,' said Tanub. 'The engineers of the *Delphinus* said it was impossible. As you saw – they are wrong.'

'A glass-blowing culture,' hissed Stetson. *'That's explain a lot of things.'*

Slowly, the disguised sled crept through the jungle. Once, a scout swooped down into the headlights, waved. Orne stopped on Tanub's order and they waited almost ten minutes before proceeding.

'Wild ones?' asked Orne.

'Perhaps,' said Tanub.

A glowing of many lights grew visible through the giant tree trunks. It grew brighter as the sled crept through the last of the jungle, emerged in cleared land at the edge of the city.

Orne stared upward in awe. The city fluted and spiralled into the moonlight sky. It was a fragile appearing lacery of bridges, winking dots of light. The bridges wove back and forth from building to building until the entire visible network appeared one gigantic dew-glittering web.

'All that with glass,' murmured Orne.

'What's happening?' hissed Stetson.

Orne touched his throat contact. *'We're just into the city clearing, proceeding towards the nearest building.'*

'That is far enough,' said Tanub.

Orne stopped the sled. In the moonlight, he could see armed Gienahns all around. The buttressed pedestal of one of the buildings loomed directly ahead. It looked taller than had the scout cruiser in its jungle landing circle.

Tanub leaned close to Orne's shoulder. 'We have not deceived you, have we, Orne?'

'Huh? What do you mean?'

'You have recognised that we are not mutated members of your race.'

Orne swallowed. Into his ears came Stetson's voice. *'Better admit it.'*

'That's true,' said Orne.

'I like you, Orne,' said Tanub. 'You shall be one of my slaves. You will teach me many things.'

'How did you capture the *Delphinus*?' asked Orne.

'You know that, too?'

'You have one of their rifles,' said Orne.

'Your race is no match for us, Orne . . . in cunning, in strength, in the prowess of the mind. Your ship landed to repair its tubes. Very inferior ceramics in those tubes.'

Orne turned, looked at Tanub in the dim glow of the cab light. 'Have you heard about the I-A, Tanub?'

'I-A? What is that?' There was a wary tenseness in the Gienahn's figure. His mouth opened to reveal the long canines.

'You took the *Delphinus* by treachery?' asked Orne.

'They were simple fools,' said Tanub. 'We are smaller, thus they thought us weaker.' The Mark XX's muzzle came around to centre on Orne's stomach. 'You have not answered my question. What is the I-A?'

'I am of the I-A,' said Orne. 'Where've you hidden the *Delphinus*?'

'In the place that suits us best,' said Tanub. 'In all our history there has never been a better place.'

'What do you plan to do with it?' asked Orne.

'Within a year we will have a copy with our own improvements. After that – '

'You intend to start a war?' asked Orne.

'In the jungle the strong slay the weak until only the strong remain,' said Tanub.

'And then the strong prey upon each other?' asked Orne.

'That is a quibble for women,' said Tanub.

'It's too bad you feel that way,' said Orne. 'When two cultures meet like this they tend to help each other. What have you done with the crew of the *Delphinus*?'

'They are slaves,' said Tanub. 'Those who still live. Some resisted. Others objected to teaching us what we want to know.' He waved the gun muzzle. 'You will not be that foolish, will you, Orne?'

'No need to be,' said Orne. 'I've another little lesson to teach you: I already know where you've hidden the *Delphinus*.'

'*Go, boy!*' hissed Stetson. '*Where is it?*'

'Impossible!' barked Tanub.

'It's on your moon,' said Orne. 'Darkside. It's on a mountain on the darkside of your moon.'

Tanub's eyes dilated, contracted. 'You read minds?'

'The I-A has no need to read minds,' said Orne. 'We rely on superior mental prowess.'

'*The marines are on their way,*' hissed Stetson. '*We're coming in to get you. I'm going to want to know how you guessed that one.*'

153

'You are a weak fool like the others, gritted Tanub.

'It's too bad you formed your opinion of us by observing only the low grades of the R&R,' said Orne.

'*Easy, boy,*' hissed Stetson. '*Don't pick a fight with him now. Remember, his race is arboreal. He's probably as strong as an ape.*'

'I could kill you where you sit!' grated Tanub.

'You write finish for your entire planet if you do,' said Orne. 'I'm not alone. There are others listening to every word we say. There's a ship overhead that could split open your planet with one bomb – wash it with molten rock. It'd run like the glass you use for your buildings.'

'You are lying!'

'We'll make you an offer,' said Orne. 'We don't really want to exterminate you. We'll give you limited membership in the Galactic Federation until you prove you're no menace to us.'

'*Keep talking,*' hissed Stetson. '*Keep him interested.*'

'You dare insult me!' growled Tanub.

'You had better believe me,' said Orne. 'We –'

Stetson's voice interrupted him: '*Got it, Orne! They caught the* Delphinus *on the ground right where you said it'd be! Blew the tubes off it. Marines now mopping up.*'

'It's like this,' said Orne. 'We already have recaptured the *Delphinus.*' Tanub's eyes went instinctively skyward. 'Except for the captured armament you still hold, you obviously don't have the weapons to meet us,' continued Orne. 'Otherwise, you wouldn't be carrying that rifle off the *Delphinus.*'

'If you speak the truth, then we shall die bravely,' said Tanub.

'No need for you to die,' said Orne.

'Better to die than be slaves,' said Tanub.

'We don't need slaves,' said Orne. 'We –'

'I cannot take the chance that you are lying,' said Tanub. 'I must kill you now.'

Orne's foot rested on the air sled control pedal. He depressed it. Instantly, the sled shot skyward, heavy G's pressing them down into the seats. The gun in Tanub's hands was slammed into his lip. He struggled to raise it. To Orne, the weight was still only about twice that of his home planet of Chargon. He reached over, took the rifle, found safety belts, bound Tanub with them. Then he eased off the acceleration.

'We don't need slaves,' said Orne. 'We have machines to do

154

our work. We'll send experts in here, teach your people how to exploit your planet, how to build good transportation, facilities, show you how to mine your minerals, how to – '

'And what do we do in return?' whispered Tanub.

'You could start by teaching us how you make superior glass,' said Orne. 'I certainly hope you see things our way. We really don't want to have to come down there and clean you out. It'd be a shame to have to blast that city into little pieces.'

Tanub wilted. Presently, he said: 'Send me back. I will discuss this with . . . our council.' He stared at Orne. 'You I-A's are too strong. We did not know.'

In the wardroom of Stetson's scout cruiser, the lights were low, the leather chairs comfortable, the green beige table set with a decanter of Hochar brandy and two glasses.

Orne lifted his glass, sipped the liquor, smacked his lips. 'For a while there, I thought I'd never be tasting anything like this again.'

Stetson took his own glass. 'ComGO heard the whole thing over the general monitor net,' he said. 'D'you know you've been breveted to senior field man?'

'Ah, they've already recognised my sterling worth,' said Orne.

The wolfish grin took over Stetson's big features. 'Senior field men last about half as long as the juniors,' he said. 'Mortality's terrific!'

'I might've known,' said Orne. He took another sip of the brandy.

Stetson flicked on the switch of a recorder beside him. 'O.K. You can go ahead any time.'

'Where do you want me to start?'

'First, how'd you spot right away where they'd hidden the *Delphinus*?'

'Easy.' Tanub's word for his people was *Grazzi*. Most races call themselves something meaning *The People*. But in his tongue that's *Ocheero*. *Grazzi* wasn't on the translated list. I started working on it. The most likely answer was that it had been adopted from another language, and meant *enemy*.'

'And *that* told you where the *Delphinus* was?'

'No. But it fitted my hunch about these Gienahns. I'd kind of felt from the first minute of meeting them that they had a culture like the Indians of ancient Terra.'

'Why?'

'They came in like a primitive raiding party. The leader

155

dropped right on to the hood of my sled. An act of bravery, no less. Counting coup, you see?'

'I guess so.'

'Then he said he was High Path Chief. That wasn't on the language list either. But it was easy: *Raider Chief*. There's a word in almost every language in history that means raider and derives from a word for road, path or highway.'

'Highwaymen,' said Stetson.

'Raid itself,' said Orne. 'An ancient Terran language corruption of road.'

'Yeah, yeah. But where'd all this translation griff put – '

'Don't be impatient. Glass-blowing culture meant they were just out of the primitive stage. That, we could control. Next, he said their moon was *Chiranachuruso*, translated as *The Limb of Victory*. After that it just fell into place.'

'How?'

'The vertical-slit pupils of their eyes. Doesn't that mean anything to you?'

'Maybe. What's it mean to you?'

'Night-hunting predator accustomed to dropping upon its victims from above. No other type of creature ever has had the vertical slit. And Tanub said himself that the *Delphinus* was hidden in the best place in all of their history. History? That'd be a high place. Dark, likewise. Ergo: a high place on the darkside of their moon.'

'I'm a pie-eyed greepus,' whispered Stetson.

Orne grinned, said: 'You probably are . . . sir.'

MYTHS MY GREAT-GRAND-
DAUGHTER TAUGHT ME

by

Fritz Leiber

One afternoon I woke in the patio feeling sun-toasted and
relaxed, my mind very clear but with the glisten of dreams
still on it. I ran my hand through my beard and decided to
chop it off, which didn't make sense as it felt silky and looked
a beautiful silver grey – when who should come around the
corner of the house but my great-granddaughter with her chin
tucked down against her chest and her big eyes boring into me
as they always do when she's prepared to confound me.

One skinny arm hugged to her side a weatherbeaten grey
book showing faintly on the cover a gold-stamped design of
three curved horns interlocking. I knew that detail because I'd
noticed the same warped-cover book lying around the house
several times lately, but never bothered to check what it was,
though I'd been meaning to.

She stopped in front of me and untucked her chin and
pushed a strand of long pale hair back from her cheek and
even yawned fakily, but I knew that was just to get me off
guard.

Then she suddenly shot at me, 'G'gramps' (she pronounces it
guh-GRAMPS) 'G'gramps,' she shot at me, 'why do the frost
giants always talk Russian?'

'Well, I guess they have some pretty tall people in Russia,' I
temporised, 'and they certainly have some pretty chilly winters,
as Napoleon and Hitler discovered to their sorrow. Hey, how
do you know these frost giants talk Russian?'

'Because they write B for V and P for R,' she explained
impatiently, 'and for G they make a little gibbet.'

'That's not talking, that's writing,' I started to object, but
she pursed her lips and bored her eyes into me again and
asked suspiciously, 'G'gramps, do you *know* Norse mythology?'

'You ought to say *dig*,' I told her. 'Why don't you talk cute
beatnik like all the other brainy little eight-year-olds with

authors for fathers, or fathers once or twice removed? Why, I've known writers to make vast fortunes just copying down what their cute teenage beatnik daughters say over the phone.'

She cut me off with, 'Oh, G'gramps, beatnik went out twenty years ago.'

'I'm very glad to hear that,' I said. 'But now about this Norse jazz, it's all very wild and doomful and warlike, and they have nine worlds, I think, but I remember Jotunheim, where the frost giants live, and Asgard – that's where our boys live – '

'Oh, so you admit they're our boys?' she interrupted.

'Well, I mean they're the heroes, sort of. They're the Aesir –'

'How do you spell that? AEC? As in Atomic Energy Commission?'

'No, AES,' I told her, 'though I suppose you could have C-cedilla.'

'Or AE could stand of American Empire,' she suggested.

'Look, I'm telling this,' I told her. 'There are these Aesir – Odin, Thor & Company – and they live in Asgard, boozing it up and being athletic. Leading off from Asgard is the bridge Bifrost (you say that Beef Roast and not By Frost) with Heimdall to guard it – '

'The launching orbit,' she interrupted excitedly. 'Bifrost is the launching orbit and Heimdall is the big radar station that guards against missiles from Jotunheim and the other countries.'

'That's too science-fictiony,' I objected, 'though I do seem to remember that Heimdall could see for a hundred miles in every direction and even hear the grass grow – '

'Sonar too,' she said. 'Radar and hyper-sonar.'

I chuckled in my throat at that, it was rather cute, though there was a little chill in the back of my neck, just behind the chuckle, because it has always seemed to me that there is something frighteningly for-our-times in the Norse notion of embattled worlds with magic weapons poised against each other and then just going ahead and destroying each other at Ragnarok.

'Go on,' she prompted. 'Tell me some more about Asgard. Tell me any story you remember.'

'Well, it's been a long time,' I objected, scratching my chin through my silky silver beard. 'I forgot what led up to it, but there was one about the dwarfs having a contest to see who could make the most wonderful gifts for the gods.'

'They're the scientists,' she said sharply, nodding her head. 'The dwarfs are the scientists and the engineers.'

'Have it your own way,' I told her. 'Well, these gifts for the Aesir – who were the gods, of course – '

'They would naturally think that,' she agreed smoothly.

I blinked at her, but went on, 'These gifts included the spear Gungnir, which would hit whatever mark it was thrown at no matter how bad the aim of the thrower – '

I thought I heard her say, 'Self-correcting homing missile,' but I went on, 'And the boat Skidbladnir – you know, it's funny but I always read that as skin-bladder – anyhow, the boat Skidbladnir, which a person could fold up and fit in his pocket – '

'Pocket battleship,' she said instantly. 'It says just that.'

And the boar Gold Bristle that flew forever, shedding light – ' I was determined to finish off my list.

'Atomic spaceship,' she said. 'Or maybe photonic.'

'And Thor's hammer Mjolnir.'

'Another missile, of course. Don't they actually have one called Thor?'

'And the gold ring Draupnir, that dropped eight rings like itself every ninth night – '

'That could be atomic transmutation,' she said thoughtfully, 'or maybe just the capitalist economic system as it dreams of itself.'

'Now look here,' I said rather loudly, for I wanted to end this nonsense before it got any more nightmarish, 'you use awfully big words and subtle concepts, even for a little girl who's outgrown beatnik.'

'I'm your own great-granddaughter, aren't I?' she countered.

Nobody could protest that comeback, so I just said, 'You sure are, honey, but you're looking pretty scrawny with all this intellection.' Really, there was something that had begun to bother me about her skinniness and the anxious intensity of her lemur-like gaze. 'Why don't you go inside and ask your g'gramma for a big peanut-butter sandwich and a glass of milk?'

'Later maybe,' she said. 'Right now I want you to tell me every last thing you remember about the Nine Worlds.' She came over and leaned straight-armed on my couch and bored with the big eyes again.

'That's asking too much,' I protested, 'especially with this science-fiction angle you've added. You seem to know more about it than I do, so why don't you tell me the answers? Why do the frost giants always talk Russian?'

She leaned two inches closer and whispered, 'Because the frost giants *are* the Russians, see?'

'Well,' I said, trying to get back into the spirit of it all, 'I have to admit that the Russians do talk guttural and ho-ho-ho harshly and lumber around in fur coats and pound on tables and knock themselves out with monster construction projects and act obtuse but menacing, just like the frost giants.'

'That's right,' she told me, nodding. 'Khrushchev was the giant Skyrmir, I'm pretty sure. Jotunheim and Asgard are Russia and America, all set to shoot missiles at each other across England and Europe, which must be Midgard, of course – though sometimes I think the English are the Vanir.'

'Say, have you been reading all this crazy stuff in that grey book?' I asked her uneasily. 'I remember now: three interlocking horns are Odin's symbol. Let me see it.'

'Later maybe,' she said, twisting the side with the book clamped to it away from my hand and then backing off a couple of steps. 'Right now we've got to dig some important things out of your memory. G'gramps, there's a tradition that Odin wandered all over Midgard, and some of the other Nine Worlds too, in disguise. Do you know who Odin might be. Like Lenin being Hresvelgr or Balder Abraham Lincoln?'

'William O. Douglas?' I suggested wildly, making another attempt to play the game. 'He travelled all over the world to see things for himself and he wrote a lot of books about it.'

'I don't think so,' she said, shaking her head, 'but maybe it's not so important to know that. After all, Odin was one of the good guys. For that matter, all the Aesir were pretty good, at least they were brave and well-intentioned, but there was one of them who wasn't . . . ' She hesitated and for some reason I shivered. 'Loki wasn't,' she said and hesitated again, and as she said 'Loki' and stared at me with those big eyes, the patio seemed to waver for a moment behind her and the sun grew dim. 'Loki was always causing trouble. He was one of the Aesir, they adopted him, but he was always working the worst mischief he could. G'gramps, who was Loki?'

'Now let's stop all this right now,' I commanded, 'or we'll be getting to Ragnarok.' I laughed and reached out to tousle her hair, but really I was a little frightened. You see, ever since I first ran across the Norse myths in third grade I've never believed for a second in that fakey tacked-on happy ending

160

about the sons of Odin and Thor establishing a new world after the other gods and the giants were dead. It's always been clear to me that Ragnarok must lie in the future, a horror overhanging us all, a doom towards which the universe is relentlessly working – any other solution would be dramatically wrong. And right now I didn't want a little girl to glimpse the dread and despair that had gripped the heart of a third-grader and never quite let go.

I must have done a poor job of concealment, though, for what she said, backing out of reach again, was, 'But G'gramps, don't you see that we've *got* to get to Ragnarok? – that that's what all this is leading up to? It all fits. The Midgard serpent, coiled around the world under the seas and never coming up till the end, is atomic submarines. The Fenris wolf, his jaws scraping earth and the stars, is spaceflight – and missiles! And Surtur, who came from Muspelheim and ended the war with a fireweapon that destroyed everything – he must have been the top general of a country, not America or Russia, that started throwing atomic bombs. But G'gramps, which country was Muspelheim? Who was Surtur? And who was the one who tricked them all into it? – who was Loki?'

Now she was the one who was advancing, her big eyes pleading but fierce, and I was the one who was backing off a little, across my couch. She seemed to have changed, or maybe it was just that I now saw for the first time that her cheeks were starved-sunken and her dress was ragged and her skinny legs were scarred.

'Who was Loki, G'gramps?' she repeated. 'If you knew, you could stop him. We can't remember, we've got amnesia for that part. We sent back the book and the myths, so you'd know what was coming and figure out the rest, and stop it from happening, but that didn't do any good, so we had to try to come back ourselves. G'gramps, *please* – '

She reached out her hand, brushing my beard, and shook my shoulder. Her fingers were ice.

'G'gramps, who was Loki?'

'Stop it, I don't know!' I cried out, flinching away from her. *'I don't even know your name?'*

At that a shadow and a strong vibration passed across everything and when I opened my eyes again, she was gone.

My beard was gone too, though I had to rub my chin several times to convince myself of that.

Then I remembered that I never had a beard, certainly not a

silver one. I also remembered that I don't have a great-grand-daughter. I have one grandchild, a girl, but she's only two.

Oh, one other thing: my wife and a couple of friends remember seeing that grey weathered book with the Odin symbol around the house, but none of them ever looked into it. And now we can't find it anywhere.

So there you are, that's the entire experience, just as it happened. No, wait a moment, I have one slight correction to make — a correction that keeps me wondering.

I don't have a great-granddaughter . . . yet.

COMMENT ON

MYTHS MY GREAT-GRANDDAUGHTER

TAUGHT ME

The Place: a third- or fourth-grade classroom in grimy, red Ravenswood Grammar School buried in the brick wilderness of Chicago's north side.

The Time: 1918 or 1919. The World War is ending. The great influenza epidemic is looming or receding. It should be late afternoon, last class of the day, for the gloomy orange sunlight slanting through the high windows hardly picks out the chalk motes in the air.

The long blackboard is at a distance, so my desk must be near the back of the room. A thin figure stands before it, but her face will not come clear, nor can recollection make more than small, ghostly blobs of the bent shoulders and heads of the pupils between me and the teacher.

But the small book held stealthily open below my desk and near my knees is spotlighted by memory. It has a red cloth binding imprinted with black, both colours somewhat faded, the corners rubbed pale. The paper, slightly soiled, is thin, tough, slippery textbook stock.

Equally vivid across the decades is the feeling of sick despair and muted but unbounded fright which drowns me.

I have just been discovering the myths of the Norse gods: flaring Valhalla, the Valkyries, Odin riding the stormy sky on eight-legged Sleipnir, mysterious and ever-ingenious Loki, his and Thor's courageous journey through the snows to chal-

162

lenge the Frost Giants, Balder the Brave and Beautiful, Heimdall the watchman on the rainbow bridge traversing the churning, black clouds – a band of great friends defying with steady nerves and laughter a murky, unfathomable universe filled with monsters. Perhaps for the first time my sense of wonder and even worship, untouched by harsh, sand-blown Biblical stories and the bright, limited perfection and lush sexuality of Classical legend, has been roused. These are the gods for me! I have become so excited that I have continued my reading, begun during a study period, into the next class.

And now I find out that my gods must all die in the cosmic battle of Ragnarok. The world of Norse myth and the real world fuse. I am staring across the desks at the grey, empty blackboard and I am filled with a vague hopelessness and apprehension like the onset or slow departure of the 'flu.

I was easy to scare in those days. I was still afraid of the dark. For weeks after seeing the stage play of *The Cat and the Canary* I watched warily over-shoulder for a secret panel to open in the wallpaper and a green, long-taloned hand thrust out. Several years later I was so depressed by Lovecraft's grimly tragic *The Colour Out of Space* that I almost gave up reading the magazine Amazing Stories. But Norse mythology turned out to have deeper roots in the universe, in literature, and in myself; one of its enduring attractions for me was its likeness to a wild, shimmering scene in a huge, dark theatre – I was the child of Shakespearean actors, though at that time I was living with aunts, far from the glories of the stage.

The earth revolved. I re-encountered Ragnarok as Gotterdammerung in Wagner's Ring operas with their eerie, yearning music; I was thrilled in spite of the ponderous recommendations of my Chicago German relatives, which generally turned me against things. I reread the northern myths in Bulfinch and in Padraic Colum's more polished versions. Finally I reached their source in the *Elder Edda*. This happened at about the same time as I was reading all of Ibsen and I have ever since been drawn towards the products of Scandinavian creativity: the plays of Strindberg, the theology of Kierkegaard, the art of Edward Munch, Jensen's *The Long Journey,* Anker-Larsen's mystical novels such as *The Philosopher's Stone,* and recently the films of Bergman.

With the *Elder Edda* I was also absorbing Spengler's *The*

Decline of the West and its gloomy vision of the lives and inevitable deaths of cultures and Western or Faustian man's vaulting drive towards spatial and temporal infinity – an urge worthy of Odin, Heimdall, Frey, and the rest of the Aesir.

At the same time I was encountering adventures of the Viking sort in the boyish, wild, poetic sword-and-sorcery stories of Robert E. Howard and in the character of Sigurdson in Talbot Mundy's *Tros of Samothrace*. My own Fafhrd became another such. For now I was writing. Occasional references to Norse myth cropped up in fantasy and science fiction: John Campbell's *Cloak of Aesir* and my own *Roots of Yggdrasil* – at any rate that was my title until Campbell changed it to *Destiny Times Three*. Occasionally the Norse gods turned up in a body, usually for romantic, swashbuckling, or humorous purposes – notably so in the first half of L. Sprague de Camp's *The Incomplete Enchanter*. I enjoyed these stories, though something inside me whispered, 'It's also deeper than that.'

From the horrors of World War Two grew scientific wonders which soon seemed to be leading towards horrors again.

One day in 1962 I was particularly worried – grandiose conceit! – about the future of the world and the threats of atomic war. I believe I was feeling particularly sympathetic towards Dr Oppenheimer and very angry with Dr Teller in that easy way in which we can be privately angry with public figures or nations. My mind leaped back to that instant in Ravenswood Grammar School – yes, the feeling was right and so was the metaphor! Ragnarok equals atomic doom! Come to think of it, there were many striking parallels between Norse magics and the scientific weapons of modern war – though I had already learned, by the negative example of Hans Bellamy's *Moons, Myths, and Man*, that you can prove anything from mythology. Bellamy was one of Velikovsky's many precursors. But forget that, I told myself, you're writing a story, not fashioning a scientific theory.

Let's see, it would have to be a science-fiction or at least science-fantasy story, for Ragnarok must figure as an actual atomic holocaust to enshroud our real world. Time-travel seemed indicated. There have been stories of time-travellers who came back to change the present, or alert people in the present, in order to alter the future favourably, averting some onrushing doom. What if the Norse myths had been sent back as such a warning?

Let's see again, this couldn't possibly be 'hard' science fiction, or an action-packed romance, or any sort of long story. No matter how many 'striking parallels', the idea was full of unpatchable holes. The most I could hope to convey for a moment was the wonder of those parallels and my own feelings about Norse myth and atomic war. While romance, with its swords and maidens and hoofbeats, would take the reader away from the real world. No, my story must be dead serious yet light as thistledown.

The most disarming, homely literary form seemed indicated. What about those little anecdotal fantasies which Billy Rose and other newspaper columnists have on occasion written to fill their space – something comic and topical with a snapper at the end? Yes, that would do it! – this story would begin with a lazy after-Sunday-breakfast atmosphere and innocently yet slyly step, rather than 'build', towards a moment of dread. And who steps more innocently yet slyly than a little girl? So I had one character, my time-traveller. The other had to be me – those columnists always write first person. Must get in a bit of fun-poking – it turned out to be at beatniks and alphabets and authors like the lucky one of the *Gidget* books – in order to work towards some initially light mockery of Russia and America. Then hang a catchy ridiculous title on it – and hope Dvorak would forgive me.

FRITZ LEIBER

COMMENT ON
SYNDROME JOHNNY

Evolution is a Good Thing. But Evolutions's method of improving a race is usually violent death or sterility, or some unpleasant partial mixture of the two, as a way of pruning off inferior branches.

Assuming you approve of Evolution and hope for a better future for mankind, how would you feel if confronted by someone who wanted to commit evolution on you?

Are you an idealist? Evolution is a source of intelligence and beauty. Deers and wolves have evolved large shining eyes, keen senses, swift muscles, and ready emotions, in the race against each other. Back in the depth of time they would all have remained gophers if one kind of gopher had not started chasing another with the intention of catching an easy meal. When viewed from a distance, when viewed across the sweep of centuries, evolution is a wonderful process.

How about viewing it up close? The current population explosion came from well-meant separation of sewage and drinking water, cutting down water-carried diseases, increasing the life-chances of children in crowded lands. It has left the people of the poor lands up to their necks in children; too busy trying to feed and care for the hordes of young ones to listen to any birth control information, too busy to learn to read, too busy to teach the children, too poor to buy devices either for birth control or for time saving, too poor for farm gadgets that might relieve the constant work and increase the food supply. This kind of crisis can destroy a thousand years of civilisation in two generations. But Nature's answer to this kind of crisis has traditionally been the plague. Striking at the most crowded and hunger-weakened places, the epidemic takes one person out of two, or two out of three and leaves the survivors enough land to raise food, enough room in the houses to sit down, a little time to rest, to think, to remember and learn ways to keep that desperate hunger from coming again.

166

A virus which kills half a population might be a blessing to the survivors and their descendants, but a man who aids such a virus to kill is a murderer, breaking the human taboo that we must not be made to fear each other.

I decided to write about such a man. His intentions were good.

KATHERINE MACLEAN

SYNDROME JOHNNY

by

Katherine MacLean

The blood was added to a pool of other blood, mixed, centrifuged, separated to plasma and corpuscles, irradiated slightly, pasteurised slightly, frozen, evaporated, and finally banked. Some of the plasma was used immediately for a woman who had bled too much in childbirth.

She died.

Others received plasma and did not die. But their symptoms changed, including a syndrome of multiple endocrine unbalance, eccentricities of appetite and digestion, and a general pattern of emotional disturbance.

An alert hospital administrator investigated the mortality rise and narrowed it to a question of who had donated blood the week before. After city residents were eliminated, there remained only the signed receipts and thumbprints of nine men. Nine healthy unregistered travellers poor enough to sell their blood for money, and among them a man who carried death in his veins. The nine thumbprints were broadcast to all police files and a search began.

The effort was futile, for there were many victims who had sickened and grown partially well again without recognising the strangeness of their illness.

Three years later they reached the carrier stage and the epidemic spread to four cities. Three more years, and there was an epidemic which spread around the world, meeting another wave coming from the opposite direction. It killed two out of four, fifty out of a hundred, twenty-seven million out of fifty million. There was hysteria where it appeared. And where it had not appeared there were quarantines to fence it out. But it could not be fenced out. For two years it covered the world. And then it vanished again, leaving the survivors with a tendency towards glandular troubles.

Time passed. The world grew richer, more orderly, more peaceful.

A man paused in the midst of his work at the U.N. Food and Agriculture Commission. He looked up at the red and green production map of India.

'Just too many people per acre,' he said. 'All our work at improving production . . . just one jump ahead of their rising population, one jump ahead of famine. Sometimes I wish to God there would be another plague to give us a breathing spell and a fair chance to get things organised.'

He went back to work and added another figure.

Two months later, he was one of the first victims of the second plague.

In the dining hall of a university, a biochemical student glanced up from his paper to his breakfast companion. 'You remember Johnny, the mythical carrier that they told about during the first and second epidemics of Syndrome Plague?'

'Sure. Syndrome Johnny. They use that myth in psychology class as a typical example of mass hysteria. When a city was nervous and expecting the plague to reach it, some superstitious fool would imagine he saw Syndrome Johnny and the population would panic. Symbol for Death or some such thing. People imagined they saw him in every corner of the world. Simultaneously, of course.'

It was a bright morning and they were at a window which looked out across green rolling fields to a towering glass-brick building in the distance.

The student who had gone back to his paper suddenly looked up again. 'Some Peruvians here claim they saw Syndrome Johnny –'

'Idiotic superstition! You'd think it would have died when the plague died.'

The other grinned. 'The plague didn't die.' He folded his newspaper slowly, obviously advancing an opening for a debate.

His companion went on eating. 'Another of your wild theories, huh?' Then through a mouthful of food: 'All right, if the plague didn't die, where did it go?'

'Nowhere. *We have it now.* We all have it!' He shrugged. 'A virus catalyst of high affinity for the cells and a high similarity to a normal cell protein – how can it be detected?'

'Then why don't people die? Why aren't we sick?'

'Because we have sickened and recovered. We caught it on conception and recovered before birth. Proof? Why do you think that the countries which were known as the Hungry

169

Lands are now well-fed, leisured, educated, advanced? Because the birth rate has fallen! Why has the birth rate fallen?' He paused, then very carefully said, 'Because two out of three of all people who would have lived have died before birth, slain by Syndrome Plague. We are all carriers now, hosts to a new guest. And' – his voice dropped to a mock sinister whisper – 'with such a stranger within our cells, at the heart of the intricate machinery of our lives, who knows what subtle changes have crept upon us unnoticed!'

His companion laughed. 'Eat your breakfast. You belong on a horror programme!'

A police psychologist for the Federated States of The Americas was running through reports from the Bureau of Social Statistics. Suddenly he grunted, then a moment later said, 'Uh-huh!'

'Uh-huh what?' asked his superior, who was reading a newspaper with his feet up on the desk.

'Remember the myth of Syndrome Johnny?'

'Ghost of Syndrome Plague. Si, what of it?'

'Titaquahapahel, Peru, population nine hundred, sent in a claim that he turned up there and they almost caught him. Crime Statistics rerouted the report to Mass Phenomena, of course. Mass Phenomena blew a tube and sent their folder on Syndrome Johnny over here. Every report they ever had on him for ninety years back! A memo came with it.' He handed the memo over.

The man behind the desk looked at it. It was a small graph and some mathematical symbols. 'What is it?'

'It means,' said the psychologist, smiling dryly, 'that every crazy report about our ghost has points of similarity to every other crazy report. The whole business of Syndrome Johnny has been in their "funny coincidence" file for twenty years. This time the suspect hits the averaged description of Johnny too closely: A solid-looking man, wide-boned, five-eight, one eighty, unusual number of visible minor scars, especially on the face and hands, and a disturbing habit of bending his fingers at the first-joint knuckles when he is thinking. The coincidence has gotten too damn funny. There's a chance we've been passing up a crime.'

'An extensive crime,' said the man at the desk softly. He reached for the folder. 'Yes, a considerable quantity of murder.' He leafed through the folder and then thought a while,

170

looking at the most recent reports. Thinking was what he was paid for, and he earned his excellent salary.

'This thumbprint on the hotel register – the name is false, but the thumbprint looks real. Could we persuade the Bureau of Records to give their data on that print?'

'Without a warrant? Against constitutional immunity. No, not a chance. The public has been touchy about the right to secrecy ever since that police state was attempted in Varga.'

'How about persuading an obliging judge to give a warrant on grounds of reasonable suspicion?'

'No. We'd have the humanist press down on our necks in a minute, and any judge knows it. We'd have to prove a crime was committed. No crime, no warrant.'

'It seems a pity we can't even find out who the gentleman is,' the Crimes Department head murmured, looking at the thumbprint wistfully. 'No crime, no records. No records, no evidence. No evidence, no proof of crime. Therefore, we must manufacture a small crime. He was attacked and he must have defended himself. Someone may have been hurt in the process.' He pushed a button. 'Do you think if I send a man down there, he could persuade one of the mob to swear out a complaint?'

'That's a rhetorical question,' said the psychologist, trying to work out an uncertain correlation in his reports. 'With that sort of mob hysteria, the town would probably give you an affidavit of witchcraft.'

'Phone for you, Doctor Alcala.' The nurse was crisp but quiet, smiling down at the little girl before vanishing again.

Ricardo Alcala pushed the plunger in gently, then carefully withdrew the hypodermic needle from the little girl's arm. 'There you are, Cosita,' he said, smiling and rising from the chair beside the white bed.

'Will that make me better, Doctor?' she piped feebly.

He patted her hand. 'Be a good girl and you will be well tomorrow.' He walked out into the hospital corridor to where the desk nurse held out a phone.

'Alcala speaking.'

The voice was unfamiliar. 'My deepest apologies for interrupting your work, Doctor. At this late hour I'm afraid I assumed you would be at home. The name is Camba, Federation Investigator on a health case. I would like to consult you.'

Alcala was tired, but there was nothing to do at home. Nita was at the health resort and Johnny had borrowed all his

171

laboratory space for a special synthesis of some sort, and probably would be too busy even to talk. Interest stirred in him. This was a Federation Investigator calling; the man's work was probably important. 'Tonight, if that's convenient. I'll be off duty in five minutes.'

Thirty minutes later they were ordering in a small cantina down the street from the hospital.

Julio Camba, Federal Investigator, was a slender, dark man with sharp, glinting eyes. He spoke with a happy theatrical flourish.

'Order what you choose, Señor. We're on my expense account. The resources of the Federated States of all The Americas stand behind your menu.'

Alcala smiled. 'I wouldn't want to add to the national debt.'

'Not at all, Señor. The Federated States are only too happy thus to express a fraction of their gratitude by adding a touch of luxury to the otherwise barren and self-sacrificing life of a scientist.'

'You shame me,' Alcala said dryly. It was true that he needed every spare penny for the health of Nita and the child, and for the laboratory. A penny saved from being spent on nourishment was a penny earned. He picked up the menu again and ordered steak.

The investigator lit a cigar, asking casually: 'Do you know John Osborne Drake?'

Alcala searched his memory. 'No. I'm sorry . . . ' Then he felt for the first time how closely he was being watched, and knew how carefully his reaction and the tone of his voice had been analysed. The interview was dangerous. For some reason, he was suspected of something.

Camba finished lighting the cigar and dropped the match into an ashtray. 'Perhaps you know John Delgados?' He leaned back into the shadowy corner of the booth.

Johnny! Out of all the people in the world, how could the government be interested in him? Alcala tried to sound casual. 'An associate of mine. A friend.'

'I would like to contact the gentleman.' The request was completely unforceful, undemanding. 'I called, but he was not at home. Could you tell me where he might be?'

'I'm sorry, Señor Camba, but I cannot say. He could be on a business trip.' Alcala was feeling increasingly nervous. Actually, Johnny was working at his laboratory.

172

'What do you know of his activities?' Camba asked.

'A biochemist.' Alcala tried to see past the meditative mask of the thin dark face. 'He makes small job-lots of chemical compounds. Special bug spray for sale to experimental planta-tions, hormone spray for fruits, that sort of thing. Sometimes, when he collects some money ahead, he does research.'

Camba waited, and his silence became a question. Alcala spoke reluctantly, anger rising in him. 'Oh, it's genuine re-search. He has some patents and publications to his credit. You can confirm that if you choose.' He was unable to keep the hostility out of his voice.

A waiter came and placed steaming platters of food on the table. Camba waited until he was gone. 'You know him well, I presume. Is he sane?'

The question was another shock. Alcala thought carefully, for any man might be insane in secret. 'Yes, so far as I know.' He turned his attention to the steak, but first took three very large capsules from a bottle in his pocket.

'I would not expect that a doctor would need to take pills,' Camba remarked with friendly mockery.

'I don't need them,' Alcala explained. 'Mixed silicones. I'm guinea-pigging.'

'Can't such things be left to the guinea-pigs?' Camba asked, watching with revulsion as Alcala uncapped the second bottle and sprinkled a layer of grey powder over his steak.

'Guinea-pigs have no assimilation of silicones; only man has that.'

'Yes, of course. I should have remembered from your famous papers, *The Need Of Trace Silicon In Human Diet* and *Silicon Deficiency Diseases*.'

Obviously Camba had done considerable investigating of Alcala before approaching him. He had even given the titles of the research papers correctly. Alcala's wariness increased.

'What is the purpose of the experiment this time?' asked the small dark Federation agent genially.

'To determine the safe limits of silicon consumption and if there are any dangers in an overdose.'

'How do you determine that? By dropping dead?'

He could be right. Perhaps the test should be stopped. Every day, with growing uneasiness, Alcala took his dose of silicon compound, and every day, the chemical seemed to be absorbed completely – not released or excreted – in a way that was un-

173

pleasantly reminiscent of the way arsenic accumulated without evident damage, then killed abruptly without warning.

Already, this evening, he had noticed that there was something faulty about his co-ordination and weight and surface sense. The restaurant door had swung back with a curious lightness, and the hollow metal handle had had a curious softness under his fingers. Something merely going wrong with the sensitivity of his fingers – ?

He tapped his fingertips on the heavy indestructible silicone plastic table top. There was a feeling of heaviness in his hands, and a feeling of faint rubbery *give* in the table.

Tapping his fingers gently, his heavy fingers . . . the answer was dreamily fantastic. *I'm turning into silicon plastic myself*, he thought. But how, why? He had not bothered to be curious before, but the question had always been – what were supposedly insoluble silicons doing assimilating into the human body at all?

Several moments passed. He smoothed back his hair with his oddly heavy hand before picking up his fork again.

'I'm turning into plastic,' he told Camba.

'I beg your pardon?'

'Nothing. A joke.'

Camba was turning into plastic, too. Everyone was. But the effect was accumulating slowly.

Camba lay down his knife and started in again. 'What connections have you had with John Delgados?'

Concentrate on the immediate situation. Alcala and Johnny were obviously in danger of some sort of mistaken arrest and interrogation.

As Alcala focused on the question, one errant whimsical thought suddenly flitted through the back of his mind. In red advertising letters: TRY OUR NEW MODEL RUSTPROOF, WATERPROOF, HEAT & SCALD RESISTANT, STRONG – EXTRA-LONG-WEARING HUMAN BEING!

He laughed inwardly and finally answered: 'Friendship. Mutual interest in high ion colloidial suspensions and complex synthesis.' Impatience suddenly mastered him. 'Exactly what is it you wish to know, Señor? Perhaps I could inform you if I knew the reasons for your interest.'

Camba chose a piece of salad with great care. 'We have reason to believe that he is Syndrome Johnny.'

Alcala waited for the words to clarify. After a moment, it

ceased to be childish babble and became increasingly shocking. He remembered the first time he had met John Delgados, the smile, the strong handclasp. 'Call me Johnny,' he had said. It had seemed no more than a nickname.

The investigator was watching his expression with bright brown eyes.

Johnny, yes . . . but not Syndrome Johnny. He tried to think of some quick refutation. 'The whole thing is preposterous, Señor Camba. The myth of Syndrome Plague Johnny started about a century ago.'

'Doctor Alcala' – the small man in the grey suit was tensely sober – 'John Delgados is very old, and John Delgados, is not his proper name. I have traced his life back and back, through older and older records in Argentina, Panama, South Africa, the United States, China, Canada. Everywhere he has paid his taxes properly, put his fingerprints on file as a good citizen should. And he changed his name every twenty years, applying to the courts for permission with good honest reasons for changing his name. Everywhere he has been a laboratory worker, held patents, sometimes made a good deal of money. He is one hundred and forty years old. His first income tax was paid in 1970, exactly one hundred and twenty years ago.'

'Other men are that old,' said Alcala.

'Other men are old, yes. Those who survived the two successive plagues were unusually durable.' Camba finished and pushed back his plate. 'There is no crime in being long-lived, surely. But he has changed his name five times!'

'That proves nothing. Whatever his reasons for changing his name, it doesn't prove that he is Syndrome Johnny any more than it proves he is the cow that jumped over the moon. Syndrome Johnny is a myth, a figment of mob delirium.'

As he said it, he knew it was not true. A Federation Investigator would not be on a wild goose chase.

The plates were taken away and cups of steaming black coffee put between them. He would have to warn Johnny. It was strange how well you could know a man as well as he knew Johnny, firmly enough to believe that, despite evidence, everything the man did was right.

'Why must it be a myth?' Camba asked softly.

'It's ridiculous!' Alcala protested. 'Why would any man – ' His voice cut off as unrelated facts fell into a pattern. He sat

175

for a moment, thinking intensely, seeing the century of plague as something he had never dreamed . . .

A price.

Not too high a price in the long run, considering what was purchased. Of course, the great change over into silicon catalysis would be a shock and require adjustment and, of course, the change must be made in several easy stages – and those who could not adjust would die.

'Go on, Doctor,' Camba urged softly. ' "*Why* would any man – " '

He tried to find a way of explaining which would not seem to have any relationship to John Delgados. 'It has been recently discovered' – but he did not say *how* recently – 'that the disease of Syndrome Plague was not a disease. It is an improvement.' He had spoken clumsily.

'An improvement on life?' Camba laughed and nodded, but there were bitterness and anger burning behind the small man's smile. 'People can be improved to death by the millions. Yes, yes, go on, Señor. You fascinate me.'

'We are stronger,' Alcala told him. 'We are changed chemically. The race has been improved!'

'Come, Doctor Alcala,' Camba said with a sneering merriment, 'the Syndrome Plagues have come and they have gone. Where is this change?'

Alcalal tried to express it clearly. 'We are stronger. Potentially, we are tremendously stronger. But we of this generation are still weak and ill, as our parents were, from the shock of the change. And we need silicone feeding; we have not adjusted yet. Our illness masks our strength.' He thought of what that strength would be!

Camba smiled and took out a small notebook. 'The disease is connected with silicones, you say? The original name of Delgados was John Osborne Drake. His father was Osborne Drake, a chemist at Dow Corning, who was sentenced to the electric chair in 1967 for unauthorised bacterial experiments which resulted in an accidental epidemic and eight deaths. Dow Corning was the first major manufactury of silicones in America, though not connected in any way with Osborne Drake's criminal experiments. It links together, does it not?'

'It is not a disease, it is strength!' Alcala insisted doggedly.

The small investigator looked up from his notebook and his smile was an unnatural thing, a baring of teeth. 'Half the world died of this strength, Señor. If you will not think of the men and women, think of the children. Millions of children died!'

The waiter brought the bill, dropping it on the table between them.

'Lives will be saved in the long run,' Alcala said obstinately. 'Individual deaths are not important in the long run.'

'That is hardly the philosophy for a doctor, is it?' asked Camba with open irony, taking the bill and rising.

They went out of the restaurant in silence. Camba's 'copter stood at the kerb.

'Would you care for a lift home, Doctor Alcala?' The offer was made with the utmost suavity.

Alcala hesitated fractionally. 'Why, yes, thank you.' It would not do to give the investigator any reason for suspicion by refusing.

As the 'copter lifted into the air, Camba spoke with a more friendly note in his voice, as if he humoured a child. 'Come, Alcala, you're a doctor dedicated to saving lives. How can you find sympathy for a murderer?'

Alcala sat in the dark, looking through the windshield down at the bright street falling away below. 'I'm not a practicing medico; only one night a week do I come to the hospital. I'm a research man. I don't try to save individual lives. I'm dedicated to improving the average life, the average health. Can you understand that? Individuals may be sick and individuals may die, but the average lives on. And if the average is better, then I'm satisfied.'

The 'copter flew on. There was no answer.

'I'm not good with words,' said Alcala. Then, taking out his pen-knife and unfolding it, he said, 'Watch!' He put his index finger on the altimeter dial, where there was light, and pressed the blade against the flesh between his finger and his thumb He increased the pressure until the flesh stood out white on either side of the blade, bending, but not cut.

'Three generations back, this pressure would have gone right through the hand.' He took away the blade and there was only a very tiny cut. Putting the knife away, he brought out his lighter. The blue flame was steady and hot. Alcala held it close to the dashboard and put his finger directly over it, counting patiently, 'One, two, three, four, five – ' He pulled the lighter back, snapping it shut.

'Three generations ago, a man couldn't have held a finger over that flame for more than a tenth part of that count. Doesn't all this prove something to you?'

The 'copter was hovering above Alcala's house. Camba lowered it to the ground and opened the door before answering. 'It proves only that a good and worthy man will cut and burn his hand for an unworthy friendship. Goodnight.'

Disconcerted, Alcala watched the 'copter lift away into the night, then, turning, saw that the lights were still on in the laboratory. Camba might have deduced something from that, if he knew that Nita and the girl were not supposed to be home.

Alcala hurried in.

Johnny hadn't left yet. He was sitting at Alcala's desk with his feet on the wastebasket, the way Alcala often liked to sit, reading a technical journal. He looked up, smiling. For a moment Alcala saw him with the new clarity of a stranger. The lean, weathered face; brown eyes with smile deltas at the corners; wide shoulders; steady, big hands holding the magazine – solid, able, and ruthless enough to see what had to be done, and do it.

'I was waiting for you, Ric.'

'The Feds are after you.' Ricardo Alcala had been running. He found he was panting and his heart was pounding.

Delgados' smile did not change. 'It's all right, Ric. Everything's done. I can leave any time now.' He indicated a square metal box standing in a corner. 'There's the stuff.'

What stuff? The product Johnny had been working on? 'You haven't time for that now, Johnny. You can't sell it. They'd watch for anyone of your description selling chemicals. Let me loan you some money.'

'Thanks.' Johnny was smiling oddly. 'Everything's set. I won't need it. How close are they to finding me?'

'They don't know where you're staying.' Alcala leaned on the desk edge and put out his hand. 'They tell me you're Syndrome Johnny.'

'I thought you'd figured that one out.' Johnny shook his hand formally. 'The name is John Osborne Drake. You aren't horrified?'

'No,' Alcala knew that he was shaking hands with a man who would be thanked down all the successive generations of mankind. He noticed again the odd white webwork of scars on

178

the back of Johnny's hand. He indicated them as casually as he could. 'Where did you pick those up?'

John Drake glanced at his hand. 'I don't know, Ric. Truthfully. I've had my brains beaten in too often to remember much any more. Unimportant. There are instructions outlining plans and methods filed in safety deposit boxes in almost every big city in the world. Always the same typing, always the same instructions. I can't remember who typed them, myself or my father, but I must have been expected to forget or they wouldn't be there. Up to eleven, my memory is all right, but after Dad started to remake me, everything gets fuzzy.'

'After he did *what*?'

Johnny smiled tiredly and rested his head on one hand. 'He had to remake me chemically, you know. How could I spread change without being changed myself? I couldn't have two generations to adapt to it naturally like you, Ric. It had to be done artificially. It took years. You understand? I'm a community, a construction. The cells that carry on the silicon metabolism in me are not human. Dad adapted them for the purpose. I helped, but I can't remember any longer how it was done. Memory can't be pasted together.'

John Drake rose and looked around the laboratory with something like triumph. 'They're too late. I made it, Ric. There's the catalyst cooling over there. This is the last step. I don't think I'll survive this plague, but I'll last long enough to set it going for the finish. The police won't stop me until it's too late.'

Another plague!

The last one had been before Alcala was born. He had not thought that Johnny would start another. It was a shock.

Alcala walked over to the cage where he kept his white mice and looked in, trying to sort out his feelings. The white mice looked back with beady bright eyes, caged, not knowing they were waiting to be experimented upon.

A timer clicked and John Delgados-Drake became all rapid efficient activity, moving from valve to valve. It lasted a half minute or less, then Drake had finished stripping off the lab whites to his street clothes. He picked up the square metal box containing the stuff he had made, tucked it under his arm and held out a solid hand again to Alcala.

179

'Goodbye, Ric. Wish me luck. Close up the lab for me, will you?'

Alcala took the hand numbly and mumbled something, turned back to the cages and stared blindly at the mice. Drake's brisk footsteps clattered down the stairs.

Another step forward for the human race.

God knew what wonders for the race were in that box. Perhaps something for nerve construction, something for the mind – the last and most important step. He should have asked.

There came at last a pressure that was a thought emerging from the depth of intuition. *Doctor Ricardo Alcala will die in the next plague, he and his ill wife Nita and his ill little girl . . . And the name of Alcala will die forever as a weak strain blotted from the bloodstream of the race . . .*

He'd find out what was in the box by dying of it!

He tried to reason it out, but only could remember that Nita, already sickly, would have no chance. And Alcala's family genes, in attempting to adapt to the previous steps, had become almost sterile. It had been difficult having children. The next step would mean complete sterility. The name of Alcala would die. The future might be wonderful, but it would not be *his* future!

'Johnny!' he called suddenly, something like an icy lump hardening in his chest. How long had it been since Johnny had left?

Running, Alcala went down the long half-lit stairs, out the back door and along the dark path towards the place where Johnny's 'copter had been parked.

A light shone through the leaves ahead. He stooped and picked up a rock, and ran on.

'Johnny!'

John Osborne Drake was putting his suitcase into the rear of the 'copter.

'What is it, Ric?' he asked in a friendly voice without turning.

'*For Nina,*' Alcala thought as he swung the rock. Stone struck, crunched, sinking in. The doctor had forgotten his new strength and was dimly surprised at the fragility of bone in a skull. He raised an arm to strike again but the figure before him slowly sank down to its knees, then tilted forward on its

180

face, half kneeling. Alcala waited, but there was no further motion.

His terror ebbed, and the darkness cleared from before his eyes. A night cricket was chirping with a friendly intermittent note. Alcala hurled the rock violently away.

A police siren wailed in the distance. The crouching dead figure slowly fell over sidewise. The wail of sirens approached – the police coming to arrest a criminal who had spread disease.

Alcala was surprised to find himself unharmed. He had thought Johnny was capable, but the big scarred figure was motionless, battered head hanging limply among the twigs of a bush, big curled fingers resting on earth. A doctor sees many such dead. The worker was dead.

'Just one death can stop the killing,' Alcala said. He snarled down at the body suddenly and ferociously. 'What did you expect – gratitude?'

A FURTHER COMMENT ON
SYNDROME JOHNNY

Syndrome Johnny had a lot of adventure and trouble in his lifetime: it would have taken a much longer story to write it. With an editor waiting eagerly for a finished story, I did what I usually do when the time it would take to finish a story stretched over the horizon and out of sight – I shortened it by telling it from the viewpoint of someone who wasn't there and didn't know the hero, and hadn't much to tell.

Money is not the motive for writing, it is a motive of getting something into an envelope and mailing it out, written well or not. Money can urge me to take a first chapter of a novel and make it into a short story for a quick sale, and forget the novel. Money can urge me to quit writing and get a job. When there is a need for money, it is for money *now*. Story money is money later, novel money is money *much* later. I did not write the novel *Syndrome Johnny* but I did write the short story.

The only reason I've ever had for writing any story was because I wanted to read it. Just to read it. Thinking of some general idea like Evolution suddenly generates a fragmentary glimpse of action, a feeling of importance and suspense. It is like finding a few pages left of a burned book, and, reading them, finding it is the middle of a story. I hear a tantalising bit of a conversation, see someone falling out of a window, sense implications of vast networks of consequences. The falling man! Will he survive? What use is his destruction, what impact against the network of politics and change? Why?

There is no use for me to search other people's books for the answers. If I want to read that story I will have to write it myself.

Writing is toil. Moving forward step by step, wrestling with sentence style, spelling, description, probability, logic, complex explanations and a gap in the imagination – almost a deafness of being unable to hear the exact words they say to each other is work. But as I move forward the scene moves forward; as each page emerges, I am reading it and living it.

Now – years later, I would still like to know about Syndrome Johnny's risks and defeats while spreading death in the crowded cities of the world. Even 'Mr Brink' the grim reaper himself is sometimes met in fiction as a sympathetic character, and Johnny is a peculiarly stubborn and human character, someone I'd like to see more of.

But I'll never read it, because I didn't write it.

KATHERINE MACLEAN

DAY MILLION

by

Frederik Pohl

On this day I want to tell you about, which will be about ten thousand years from now, there were a boy, a girl and a love story.

Now, although I haven't said much so far, none of it is true. The boy was not what you and I would normally think of as a boy, because he was a hundred and eighty-seven years old. Nor was the girl a girl, for other reasons. And the love story did not entail that sublimation of the urge to rape, and concurrent postponement of the instinct to submit, which we at present understand in such matters. You won't care much for this story if you don't grasp these facts at once. If, however, you will make the effort you'll likely enough find it jampacked, chockful and tip-top-crammed with laughter, tears and poignant sentiment which may, or may not, be worthwhile. The reason the girl was not a girl was that she was a boy.

How angrily you recoil from the page! You say, who the hell wants to read about a pair of queers? Calm yourself. Here are no hot-breathing secrets of perversion for the coterie trade. In fact, if you were to see this girl you would not guess that she was in any sense a boy. Breasts, two; reproductive organs, female. Hips, callipygean; face hairless, supra-orbital lobes nonexistent. You would term her female on sight, although it is true that you might wonder just what species she was a female of, being confused by the tail, the silky pelt and the gill slits behind each ear.

Now you recoil again. Cripes, man, take my word for it. This is a sweet kid, and if you, as a normal male, spent as much as an hour in a room with her you would bend heaven and earth to get her in the sack. Dora – we will call her that; her 'name' was omicron-Dibase seven-group-totter-out 3 Doradus 5314, the last part of which is a colour specification corresponding to a shade of green – Dora, I say, was feminine, charming and cute. I admit she doesn't sound that way. She was, as you might put it, a dancer. Her art involved qualities of intellection and expertise of a very high order, requiring both tremendous natural capacities and endless practice; it was performed in null-gravity and I can best describe it by saying that it was something like the performance of a contortionist and something like a classical ballet, maybe resembling Danilova's dying swan. It was also pretty damned sexy. In a symbolic way, to be sure; but face it, most of the things we call 'sexy' are symbolic, you know, except perhaps an exhibitionist's open clothing. On Day Million when Dora danced, the people who saw her panted, and you would too.

About this business of her being a boy. It didn't matter to her audiences that genetically she was male. It wouldn't matter to you, if you were among them, because you wouldn't know it – not unless you took a biopsy cutting of her flesh and put it under an electron-microscope to find the XY chromosome – and it didn't matter to them because they didn't care. Through techniques which are not only complex but haven't yet been discovered, these people were able to determine a great deal about the aptitudes and easements of babies quite a long time before they were born – at about a second horizon of cell-division, to be exact, when the segmenting egg is becoming a free blastocyst – and then they naturally helped those aptitudes along. Wouldn't we? If we find a child with an aptitude for music we give him a scholarship to Juillard. If they found a child whose aptitudes were for being a woman, they made him one. As sex had long been dissociated from reproduction this was relatively easy to do and caused no trouble and no, or at least very little, comment.

How much is 'very little'? Oh, about as much as would be caused by our own tampering with Divine Will by filling a tooth. Less than would be caused by wearing a hearing aid. Does it still sound awful? Then look closely at the next busty babe you meet and reflect that she may be a Dora, for adults who are genetically male but somatically female are far from unknown even in our own time. An accident of environment in the womb overwhelms the blue-prints of heredity. The difference is that with us it happens only by accident and we don't know about it except rarely, after close study; whereas the people of Day Million did it often, on purpose, because they wanted to.

Well, that's enough to tell you about Dora. It would only confuse you to add that she was seven feet tall and smelled of peanut butter. Let us begin our story.

On Day Million, Dora swam out of her house, entered a transportation tube, was sucked briskly to the surface in its flow of water and ejected in its plume of spray to an elastic platform in front of her – ah – call it her rehearsal hall. 'Oh, hell!' she cried in pretty confusion, reaching out to catch her balance and finding herself tumbled against a total stranger, whom we will call Don.

They met cute. Don was on his way to have his legs renewed. Love was the farthest thing from his mind. But when, absent-mindedly taking a shortcut across the landing platform for submarines and finding himself drenched, he discovered his arms full of the loveliest girl he had ever seen, he knew at once they were meant for each other. 'Will you marry me?' he asked. She said softly, 'Wednesday,' and the promise was like a caress.

Don was tall, muscular, bronze and exciting. His name was no more Don than Dora's was Dora, but the personal part of it was Adonis in tribute to his vibrant maleness, and so we will call him Don for short. His personality colour-code, in angstrom units, was 5290, or only a few degrees bluer than Dora's 5314 – a measure of what they had intuitively discovered at first sight; that they possessed many affinities of taste and interest.

I despair of telling you exactly what it was that Don did for a living – I don't mean for the sake of making money, I mean for the sake of giving purpose and meaning to his life, to keep him from going off his nut with boredom – except to say that it involved a lot of travelling. He travelled on interstellar spaceships. In order to make a spaceship go really fast, about thirty-one male and seven genetically female human beings had to do certain things, and Don was one of the thirty-one. Actually, he contemplated options. This involved a lot of exposure to radiation flux – not so much from his own station in the propulsive system as in the spillover from the next stage, where a genetic female preferred selections, and the sub-nuclear particles making the selections she preferred demolished themselves in a shower of quanta. Well, you don't give a rat's ass for that, but it meant that Don had to be clad at all times in a skin of light, resilient, extremely strong copper-coloured metal. I have already mentioned this, but you probably thought I meant he was sunburned.

More than that, he was a cybernetic man. Most of his ruder parts had been long since replaced with mechanisms of vastly more permanence and use. A cadmium centrifuge, not a heart, pumped his blood. His lung moved only when he wanted to speak out loud, for a cascade of osmotic filters rebreathed oxygen out of his own wastes. In a way, he probably would have looked peculiar to a man from the 20th century, with his glowing eyes and seven-fingered hands. But to himself, and of course to Dora, he looked mighty manly and grand. In the course of his voyages Don had circles Proxima Centuri, Procyon and the puzzling worlds of Mira Ceti; he had carried agricultural templates to the planets of Canopus and brought back warm, witty pets from the pale companion of Aldebaran. Blue-hot or red-cool, he had seen a thousand stars and their ten thousand planets. He had, in fact, been travelling the star-lanes, with only brief leaves on Earth, for pushing two centuries. But you don't care about that, either. It is people who make stories, not the circumstances they find themselves in, and you want to hear about these two people. Well, they made it. The great thing they had for each other grew and flowered and burst into fruition on Wednesday, just as Dora had promised. They met at the encoding room, with a couple of well-wishing friends apiece to cheer them on, and while their identities were being taped and stored they smiled and whispered to each other and bore the jokes of their friends with blushing repartee. Then they exchanged their mathematical analogues and went away, Dora to her dwelling beneath the surface of the sea and Don to his ship.

It was an idyll, really. They lived happily ever after – or anyway, until they decided not to bother any more and died.

Of course, they never set eyes on each other again.

Oh, I can see you now, you eaters of charcoal-broiled steak, scratching an incipient bunion with one hand and holding this story with the other, while the stereo plays d'Indy or Monk. You don't believe a word of it, do you? Not for one minute. People wouldn't live like that, you say with a grunt as you get up to put fresh ice in a drink.

And yet there's Dora, hurrying back through the flushing commuter pipes towards her underwater home (she prefers it there; has had herself somatically altered to breathe the stuff). If I tell you with what sweet fulfilment she fits the recorded analogue of Don into the symbol manipulator, hooks herself in and turns herself on . . . if I try to tell you any of that you will simply stare. Or glare; and grumble, what the hell kind of love-making is this? And yet I assure you, friend, I really do assure you that Dora's ecstasies are as creamy and passionate as any of James Bond's lady spies', and one hell of a lot more so than anything you are going to find in 'real life'. Go ahead, glare and grumble. Dora doesn't care. If she thinks of you at all, her thirty-times-great-great-grandfather, she thinks you're a pretty primordial sort of brute. You are. Why, Dora is farther removed from you than you are from the australopithecines of five thousand centuries ago. You could not swim a second in the strong currents of her life. You don't think progress goes in a straight line, do you? Do you recognise that it is an ascending, accelerating, maybe even exponential curve? It takes hell's own time to get started, but when it goes it goes like a bomb. And you, you Scotch-drinking steak-eater in your relaxacising chair, you've just barely lighted the primacord of the fuse. What is it now, the six or seven hundred thousandth day after Christ? Dora lives in Day Million. Ten thousand years from now. Her body fats are polyunsaturated, like Crisco. Her wastes are hemodialysed out of her bloodstream while she sleeps – that means she doesn't have to go to the bathroom. On whim, to pass a slow half-hour, she can command more energy than the entire nation of Portugal can spend today, and use it to launch a weekend satellite or remould a crater on the Moon. She loves Don very much. She keeps his every gesture, mannerism, nuance, touch of hand, thrill of intercourse, passion of kiss stored in symbolic-mathematical form. And when she wants him, all she has to do is turn the machine on and she has him.

And Don, of course, has Dora. Adrift on a sponson city a few hundred yards over her head, or orbiting Arcturus fifty light-years away, Don has only to command his own symbol-manipulator to rescue Dora from the ferrite files and bring her to life for him, and there she is; and rapturously, tirelessly they love all night. Not in the flesh, of course; but then his flesh has been extensively altered and it wouldn't really be much fun. He doesn't need the flesh for pleasure. Genital organs feel nothing. Neither do hands, nor breasts, nor lips; they are only receptors, accepting and transmitting impulses. It is the brain that feels; it is the interpretation of those impulses that makes agony or orgasm, and Don's symbol-manipulator gives him the analogue of cuddling, the analogue

187

of kissing, the analogue of wild, ardent hours with the eternal, exquisite and incorruptible analogue of Dora. Or Diane. Or sweet Rose, or laughing Alicia; for to be sure, they have each of them exchanged analogues before, and will again.

Rats, you say, it looks crazy to me. And you – with your aftershave lotion and your little red car, pushing papers across a desk all day and chasing tail all night – tell me, just how the hell do you think you should look to Tiglath-Pileser, say, or Attila the Hun?

COMMENT ON

DAY MILLION

Like all of the short stories of mine that I am reasonably well contented with, *Day Million* came out of the typewriter just about as fast as my fingers could move on the keyboard. I sat down at the typewriter along about five o'clock one morning and the first draft was complete before eight; I said 'Good morning' to my family, ate something, went back to it, read it over and revised it as I typed, completing the finished version before noon, whereupon I put it in an envelope and tottered off to bed. (Given a choice, I like to write at night because the world is quieter then; this was one of the times when I was able to do what I liked.) I would be happy to say that the story was immediately accepted by the first publication to see it, but in fact No. 1 returned it because it was 'too sick'; No. 2 returned it without a reason; and it wasn't until Frank Robinson, then editing *Rogue*, saw it as third in the procession that it was accepted. (Sometimes new writers, or non-writers, get the notion that after a few sales a professional writer never gets a story rejected by anybody. This is partly true under some circumstances; the circumstances under which it is true, however, rest on a writer's willingness to write nothing that he hasn't written before. Try something new and your hard-won advantage disappears. This no longer worries me much – after all, *The Space Merchants*, which seems to be the most durable piece of writing I've had anything to do with, was rejected by every major book publisher when first offered – but I have to admit it still *nettles* me sometimes.) Anyway . . .

188

Although the actual processing time on *Day Million*, so to speak, was only a few hours, the programming and tooling-up ran quite a lot longer; I had been mulling it, or parts of it, for at least four years. The reason it took so long is that it deals with what seemed to me hard questions. It deals with the future; and in the future, even the relatively near future, geologically speaking, we aren't going to be quite the same breed of hominid we are today. Evolution is slow, but technology is rapid and we have shifted to the express.

Where the express is going is what I have tried to say in *Day Million*. Maybe not there exactly, but somewhere *like* there, or at least somewhere quite as dissimilar from here and now . . . and, dear God, how fast we're beginning to move.

FREDERIK POHL

RETALIATION

by

Mack Reynolds

There was a light flashing red. Alex hit the release button with the heel of his hand, flicked his eyes to the dial in question.

Animal heat.

He dropped both the speed and altitude levers, banked steeply and dove. His eyes went to the screen, he reached up and increased magnification ten fold. His fingers danced over buttons, searching out the appropriate chart. It flashed on to the map-screen.

Damn. The beetle was above that poorly mapped, all but unknown Balkan area where the Thrace of Greece and the Macedonia of Yugoslavia met Bulgaria. The nearest cities of any size would have been Yugoslavian Skopje, Greek Salonika, Bulgarian Plovdiv, but he was far from the ruins of any of them.

As the ground came up, his eyes shot to the dial again. Quite a bit of animal heat. Probably a man.

A man in this area? Alex pursed his lips. Possible, but not probable.

He was less than two miles in altitude, now. He increased magnification again. The vicinity was highly wooded.

He adjusted his metallic sensors, fossil fuel sensors, nuclear power sensors. For all he knew, this was a Comic trap and they were trying to suck his beetle in. Seemed unlikely, though. He hadn't spotted a Comic in this area for a goodly time.

When he was within a mile of the surface, he cut propulsion completely and hovered. His eyes went back to the chart and he enlarged it to ultimate. It still didn't give him much. The area had been fought over, ravaged, destroyed and rebuilt since the days of Philip and Alexander but it had never really been charted in the modern sense. There were the remains of a small farming town to the south; however, he

190

couldn't make out if it might be Rodopolis in what had once been Greece, or Novo Selo in Macedonia.

He scowled at the dial. There was more heat radiation than was called for by one person. Perhaps there were two or three. It was possible, no matter how unlikely. The human animal is gregarious; given any opportunity at all he will seek out his fellows, even though it might increase his chances of destruction.

He flicked his eyes over to the cocking handles of the mini-rockets, though he knew he had checked them out before take-off. Given life below, Alex was in a position to start snuffing it out like candles.

The trouble was, exactly where was he, over Comic territory or their own?

He had made that mistake with the fishing boat, off the coast of Cuba. He had thought, of course, that the two terrified occupants had been enemy civilians. It had been sickening to find his mistake later.

He zeroed-in on the source of body heat, brought the beetle up to a slow, careful speed. It might still be a Comic trap, but he could find no signs of the presence of mechanical equipment in the vicinity. He dropped lower, tense now. He was getting awfully close. He kept his right hand very near the trigger of one of the mini-rockets.

Suppose it was some peasant, miraculously saved from the holocaust. How was he to know, in this area, if the man was Greek, Macedonian or Bulgar? As he recalled, the nationalities blended into each other at this point to such a degree that even borders made precious little difference.

All of a sudden, he brought the beetle to a halt and began to chuckle. There in a small meadow, clearing would be the better term, browsed a woebegone cow.

It had been a long time since he had seen a cow. Alex looked at it for a long moment, ruefully. In his youth, he had spent some time on a farm and had loved every minute. It had been fate that had put him into an educational bracket which had wound him up as the pilot of a beetle.

He shook his head, even as he reached for the altitude lever. Had he become a farmer, he would now, without question, have been dead. And even though family, relatives, friends, sweetheart were now all passed away, life is to be lived.

He shot into patrol pattern again, resetting his sensors. His chronometer told him that he had only a few more moments to go.

When his time had elapsed, he put the beetle into orbit, threw the automatic control switch, then stood up, yawning. He stretched greatly, then massaged the back of his neck. He had a tendency to tighten up when on patrol.

Alex turned and threw the cogs on the metal door behind him. He stepped into the corridor beyond and headed for the executive officer's office.

Nick was on the desk. He said, 'How did it go?'

Alex yawned again. 'Nothing. I begin to suspect that there's nobody left at all in my area. The fallout must have got those that survived.'

Nick grunted. 'The Comics would like it, if they knew we thought so. Don't underestimate the human animal, Alex. He survives under some of the most impossible circumstances. Peter ran into a whole island of Eskimo in the northern Pacific.'

Alex was surprised. 'What did he do?'

'Blasted them, of course. They were Comics.'

Alex wondered, inwardly. Eskimo. Possibly they didn't have the vaguest knowledge of the war, nor why it was they were being killed. But Nick was right. Man had a fantastic ability to survive.

Nick said, 'You left your beetle in orbit?'

'That's right,' Alex said wearily. 'It isn't due for a check-out yet.' He turned to go, but then recalled the animal he had seen.

He said, 'You know what I saw today? A cow. I thought I was getting a heat indication of at least one man, but it was a cow. Wonder how it ever survived.'

Nick said, 'The last time I was on patrol, I saw four deer.'

'Oh? What did you do?'

'What could I do? I was over Comic territory. I blasted them.'

'Blasted them! Well, *why*?' Alex felt a sinking sensation. With so precious little major life left at all on Earth, who could wish to butcher deer?

Nick was irritated. 'I told you. It was Comic territory. Had there been any human life hiding out, surviving somehow or other, the deer would have been potential food. I killed them. In the same way as if you saw a house standing, you'd blast it,

192

so that it couldn't be used for shelter.' He hesitated for a moment, then said, 'Was she being milked?'

The other's mind had been on the deer. He said, 'How do you mean?'

'The cow. Was it being milked?'

'How would I know?'

'The udder, you ninny. If it was full, she was being milked, which would mean, in turn, that there's somebody doing the milking.'

'I didn't get any indication of further animal heat.'

'Could be in some sort of dugout. It's surprising how quickly some of the survivors have adapted to protecting themselves against us. Not that they're any smarter than our people. They've worked out a dozen ways of preserving themselves against those buzz-fighters in Comics use.'

Alex grunted. He had long been of the opinion that the higher-ups would do better to spend more effort protecting their civilians who had survived, rather than continuing to seek out the pitiful remnant of the Comics who were still alive. However, he didn't say anything. Nick had a mono-rail mind, when it came to official position. *Anything* the brass decided was gospel to Nick.

Alex said, 'I'll take another look at the cow, tomorrow, if I can find it again. Even if it is being milked, I'm not sure it's in what was formerly our own territory, or theirs.'

Nick said, 'Well, you know what the general said, when in doubt.'

Alex repressed a shudder, as he headed back for his sleeping quarters. The general had never jockeyed a beetle in his life. Had never had to blast a noncombatant. Perhaps he wouldn't be quite so devout at retaliationist, had he to follow his own orders.

In the morning, going by the twenty-four hour Earth Clock, Alex came awake slowly. There had been a time, when he had been an ambitious young officer, that he had tried to discipline himself away from this practice. Now he had given up. In truth, the half hour or so that he allowed to lapse between first stirrings of consciousness and full awakening was the happiest of his day. Happiest wasn't quite the word. There was no such reality as happiness in the life now led. But at least his semi-dream state was the most nearly satisfying.

In half control of his dream-thinking, he could steer his

thoughts in what direction he would. Back over yesteryear when there had been ambitions, appetites, goals. When there had been arts to appreciate, crafts to study, entertainments to enjoy.

There had been Anna to love. And what was Anna now? A cinder. If not a cinder, a terrified, underfed, under-clothed, under-sheltered fugitive from the Comic buzz-fighters who patrolled, even as Alex patrolled, seeking out the last remnants of life.

He had allowed his thoughts to go where he would rather they did not stray. He came fully awake and swung his legs out over the edge of the bunk.

He went through the usual routine of getting cleaned up and dressed, the never ending sameness of it all, and made his way to the mess.

As he ate the food of the hydroponic beds, the yeast cellars, he scanned the freshly printed day's bulletin.

An inspiration editorial by the general. The day would soon come when, the Comics utterly defeated, the personnel of moon-base would return to Earth and begin the task of reconstruction.

Alex grunted. He sometimes suspected that the general had fed his ideas into one of the typer-computers with standing orders that for each issue of the bulletin a new editorial be turned out, saying the same thing over and over again in a slightly altered version.

The fact was, that there was precious little chance that the Comics would ever be utterly defeated. Their super-Sputnik, as the junior officers had dubbed it, was as impregnable to attack as was the moon-base. And the truth had long since been accepted. The efforts to eliminate their mutual bases had been so costly that neither side any longer attempted it. Such fighting as took place between them, were the rare meetings above the surface of Earth, when beetle met buzz-fighter, usually through inadvertence, and fought it out.

If the truth were known, the general didn't even encourage that. The two fighting craft were so equally matched that one side's losses balanced the other's, and they were running short on the beetles they need to prosecute the retaliation.

Which brought him to another item in the bulletin. A sneak landing had been made hurriedly in the Antarctic and a sizeable amount of supplies loaded upon one of the freighter-craft. The supplies had been left over from the days when the nations had in considerable co-operation been exploring that remote continent.

Alex grunted. So that's where so many of the beetles had been, protecting the scavenging raid. It was a minor victory. In fact, more than balanced by the Comic Raid earlier when they had dispatched an equivalent space freighter to one of the Pacific islands where they had managed to locate a supply of fuel.

He wondered at the need of secrecy here on the moon-base. It was hard to believe that any Comic agent might be among them. And even if there was, how in the world could such an agent ever get a message to the enemy? No, Alex suspected that their rigid security measures were nonsense, left-over methods of an earlier period. The military mind was slow to change, even in the age of space war.

And here was the story of Peter's successful attack upon the Eskimo. Evidently there had been at least a score of them. Alex shook his head. How could it possibly have been known that they were from Comic territory, originally? The Eskimo were nomadic. Food supply, such as it was, would dictate that they move as much as a hundred miles in a week.

It was the same problem he had faced on the patrol yesterday.

Even had he spotted a survivor of the world debacle, how could he know whether the person was originally a resident of Comic territory? In desperate search of food and shelter, and protection from the ruthless attacks of beetles and buzzfighters, such a refugee might travel many a mile from his place of origin.

The speaker called his name.

He was to report for immediate patrol.

That was only mildly surprising. The men who had covered the Antarctic sneak landing had probably been on duty for long hours beyond the usual. They would need rest. He was comparatively fresh.

He came to his feet, adjusted his tunic on the off chance that he might meet one of the brass hats in the corridors and be dressed down for sloppy appearance, and started for the cubicle which he usually occupied when piloting a remote-control beetle.

At this hour he met only one other person. One of the

195

women scientists. He saluted her, as regulations called for, but she ignored him and bustled on.

It came to Alex, sourly, even as he continued, that this horse-faced, cow-figured specimen was probably one of the few remaining females of his species who might survive to help replenish the Earth. If any at all survived. Briefly, he wondered if the high-ups had decided upon a programme of breeding. If they had, it should best get underway even whilst they were still here on Luna. Most of these women scientists were by no means youngsters. Some must already be past the menopause.

He reached the executive officer's preserve, reported, got his assignment, which was identical to yesterday's, saluted, and continued to his cubicle. He wondered how many beetles were out today. He hadn't seen any of the other fellows in the corridors, or in the mess. Probably everybody who could be spared was on patrol. The Comics were probably in a tizzy over the Antarctic raid, and would be speeding up their retaliation.

He hung his jacket up and seated himself at the control chair, before the screens, the panels, the dials, switches, triggers, gauges and all the rest of it. And even as he went through the standard routine of taking over the beetle, now in fast orbit, his memory went back to the long studies that had been involved in learning this business of eliminating every unit of human life in the lands of the enemy. At the time of his training, he had never expected it to ever come to this. But, then, he doubted if anyone else had, either.

At the very last, he threw the cocking handles of the mini-rockets, threw off the automatic control, and accepted the piloting of the vicious little beetle.

It was a full hour later, an hour of carefully scanning over a large area of southern Europe, when he came to the vicinity where he had spotted the cow the day before.

He had little doubt that he could find the animal again. And yes, there it was. The indicator flashed animal heat.

He increased the magnification of his viewing screen, and sent the beetle darting towards the little meadow the cow had been grazing in the day before.

For the moment, engrossed in his object, he had failed to keep a constant eye on his other screens and scanning devices. Thus it was that his first warning of attack was a flashing ball of fire which, he realised, must have missed the miniature craft

196

he was piloting from afar, by a scant half mile.

Automatically he upped the speed lever, and pulled the directional stick backward, slamming for altitude. He banged open all screens, darted his head around, seeking the source of the attack. The nuclear power sensor was flashing green warning, the alarm siren was whining. Impatiently, he brushed them both to inoperation. He decreased the magnification on all screens, desperately seeking the foe over the broadcast area, even as he took standard evasive action.

Wherever and whoever his enemy, the Comic wasn't the man he might be. Alex's beetle should have been crisped by now. As it was, he hadn't even been nicked.

And, yes, there it was! A one man buzz-fighter, of course.

It was their one big advantage over the Comics. The enemy craft contained a living pilot who died in defeat. The beetles, piloted remotely from the moon-base, could be destroyed surely enough, but it was impossible for a pilot to be lost. War in air and space had come a long way since the Fokkers and Spads of World War One fought it out over the Western Front.

The buzz-fighters, comparatively large and cumbersome, must needs come down from their artificial satellite base before taking over their retaliation patrols. It was a time consuming, man consuming matter and Alex had a secret admiration for the stamina involved.

Even as they began their jockeying of death, roaring about the sky in great screaming of agonised machinery, great roaring of rockets and jets, he realised that the other must have spotted Alex's beetle towards the end of a patrol, and comparatively was physically exhausted.

Only that would account for the fact that the foe's reactions were obviously slow. Ordinarily, a buzz-fighter gave as much as it took. Indeed, it had some advantages over the tiny beetle. For one thing, it mounted a heavier firepower, a greater supply of bolts. The beetle's sole armament was the two mini-rockets, nuclear charged and capable of blasting a fairly good-sized town. Alex didn't know how many bolts the buzz-fighter boasted, but he knew it was considerably more than two.

He dropped sharply in a feint, came up roaring from below.

He had blisters of cold sweat on his forehead, could feel his shirt sticking to his back. He inevitably perspired in action. Safe, hundreds of thousands of miles away from the combat he might be, but in action you largely forgot that. Not com-

197

pletely though. At least in your subconscious you knew you were untouchable. But how about that enemy pilot? If his craft took a bolt, then all was over. At most, Alex would get a reprimand for being inept.

For the briefest of split seconds, the buzz-fighter was in his sighter screen, past the cross hairs, but in it. He slashed his fist out at the trigger button and his screen blurred momentarily as the beetle's weight dropped suddenly with the release of the mini-rocket.

Then there was glare!

A near hit? Had the missile's sensors caught enough of the enemy's heat to detonate?

Or was it another fluke blast? The mini-rockets Armament was turning out these days weren't up to original standards. Which wasn't surprising in view of the improvising they had to do, what with limited materials.

He came around in a roar – a roar tens upon tens of thousands of miles from his ear – and banged the screens to increased magnification.

And stared.

He had never seen before a buzz-fighter merely crippled. On all other occasions when he had come against the enemy fighters, they had flared up like magnesium upon being hit. Flared up from the atomic attack in such wise that there could be no question of survival on the part of the Comic pilot.

But now this one was fluttering to earth, like a wounded airborne bird.

He kicked controls around and headed for it.

He had a double problem. He had exactly one mini-rocket left and couldn't waste it. The enemy pilot must be destroyed beyond any doubt. There were a limited number of Comic pilots left, and each one departed hastened the day when the war could be considered over and the general's oft proclaimed return to earth became a reality.

But there was also the chance that the enemy was still in condition to mount a counter-attack on his diminutive enemy. Alex had no way of knowing whether or not the other was still conscious, but he must assume that he was. The buzz-fighter had caught only the edge of the mini-rocket blast and had evidently had delicate equipment so smashed that it was no longer fully operative.

He came in with care. Since the brief battle had been fought

198

in the same area he had patrolled the day before, the buzz-fighter managed to sink to a landing in the meadow in which Alex had spotted the cow the previous day.

He banked around quickly, and dropped the beetle's speed. Perhaps the other was dead. In which case, the thing was to make every effort to get a full size combat unit down here with a freighter-craft and try to capture the buzz-fighter intact, before the lads on the super-Sputnik caught on and fired a real flattener to blast this whole section of the Balkans. The technicians and scientists there at moon-base had never had the opportunity to take apart a buzz-fighter. Given such a chance, it might lead to some discovery that would make a decisive difference in the prosecuting of the war.

But no. Even as he manoeuvred his diminutive fighter into the clearing, a figure broke from the side of the enemy craft and dashed for the woods. At the same split second, the buzz-fighter began to glow in heat, and rapidly crumbled into a mass of flaming nothingness.

The Comic had sabotaged his craft. Alex swore, but his obscenities broke off in the middle.

The other was garbed in shorts and halter, and blonde hair was streaming behind even as she ran for what little protection the trees might offer.

Meaninglessly, as he darted his beetle after her, the thought came to his mind, was the briefness of clothing due to heat in the buzz-fighter, or was it a matter of saving weight?

There was something strangely familiar in her desperate flight, and then it came to him. She ran as Anna ran. As Anna had once run. Her figure, too, was Anna's. Youthful, firm, but all rounded woman. This enemy pilot could be no more than in her mid-twenties.

He had heard that the Comics used women as well as men in the war in space and air, but he had secretly thought it propaganda, as he thought most of the atrocity stories. Evidently, it was true enough. Comic manpower was evidently as short as his own side's.

She was nearly to the edge of the clearing, running desperately hard.

She must have known, as he so well knew, that her flight was meaningless. A bolt from his beetle would blast everything in an area the diameter of a mile, reducing it to nothing. But life is so much to be lived, even the last ultimate minute.

Suddenly he pulled back the control stick and, pointing the beetle skyward, hit at the same moment both the remaining mini-rocket trigger and the speed lever. The bolt went arching off into the depths of space, and the beetle headed home.

He threw it into automatic and came to his feet, rubbing the back of his neck as hard as he could press fingers into the flesh.

He went out into the corridor and headed towards the exec's office. Nick was on the desk, as he had been the day before.

Nick looked up. 'Thought you were on patrol over the Balkans.'

'I was. I fired both my bolts. I've got the beetle on automatic coming in for fresh mini-rockets.'

Nick looked at him. 'Two bolts to finish off a cow?'

'A buzz-fighter jumped me, while I was going in to blast the animal. I managed to hit it.'

Nick was immediately doubly alert. 'Wonderful!' He reached for a report pad. 'Absolutely sure of destruction?'

'Yes,' Alex said. 'It burnt to a crisp.'

'Wonderful!' Nick crowed, writing rapidly. 'You'll get another citation.'

Alex said wearily, 'I feel pooped, I think I'll take a nap.'

Before he turned to leave, Alex said slowly, 'Nick, why do we call them Comics?'

'Eh?' The other continued writing the report.

'The enemy, over in that super-Sputnik of theirs, the artificial satellite.'

Nick thought about it, finally shrugged his shoulders. 'I don't know. I suppose it's derived from the fact that in the old days we used to ridicule them by saying their young people, their students, spent more time reading cartoon books, comic books, you know, than they did studying the sciences.'

'Oh,' Alex mused. 'I wonder what they call us.'

Nick said stiffly, 'I would hardly know, but probably something unworthy of our admitted idealistic goals.'

Alex made his way to his quarters and slumped down on his bed. His face worked as he stared up at the ceiling. Somehow, he thought that she would survive. The cow was there.

Lieutenant Alex Moiseyevich Menzhinsky knew he was a traitor. The thing was – she ran so very much like Anna had run, back when there was an Anna, back when they'd both been youngsters on the collective.

200

COMMENT ON
RETALIATION

Almost a quarter of a century ago, I was standing watch on the bridge of an army transport in the south Pacific. The radio man – and even now I can recall the strange look upon his face – brought a news item. Hiroshima had just been vapourised by what the brief item named an atomic bomb.

It had been a-building a long time, but I think that it was then, as I leaned on the ship's rail and stared off in the general direction of Japan, that I stopped primarily being an American, a citizen of the United States, and became first a member of the human race.

You know. A bleeding heart. A do-gooder. Synonymous with crackpot.

We have various other snide terms to denote he who believes that the present socio-economic systems that prevail in the world are antiquated and need radical change. That war is a monstrosity that can and must be ended if the race is to continue. That poverty is an anachronism that could be quite easily eliminated on a worldwide basis.

However, I like to believe that it was not my emotions that led me to take my stand. Throughout my adult life my pursuits have been in political economy, history, anthropology; the social sciences, rather than the physical ones, in which I am largely at sea.

Following the war, I spent more than fifteen years making my way about the world doing travel articles for the men's magazines, touching on some sixty countries. These embraced a wide range of politico-economic systems. Fascist countries, such as Spain and Portugal; monarchies, such as the Arab states; communist dictatorships, including all the European ones, save only Albania; off-beat experiments, such as Israel; pseudo-socialism, such as that of Scandinavia; various levels of capitalism, from more or less classic Switzerland to the State capitalism of the United States and Great Britain; not to speak of the chaotic mishmashes to be found in the newly liberated colonies.

Through that period, from time to time I found myself in the midst of this military revolt, that minor war, the other attempted revolution.

And emerged from it all strong in the belief that man has evolved to the point where he can no longer think in terms of being an American, an Englishman, a Russian, a Chinese, a Bolivian . . .

No longer can he afford the skip of heart when 'Old Glory' is paraded down the street, a tear in the eye when the band plays *God Save the Queen*, a patriotic stirring when the soldiers goose-step past the *Deutschland Über Alles*.

In the near future, the race, in my belief, will evolve a new socio-economic system which will eliminate national boundaries, wars, poverty and class divided society – including the 'New Class' of the communist bureaucracies. We will do this, or we will die.

Do you wish a blueprint of the new society for which I propagandise?

I do not have one.

My purpose, in the science fiction I write, is to stimulate imagination so that many minds will perhaps be directed towards the problem. It is astonishing how few persons consider the possibility that the socio-economic system under which they live might be changed, and even for the better. So much are we conservative creatures of habit that to tell, say, a Moroccan, an American, or a Russian, that his lot might be improved if feudalism, capitalism, or communism, as the case may be, were overthrown and a new socio-economic system established, would be to tell him what he *knows* is nonsense. His belief that his socio-economic system is the best possible is as ingrained as is his religion.

Of course, when it applies to the other fellow, it is easier to comprehend. Obvious indeed, that the Russians should overthrow their dictatorial bureaucracy – to the American. And obvious that capitalism should be abolished in America – to a Russian. And both can see that the Moroccan isn't going to get anywhere until he revolts against that sultan-king and his parasitical feudalistic family.

So my stories are devoted almost exclusively to extrapolation in the fields of the social sciences. Delving into what might happen if anarchism, technocracy, syndicalism, communism, in all its varieties, or socialism, in its range from the pink or garden variety of England's Labour Party to the Marxian socialism of America's DeLeonists, were ever to be established.

Somewhere in here, a reader is saying, 'This is fine, Reynolds using capitalism and communism interchangeably as examples of social systems calling for overthrow. But he's lucky he's living in a country where he is free to write what he believes. Suppose he was a Russian?'

Actually, I wish that was more true than it is. That freedom to write what one believes.

In truth, the Russian author, too, can write what he will. But since the publishing houses are State owned, it is unlikely that it will be printed if his beliefs do not conform. And he may even be harassed by the government.

In the West, the writer can write what he wishes, but he, also largely, might as well tear it up afterwards if it doesn't conform. Because the publishing houses are privately owned and print that which the owners want to print, nothing more. And the off-beat writer may even be harassed by such as MacCarthy, the Un-American Activities Committee, the John Birch Society, the F.B.I. I have a writer friend who is forbidden a passport because he fought in Spain; a life-long anti-communist, he leans towards syndicalism.

Even in science fiction we are not as free as many think.

A few years ago, I wrote a humour story entitled *Russkies Go Home!* which involved a future in which the Soviets had achieved their goals and were so affluent that they had become the objectionable tourists of the future. As individuals, the Russians were portrayed as the friendly, compatible people I have ever found them in my Russian travels.

Science fiction editor Horace Gold decided to buy the story and asked that it be expanded, a request pro writers paid on a word basis love to receive. However, by the time the yarn was lengthened, the U-2 affair, or some such, had developed and Horace, though professing still to like the story, wrote that it had become 'a casualty of the Cold War'. In this case, the story was accepted elsewhere.

It is not a lone example, many of my things have been rejected as 'too controversial'.

But science fiction still is the most nearly free of all fiction fields and ideas such as those in *Retaliation* can still be expressed.

Indeed, it has been to my astonishment that so few of the writers in our genre have extrapolated in the field of evolution of society. A story teller of the ability of Isaac Asimov will spin his yarns of the FOUNDATION, set a few thousand years hence. And what socio-economic system has evolved by then? Something new? Certainly not! They haven't even got capitalism. They've gone back to feudalism. The same applies to the WEAPONS SHOPS series of Van Vogt. The worlds of tomorrow have progressed in most satisfying fashion in every science, save the social sciences. Wars are still being fought, now on a galaxy wide basis, whole star systems going up into cinders; feudalistic barons swagger about toting atomic swords; the poor are still with us, evidently man, despite his progress, having not been able to achieve to the point of adequately feeding, clothing and sheltering himself.

Really, gentlemen!

It is understandable that our Russian colleagues dare not try to envision a world of the future in which what they call communism has been superseded by a superior system. At best, they wouldn't be published, at worst they'd be clobbered.

But in spite of what I have said above in regard to conforming editors, we in the West do not labour under their handicap. We are free to picture a tomorrow which has risen above our dog eat dog society. A tomorrow that no longer knows war, exploitation of man by man, corrupt politicians, the ulcer-breeding rat race for false status, and the multitude of other evils that are our present socio-economic system.

We are on our mettle! Why cannot we be the vanguard in the social sciences as well as the physical ones? Cartmill foresaw nuclear weapons, Clarke the communications satellite; there are a hundred other examples from the days of Verne and Wells to the present. Why do we hesitate to deal with extrapolation in socio-economics, or, when we do, cry disaster?

MACK REYNOLDS

PIRATES OF THE ASTEROIDS

by Isaac Asimov

An ever-increasing mystery lures David Starr into a perilous journey across a galaxy to destroy a marauding band of space privateers. Twenty-five years ago these vermin had killed his parents. All his life he had waited for the moment of vengeance. Now, that moment was very near.

THE NEW ENGLISH LIBRARY

DUNE
by Frank Herbert

DUNE is the finest, most widely acclaimed science fiction novel of this century. Huge in scope, towering in concept, it is a work which will live in the reader's imagination for the rest of his life.

'DUNE seems to me unique among science fiction novels in the depth of its characterisation and the extra-ordinary detail of the world it creates. I know nothing comparable to it except THE LORD OF THE RINGS.'
—*Arthur C. Clarke*

'Certainly one of the landmarks of modern science fiction . . . an amazing feat of creation.' —**Analog**

NEW ENGLISH LIBRARY

NEL BESTSELLERS

Crime

T017 648	HAVE HIS CARCASE	*Dorothy L. Sayers*	60p
T020 983	UNNATURAL DEATH	*Dorothy L. Sayers*	45p
T017 095	LORD PETER VIEWS THE BODY	*Dorothy L. Sayers*	40p
T019 608	HANGMANS HOLIDAY	*Dorothy L. Sayers*	40p
T021 548	GAUDY NIGHT	*Dorothy L. Sayers*	60p
T019 799	THE NINE TAILORS	*Dorothy L. Sayers*	40p
T012 484	FIVE RED HERRINGS	*Dorothy L. Sayers*	40p

Fiction

T017 087	BEYOND THIS PLACE	*A. J. Cronin*	50p
T018 539	A SONG OF SIXPENCE	*A. J. Cronin*	50p
T018 202	THE GREEN YEARS	*A. J. Cronin*	50p
T016 544	THE CITADEL	*A. J. Cronin*	75p
T016 919	THE SPANISH GARDENER	*A. J. Cronin*	40p
T020 967	BISHOP IN CHECK	*Adam Hall*	35p
T015 467	PAWN IN JEOPARDY	*Adam Hall*	30p
T021 270	THE RATS	*James Herbert*	40p
T018 156	SAMSON DUKE	*Seymour Kern*	40p
T017 737	COLOSSUS	*Stephen Marlowe*	90p
T019 152	A PORTION FOR FOXES	*Jane McIlvaine McClary*	75p
T015 130	THE MONEY MAKER	*John J. McNamara Jr.*	50p
T014 932	YOU NICE BASTARD	*G. F. Newman*	50p
T022 536	THE HARRAD EXPERIMENT	*Robert H. Rimmer*	50p
T019 381	THE DREAM MERCHANTS	*Harold Robbins*	90p
T022 986	THE CARPETBAGGERS	*Harold Robbins*	£1
T016 560	WHERE LOVE HAS GONE	*Harold Robbins*	75p
T019 829	THE ADVENTURERS	*Harold Robbins*	95p
T020 215	THE INHERITORS	*Harold Robbins*	80p
T020 347	STILETTO	*Harold Robbins*	40p
T015 289	NEVER LEAVE ME	*Harold Robbins*	40p
T020 339	NEVER LOVE A STRANGER	*Harold Robbins*	80p
T011 798	A STONE FOR DANNY FISHER	*Harold Robbins*	60p
T015 874	79 PARK AVENUE	*Harold Robbins*	60p
T011 461	THE BETSY	*Harold Robbins*	75p
T020 894	RICH MAN, POOR MAN	*Irwin Shaw*	90p
T018 148	THE PLOT	*Irving Wallace*	90p
T020 436	THE NAKED COUNTRY	*Morris West*	30p

Historical

T018 229	THE CUNNING OF THE DOVE	*Alfred Duggan*	50p
T017 958	FOUNDLING FATHERS	*Alfred Duggan*	50p
T010 279	MASK OF APOLLO	*Mary Renault*	50p
T015 580	THE CHARIOTEER	*Mary Renault*	50p
T019 035	BURKE AND HARE – THE TRUE STORY	*Hugh Douglas*	40p
T020 169	FOX 9. CUT AND THRUST	*Adam Hardy*	30p
T017 044	SWORD OF VENGEANCE	*Alexander Karol*	30p

Science Fiction

T014 576	THE INTERPRETER	*Brian Aldiss*	30p
T015 017	EQUATOR	*Brian Aldiss*	30p
T014 347	SPACE RANGER	*Isaac Asimov*	30p
T015 491	PIRATES OF THE ASTEROIDS	*Isaac Asimov*	30p
T019 780	THROUGH A GLASS CLEARLY	*Isaac Asimov*	30p
T020 673	MOONS OF JUPITER	*Isaac Asimov*	35p

T011 631	MASTER MIND OF MARS	Edgar Rice Burroughs	30p
T015 564	LOST ON VENUS	Edgar Rice Burroughs	35p
T010 333	REVOLT IN 2100	Robert Heinlein	40p
T021 602	THE MAN WHO SOLD THE MOON	Robert Heinlein	40p
T016 900	STRANGER IN A STRANGE LAND	Robert Heinlein	75p
T022 862	DUNE	Frank Herbert	80p
T012 298	DUNE MESSIAH	Frank Herbert	40p
T015 211	THE GREEN BRAIN	Frank Herbert	30p

War

T013 367	DEVIL'S GUARD	Robert Elford	50p
T020 584	THE GOOD SHEPHERD	C. S. Forester	40p
T011 755	TRAWLERS GO TO WAR	Lund & Ludlam	40p
T012 999	P.Q.17 – CONVOY TO HELL	Lund & Ludlam	30p
T014 215	THE GIANT KILLERS	Kenneth Poolman	40p
T022 528	THE LAST VOYAGE OF GRAF SPEE	Michael Powell	35p

Western

T016 994	No. 1 EDGE – THE LONER	George G. Gilman	30p
T016 986	No. 2 EDGE – TEN THOUSAND DOLLAR AMERICAN	George G. Gilman	30p
T017 613	No. 3 EDGE – APACHE DEATH	George G. Gilman	30p
T017 001	No. 4 EDGE – KILLER'S BREED	George G. Gilman	30p
T016 536	No. 5 EDGE – BLOOD ON SILVER	George G. Gilman	30p
T017 621	No. 6 EDGE – THE BLUE, THE GREY AND THE RED	George G. Gilman	30p
T014 479	No. 7 EDGE – CALIFORNIA KILLING	George G. Gilman	30p
T015 254	No. 8 EDGE – SEVEN OUT OF HELL	George G. Gilman	30p
T015 475	No. 9 EDGE – BLOODY SUMMER	George G. Gilman	30p
T015 769	No. 10 EDGE – VENGEANCE IS BLACK	George G. Gilman	30p
T017 184	No. 11 EDGE – SIOUX UPRISING	George G. Gilman	30p
T017 893	No. 12 EDGE – THE BIGGEST BOUNTY	George G. Gilman	30p
T018 253	No. 13 EDGE – A TOWN CALLED HATE	George G. Gilman	30p
T020 754	No. 14 EDGE – THE BIG GOLD	George G. Gilman	30p

General

T021 009	SEX MANNERS FOR MEN	Robert Chartham	35p
T019 403	SEX MANNERS FOR ADVANCED LOVERS	Robert Chartham	30p
W002 835	SEX AND THE OVER FORTIES	Robert Chartham	30p
T010 732	THE SENSUOUS COUPLE	Dr. 'C'	25p

Mad

S004 892	MAD MORALITY		40p
S005 172	MY FRIEND GOD		40p
S005 069	MAD FOR BETTER OR VERSE		30p

NEL, P.O. BOX 11, FALMOUTH, TR10 9EN, CORNWALL

Please send cheque or postal order. Allow 10p to cover postage and packing on one book plus 5p for each additional book.

Name ....

Address...

....

Title ....
(NOVEMBER)